"...an aviation-fueled rip-roaring read...filled with romance, suspense, wonder and danger..."
Brooks Wachtel, Creator of History Channel's "Dogfights"

"...tells at once an exciting, entertaining and dramatic story... a tragic romance in the Nazi-era and the war... offers big emotions and heavy strokes of fate..."
Bavaria Media International

"...thrillingly portrayed...propulsive war tale... vividly captures the fast-paced terror of combat in the air, and the peculiar mixture of precision and bravado displayed by the best pilots..."
Kirkus Reviews

"...themes of friendship, romance, love, war, and loyalty...woven into a perfect story made more intriguing by numerous twists and turns... Action-packed... Astonishing...!"
Online Book Club

ACES

Michael January

Winged Lion Publications

ACES

Library of Congress Cataloging on Request
ISBN-13: 978-0-9985663-06

So it was that war in the air began...
The sky rained heroes upon the astonished earth.
H.G. Wells

CHAPTER ONE

Cleveland Aerodrome 1935

The thrilled crowds at the annual National Air Races cheered and pointed from the packed viewing stands or gathered around the field with blankets and picnic baskets spread on the grass. Some stood on the hoods of their Ford Coupés and running boards of their Chevy Rumbles to get a better view of the racers as they zoomed over the field, down to the distant pylon a mile away and back again.

Lacy held her breath as the roar of an airplane boomed overhead. It was shocking and a bit frightening. The skies above were filled with the buzzing roar of sleek mono-winged Ryans, high-winged Curtiss, and stubby GeeBee Super air racers, specially designed aircraft driven by propeller blades whirling at a thousand revolutions per minute. Dodging, swooping, and dicing with one another, they chased around the red & white checkered pylons above the narrow gash of asphalt of the Cleveland Aerodrome. She had not wanted to come to Ohio, halfway across the country. These machines scared her, but she was affected by the excitement of the crowd around her, and two of the hurtling machines were in the hands of boys she loved.

Lacy Dunbrough was just eighteen, shading her eyes as she peered up at the roaring planes from the racing paddock, clinching her silk scarf in excitement and fear. The yellow gleaming Packard twelve-cylinder Phaeton she had driven from New Jersey was parked like a showroom display, surrounded by planes being worked on by mechanics. Leaning on the car were a collection of young men, college students, Ivy League by their clothes and manner, watching the race and swigging from beer bottles or silver whisky flasks.

"Oh, God...be careful...!" she cried out loud as she watched the planes.

It was hard to tell for which pilot she was praying as the loudspeaker echoed across the field with the rasp of the race announcer's voice, "Von Steuven takes the lead in GeeBee number three. Miller in second in the Ryan and Carlton coming up in third..."

The GeeBee, a stubby pure racing plane with rather the appearance of a flying bullet with bumble bee sized wings led the racers around the course. In the cockpit, a cramped space inside closed glass, the handsome twenty-year-old face with a shock of Nordic blond hair and electric blue eyes behind the goggles, Michael "Miki" von Steuven, gripped a firm control on the stick. He looked over his shoulder to the silver Ryan just off his right wing. As he approached the pylon, he counted beats in his head with one eye on the ground, seventy feet below, and coolly threw the stick to the left, arcing the little plane into a tight bank around the pylon.

In the Ryan, with its open cockpit and single wing, Aaron Miller kept his intense gaze focused on the stubby tail of the GeeBee ahead, his brown-hazel eyes protected by goggles from the stinging wind hitting his face at two hundred and fifty miles-per-hour. His dark unruly hair was made more out of control by the bluster as the wind whistled in the support wires. His vision was sharp enough to detect the air currents enveloping the wings of his rival, while still able to pick out faces in the blur of the crowds below. If Miki had timing, Aaron had an uncanny anticipation. He snapped his stick back to gain a few precious feet of altitude, pressed hard into the seat, before yanking it over into a diving banking turn to gain speed in his heavier plane.

Coming out of the turn around the pylon with his wingtip just forty feet from the earth he pulled the stick back again. The Ryan rose up to even outside of the lead plane, the GeeBee's wheels spinning in the wind just inches from his head before they straightened out to level. Wingtip to wingtip, they zoomed across the runway toward the next pylon.

The two planes dodged and diced, with wings and fuselages inches apart and evenly matched, two top competitors, daredevils with no fear. They roared around a pylon, wingtips actually touching cloth as the GeeBee took the inside line while the Ryan arced across to the outside.

Lacy clung tighter to the scarf in her hands, almost that she might tear it, destroying the silk which would cost anyone in the Depression crowd around them a suit of clothes. She was thrilled with the excitement of it despite herself. Even in their planes hurtling past she could tell them apart. Miki deliberate, never deviating from his course, smooth and steady. Aaron, free and wild, flinging his machine on the edge, unpredictable, seeming at any moment as if he might veer out of control, with doom the result of the slightest flicker of breeze.

As the two lead planes roared across the field, dead even, they raced up on another plane, a back-marker, a Beech bi-wing.

The loudspeaker called out the positions, "Von Steuven and Miller, dead on neck and neck come up on

Bullard, two laps down. This could be the race! Whoever gets past Bullard clean will take the Thompson Trophy for 1935!"

In the GeeBee cockpit Miki's steel eyes of pure focus fixed on the plane they were overtaking, glancing to Miller's Ryan on his wingtip. In the Ryan, Aaron glanced to meet Miki's gaze in the cockpit. He jogged his stick, inching his wingtip ever closer to the GeeBee's fuselage, flying almost as one plane. There was no way they could make it together.

Lacy could hardly breathe as she watched them, almost seeming welded together in the sky, like mating dragonflies.

"God, Aaron...!" she cried, then, "Miki!" She gripped the arm of one of the college boys next to her, digging her fingers, but he didn't notice as he was caught in the excitement, shouting with his buddies.

"Go low! Take him, Aaron!" shouted one.

"Hold it in there, Miki!" shouted another.

Their friends also counted on the contrast, as if one could choose head or tails, two sides of a coin. Lacy admired one, but craved the other, in way she couldn't explain. One so much like the world she knew, the other, a dangerous rebellion.

Miki closed in on the tail of the Beech, counting his beats, he threw his stick over to the left to take him inside.

As Miki made the maneuver, Aaron was counting on it, expecting it. He pulled his stick back, rising up to cross over the Beech. Just inches from the slower biplane, the two racers split, the GeeBee arcing low into the turn, the Ryan zooming high, turning right over the top of the Beech, the banking wingtip almost catching its tail wires.

They both made it past the wood and strut biplane into the turn, but just as they cleared, the third place GeeBee of Rick Carlton roared up, also trying to make it past. Thinking he was clear of the two leads who had passed him, Jim Bullard in the Beech banked, cutting into the line of Carlton's charging GeeBee. The following plane was in his blind spot and the GeeBee slammed into the Beech.

The two planes tangled in a mass of smashing cloth, wood and wires. On the ground, spectators could only watch in instant shock as the two planes both tumbled through the sky, pieces flying off as they twirled like dying birds and slammed into the ground, exploding in a ball of aero fuel flames, spreading across the field in a fiery trail.

Lacy gasped with the college boys and the stunned crowd around her in shock at the crash. She covered her face, sure that it was the boys she knew who had suddenly, without a breath of warning, died. Then, one of the college boys, Jerry Donovan, red-haired and freckle-faced, shook her with excitement. He pointed to the sky where Miki's GeeBee and Aaron's Ryan were still racing to the finish line.

Miki flew just inches from the ground. Pulling up, he took a second to look back to see the burning wreckage of Bullard and Carlton falling into the distance. As he did, Miller's Ryan swooped from above, over his cockpit shield, gaining speed.

Only a length ahead, Miki had to rise to clear the ground markers as they charged toward the flagman waving the checkered banner at the finish line while

Aaron eased his stick forward in a full throttle power dive, just zooming over the top of the GeeBee.

The two planes streaked past the waving flag, with Aaron's Ryan just half a nose ahead of the GeeBee.

The announcer shouted excitedly, echoing through the loudspeakers, "Miller takes the trophy by a prop spinner! What a race! Albert comes across the line in third, Brown lagging in fourth."

As the other planes crossed the invisible finish line, zooming past the flag tower, ambulances and firetrucks rumbled across the field with a wail of sirens toward the column of rising smoke at the distant edge of the field.

The Ryan and GeeBee touched down on the narrow asphalt, wingtip to wingtip, wheels dancing on the pitted tarmac. Aaron Miller and Michael von Steuven could look across the narrow divide to each other as they matched move for move, easing onto the runway before the Ryan's heavier weight carried it longer on the rollout.

The two planes taxied toward into the paddock area as the excited crowd was held back from the spinning props. The engines sputtered to a stop and the congratulatory throng of fans surged around the planes. They most excitedly surrounded the Ryan, clambering over the wing, almost threatening to bend the struts as they pulled Aaron from the cockpit.

Miki popped open the fuselage door of the GeeBee and slid out to the ground, extricating his long legs from the tight space. He was surrounded by a smaller group of fans, who cheerfully slapped him on the back but more reserved, perhaps respectful.

The college boys hurried over with Lacy, pushing through the crowd to greet their friend. Jerry Donovan was at the front of them, the rowdiest of the boys, unmistakable in his Irish ginger complexion.

"Hey, you old Kraut-eater," Donovan slapped Miki on the back and feinted a couple of boxing jabs, "you just lost me fifty bucks!"

Miki grinned, pulling off his goggles, answering back in his clipped German accent, "Maybe you can win it back from Aaron at billiards."

"Damn straight! The 'Brick' can fly, but he can't shoot a straight cue worth a brass nickel."

Miki noticed Lacy standing back a pace. He smiled at her.

"Glad you came, my dear?" he asked. She had not wanted to come. She had protested that she didn't like the danger they put themselves in. Aaron had asked her to come see them race before, but it wasn't until Miki asked that she agreed to make the trip to Ohio from New Jersey with the college boys. She couldn't explain why she wouldn't come when it was Aaron who had asked, maybe she felt there was something safer when it was Miki, not with the risk of the racing, but with her feelings.

Lacy lurched forward and wrapped her arms around Miki's waist, stroking a hand on his chest, what the others thought be damned.

"You scared the life out of me, Miki! How can you and Aaron fly so close? I thought that crash was you!"

Miki looked past the crowds, across the field to the burning wreckage of the two planes.

"Bullard and Carlton," said Donovan, confirming the heavy news with a weight of unspoken loss.

Miki seemed to take it hard a moment, but then set it aside in some locked place. He had only known them as competitors, but they took the same risks as he did. He was sad at their fate, but had the ability to put away the distractions of the dangers they faced and summed up as much the loss of friends as the mistake which had caused them to die in a single word, short and pointed.

"Hell," he said.

It was the one thing about Miki that held her back. She knew he felt things, deeply even, but had something untouchable in him, an insulation for his emotions, a box with a lost key.

They could hear a cheer rising from the crowd and looked over as Aaron was hoisted onto the winner's platform, underneath the Thompson Trophy banner stretched above waiting executives of the Thomson Products company who had sponsored the unlimited and amateur class of racing planes at the National Air Races since 1929. Miki and Aaron were flying in the amateur entry class of up-and-coming air pioneer racers.

Aaron peered across the heads of the throng of well-wishers to see Miki with Lacy and the boys. He waved for his friend to come over and join him on the stand.

Miki pushed through the crowd and jumped up on the platform. They grinned as they shook the bottles of champagne and sprayed the crowd as the loudspeakers echoed across the field.

"Ladies and Gentleman, the 1935 Thompson Trophy will be presented to Aaron Miller by 5-time Thompson winner, now Air Reserve Major, James R. Doolittle."

Jimmy Doolittle, a compact and rangy flier with an intense energy stepped up on the platform in his Air Corps major's uniform. He was now 38 years old and retired from his air racing career. His name was etched on the trophy five times. He had also won the Bendix long distance prize and the Schneider Sea Plane Trophy. He stepped forward to the microphone as the crowd cheered the legendary racing hero.

"On behalf of the Thompson Machine and Mechanics Company," he intoned with a glance to Aaron, standing next to him, "I present the First Place A-class trophy to Aaron Miller."

The great trophy stood on the platform behind them. It was half the size of a man, made of heavy bronze in the shape of a cliff with billowy clouds and nested eagles. The mythological figure of Icarus, the first man to fly, and the milestones of man's attainment of speed were formed in relief around it. Aaron's name would be added in etch to a brass plate at the base with the other winners.

Doolittle handed Aaron a plaque and shook his hand, standing in front of the display monument for photographers to flash photo bulbs. After a series of photographs from all angles so the press from local and national papers got their covers, Doolittle returned to the microphone.

"These young men you've seen here represent the pinnacle of flying skill today." He waited for the cheers to die as he had something more to say than just presenting a trophy, for sports heroes become spokesmen.

"They, and many of you out there, boys of skill and courage, will be the backbone of technological advancement and American air power as we face an increasingly troubled world. And I hope to see many of those eager faces I'm looking at now over at the Army Air Corps recruiting table." And even as he spoke, the tables set up to turn eager young flying fans into pilots grew crowded.

Doolittle turned away from the microphone and shook Aaron's hand.

"Good flying, son. Maybe I'll see you at the table?"

"I'm really honored to shake your hand, Major. You're one of the reasons I fell in love with flying. But I've got another year of undergrad and a law degree to finish."

Doolittle smiled, maybe a little disappointed, but he understood. He himself was in the reserve, dividing his time as a consultant for Shell Oil. Whether aviation would advance in the private world or in war was the same to him.

"What the world needs, a few more lawyers," he joked. "Good luck, son." He shook Aaron's hand warmly, then turned to shake Miki's hand, but more in courtesy than enthusiasm.

"Nice flying, son," he said, and turned away from him without another word.

Aaron noticed the cold shoulder, watching Doolittle go down the steps.

"He knows you're not a citizen. Foreigner, you know... Don't worry about it."

Miki smiled, pleasant, but hiding maybe a darker twinge. He knew what the American flying hero thought of him. He was flying the GeeBee Doolittle had won with two years before.

"It doesn't matter," he said, with the pointed consonants of his North Westphalian accented English more pronounced.

Aaron noticed Lacy pushing through the crowd and he dropped off the platform to grab her up in his arms, lifting her off the ground in a bear hug in his flight overalls and swinging her around.

"Aaron!!" she giggled. "You're making me dizzy!"

He swung her around and around, making airplane sounds until they fell to the ground with Aaron on top of her.

"Crash and burn!" he shouted, joking in his offhand manner and kissed her on the ground.

Aaron was almost two years older than Lacy, already a junior at Princeton when they met. There were a lot of local girls who hung around the school, looking for husband prospects among the prep school boys who would be leaders of the world, but Lacy was different. She was the daughter of an alumni trustee and they were a most unlikely couple. As he kissed her, Lacy grew conscious of the public around them.

"Aaron, people are watching."

"Oh, so very sorry," he said, but wasn't sorry in the least. He enjoyed teasing her, "Quite improper of me." He kissed her again, then hopped up and held out his hand. She took it and he pulled her up to him. He made a show of bowing and kissing her hand.

She snapped her hand away, still giggling, "Stop that. Don't make fun." She pretended at irritation, but in truth she liked it, his foolishness. It was a freedom from the opinion of others that was liberating. She had only known a life where appearances and what others thought were everything.

"I can't help it I'm a lowlife gutter rat from the wrong side of the tracks," he joked, with his cloaked smile that meant he was hardly joking.

"You are not." Now, she was annoyed. She hated when he brought up the issue. She didn't want to think about it. "You're richer than the rest of us put together.

None of that matters to me in the least, anyway." But it did. It always did.

Donovan stepped up to intervene. "It matters to me. You lost me fifty bucks, Brick! And I want to win it back. Five bucks a ball!"

They all called him "Brick". He got the nickname when he first came to Princeton and one of them asked how he got in. He obviously wasn't one of them. No prep school, no history or connections. "How did they let you in?" It was Wilson who had asked, and that had been his answer, a single word with a bemused smile, "Brick." It took them awhile to figure out what he meant.

"You're on, my friend," said Aaron, shouting to the crowd, "Ladies and Gentlemen, I have a challenge from the Irish. He wins, I'm out fifty. I win, Donovan buys the drinks!"

The college boys cheered, and Donovan gulped. Aaron's eyesight and aim were as good as his flying was brash and bold.

A billiard ball rolled across the green felt table and cracked into a set of balls, sending them scattering about like those electron diagrams they studied. Donovan groaned as Aaron made shot after shot, caroms and cue English as if he could see the angles laid out on the table. As he banked three cushions for the last winning shot, Donovan groaned.

A whoop was raised from the club filled with air racers, as well as the college boys, and a few girlfriends who had come a thousand miles by car and train to watch their classmates fly in the races. Several crowded around Donovan, slapping him on the back, almost as if he had won, but it was they who had won drinks from him, as he gamely pulled money out of his pocket.

When he tried to pay, the barman shook his head and wouldn't take his money. Donovan was confused a moment, but Aaron was grinning that Cheshire Cat smirk of his with the dimple depressions at the corners. He knew Donovan didn't have the money he did.

"Get it next time." Aaron whispered in his ear.

Miki noticed the exchange. He tried to hide his own smile from Donovan. He stepped to challenge Aaron.

"No next time," he said. "It is always now. We still play for who pays. One beer."

Aaron grinned, "You're on! You bloody Baron!"

They sat at a table across from each other. They were both as unlikely to be friends as they were to be students at Ivy League Princeton University. Aaron Miller was the only son of a Polish immigrant bricklayer from Brooklyn who had built a construction supply empire in the New York skyscraper building boom which followed 1918 into the Roaring Twenties, while the "Baron" Michael Albrecht von Steuven was a scion of the ancient counts of Westphalia. The German nobility had lost their official recognition after the First World War, their titles abolished in the Weimar constitution, but with a wink and a nod, their heritage incorporated into the name. His father's lineage was only a minor offshoot of the former imperial ruling class, but their lands held the iron ore which had built the railways and cannons of the German industrial revolution and had now sent his son off to an American college. Aaron was a Jew, from his mother's side.

One of the college boys, a rather slight kid with ears that stuck too wide, brought over two large mugs of beer and plunked them down on the table between Aaron and Miki. Robert Wilson was nineteen, the same as Donovan, a year behind Aaron and Miki, and he admired them.

"Forget that old airplane trophy. Here's the competition that really counts."

Lacy watched Aaron and Miki from the far end of the table, their eyes meeting in total focus as they picked up the mugs.

"To Bullard and Carlton," Aaron toasted, "absent friends."

"Absent friends," said Miki. They clinked mugs in solemn memorial. Then, Miki glanced to Lacy, with a wink, "Winner gets the girl."

"You're on, buddy boy!" agreed Aaron.

"Go!' Wilson shouted.

They began to chug them down.

"Go! Go! Go!"

As they drank, a couple of the college boys stood together behind Lacy, linking arms and began to sing the Princeton Fight Song, like a glee club in the midst of the chanting and chugging.

"Fight for Old Nas-sau! Fight for our ivy halls... Fight for Old Nas-sau! Princeton stand proud and tall... Harvard and Yale will turn their tails when we fight for Old Nas-sau!!"

Aaron gulped down the last of the mug and slammed it on the table. Miki slammed his down a second later. The college boys slapped Aaron on the back.

Miki nodded in honored submission, "Two victories, Aaron. I bow my head." To add to the ceremony, he stood, wavering just a little drunk, bowed, and clicked his heels together.

"Next year, buddy. Next year!"

Suddenly, a very gruff and beefy mechanic bulled forward through the crowd to Miki, pressing close with beer breath and hate in his eyes. He was Jim Bullard's crew chief, from Cincinnati.

"Hey, Red Baron!" he shouted, challenging. He too was a little drunk. "Von Hindenburg or whatever your name is! Why don't you go back where you came from?!"

Miki looked to the man, calm, taking things in stride. He faced him square on but did his best to offer a smile.

"Forgive me, sir, if my name offends you. Perhaps you will allow me to buy you a beer."

"Lousy goddam Hinnie!" The mechanic would not be mollified. "My old man was killed in '18 at the Marne by some heel-snapping jackboot Prussian scum! I wouldn't let you by me a piss!"

Miki maintained his even temper. He always did. It was one of his knacks for survival. "My friend, I was three years old in 1918. But you have my apologies anyway for your father. And I am happy to say that I am not Prussian, but Westphalian by birth and a German by nationality."

"I don't give a goddamn what variety of Wiener Schnitzel you are, Heinrich... still smell like Kraut puke to me!" The mechanic hauled back and threw a telegraphed fist which Miki easily managed to dodge.

Aaron was up from his chair in a flash, flying across the table and jumping the mechanic to defend his friend.

They brawled about the club room, flinging into tables, knocking pictures of past airplanes and fliers off the walls. The local mechanic with two inches in height on the kid from Brooklyn flung ham fists, while Aaron returned boxing trained body shots.

"Aaron!!" Lacy shouted, worried for him. "Somebody stop this!"

Donovan leaned close to her with a grin, "Let him work off some steam."

Lacy pleaded to Miki, "Michael."

With a sigh, he nodded to her, "I am a pacifist, you know. But..." Called to duty, he picked up an empty beer mug and carried it to the bar. While Aaron and the mechanic continued their fighting, rolling on the floor and flinging wild punches, Miki ran the beer tap, filling the mug.

He carried it over to where Aaron had the mechanic on his back on the floor.

"This one's on me, my friend," he said, then poured the beer onto the mechanic's face, into his open mouth, gasping for breath until he almost drowned.

When the mechanic was subdued, coughing up beer, Aaron got off of him. Miki now picked up a wooden captain's bar chair. He set it on top of the mechanic, trapping him between the legs and sat on it, holding the man to the floor. While the mechanic struggled, Miki raised the mug and sang with bemused gusto, "Fight for Old Nas-sau! Fight for our ivy halls..."

The college boys joined him, "Fight for Old Nas-sau! Princeton stand proud and tall..."

Aaron, Donovan, Wilson, and even Lacy joined in, "Harvard and Yale will turn their tails when we fight for Old Nas-sau!!"

The Packard cruised along the highway through the western Pennsylvania hills, its powerful twelve cylinder engine pulling it along. The top was down and Lacy was at the wheel. The steering wheel was large in her hands and the heavy machine felt like it had its own will as she handled it around the bends. She was more used to the Lincoln Le Baron roadster from the family garage, but it wouldn't have fit them all. She would have let one of the boys drive, but she had promised her father she would be responsible, and the boys could be, well, boys. And her younger brother, Edward, who had tagged along as chaperone, didn't have a license yet.

Miki sat in front, leaning on the door, letting the wind tousle his hair and blow in his face. Lacy glanced over at him a moment. She thought he looked like a big puppy dog. Donovan sat between them. Eddie was in the back, squeezed between Anderson and Wilson. The college boys kept pinching young Eddie between them, which nettled him to no end.

"Would you leave him alone," Lacy had to scold in the open air. She could see her little brother squirming. They were already halfway, but it would be a long drive back.

A distance behind them, a stake truck carried Miki's GeeBee Racer with its little wings detached. It came in and out of view in the mirrors as the car wound through the low green dales. Miki had been talking about how he would have to find a buyer for it. How the plane was two seasons old now, and he would have to hire a designer and get a sponsor for something new, but Lacy wasn't listening closely.

Miki looked at the speedometer. Lacy was driving at a sensible forty-eight miles an hour.

"Faster! Faster!" he said, teasing her.

"I'm going fast enough," she answered. She had promised her father she wouldn't push the motor over fifty, knowing full well it could break a hundred.

"Turtles go faster," added Donovan. "We should be back to New Jersey by October!"

As the car topped a rise, they could see the smoke stacks in the distance toward King of Prussia and Philadelphia.

"Aren't your father's mills here?" Miki asked, interested.

"Farther on, I think," Lacy said. "They're around Scranton."

"Didn't we see a sign for Scranton back a few miles?" Donovan asked. He was teasing.

"Scranton isn't anywhere near here," Lacy said, hiding a little annoyance. They had been joking about her behind the wheel ever since they left.

She shrugged, "I don't pay much attention to dad's businesses. He has accountants for that. And lawyers. And so on and so on. He had to close two plants after the crash in '29."

"Is he still planning to go over to Europe?" Miki asked. "To Essen?"

"Yep. In a couple of months, I think." She knew it was supposed to be a big trip, with several executives going. They were taking the Normandie, which had just broken the Atlantic crossing speed record.

"My father is looking very much forward to meeting him."

"And I think daddy is looking very much forward to signing that contract!" She glanced over to Miki, grinning with a wry amused twinkle.

Suddenly, they were overtaken by the roar of an airplane engine overhead, as if from nowhere. They all looked up as Aaron's Ryan zoomed past them, dropping low over the road ahead, almost as if it was going to land.

18

An oncoming truck in the opposite lane almost had to swerve off the road, but the sleek plane pulled up in time and rose in a sharp bank around.

"I think we are under attack," said Miki, laughing.

Lacy didn't find it so funny.

They waved as the plane zoomed past them the opposite way, then arced around, swooping over the tree tops cleared back from road's edge.

Flying along the road in his plane's open cockpit, Aaron throttled back so that he could pace the car below. They had left well before him and he wasn't sure if could catch them, or even find them, but he had. He thought Miki was the practical one, shipping his plane back. Finding a landing strip and a mechanic between Cleveland and Lawrenceville would have been tricky if there was a problem, but the Ryan was more reliable over distance, anyway.

Aaron looked over the wing, down at the car. He could see Miki and Lacy, with Donovan between them.

Miki could look up to see Aaron's plane at not more than three hundred feet, following them. The plane's shadow paced them evenly on the roadside vegetation in the late, low hazy sun. He knew Aaron was watching them. He deliberately reached over to touch Lacy's shoulder.

"Wave," he said.

"I did."

"Do it again." Miki made a point of keeping his hand on her shoulder. Lacy turned partially to make a big wave of her arm toward the plane. Miki waved, too, but kept his hand on her arm.

Aaron saw them waving from the car below, but what he mostly noticed was Miki touching her. He suddenly pushed the throttle forward. The plane nosed into a low dive, its engine roaring into a whine.

"What's he doing?" Lacy asked.

"Head down!" warned Miki. He knew what was coming.

The plane dove for the car as if it were an angry hornet, roaring low just over the top, making Lacy almost lose control. They all ducked by instinct. The plane surely missed them by fifty feet, but it felt like inches with the roar of the engine and the rush of air vortex from the wings. Then, as it passed over, Aaron pulled up into a loop, rising high into the sky and disappeared into a cloud.

The passengers in the car looked around, but the plane was gone.

Miki laughed.

Lacy was surprised and a little shaken, "What was that about?"

Miki took his hand off her arm and looked out to the passing scenery with a private smile. "Nothing," he said casually, but secretly very pleased.

Aaron flew the Ryan onward through the puffy clouds over the fields and hills of Pennsylvania. He soared lazily, totally free in the air. He thought about how he might nettle Miki when they were all back home. He would come up with something, but it was hard to stay mad or think of revenge while soaring like an eagle on silver wings.

~~~

CHAPTER TWO

Princeton

Early morning mist clung to the glassy flat surface of the narrows of Lake Carnegie where it formed from the dam of Millstone Creek and cradled the university campus just off its shore. The calm mirror of the water was sliced by the prows of two four-man rowing sculls, as two Coxswains called out.

"Stroke! Stroke!"

The two boats glided through the water as the rowers pulled, the prows shoving forward in surging thrusts as the oars dipped and rose again, sweeping forward, and dipped once again with rhythmic precision.

In one of the sculls, Aaron and Donovan were rowing in second and third position. Wilson was Coxswain, calling the count.

"Come on fellas, put your backs into it. Stroke. And no more brew for you, Miller. Now, stroke…"

The boys pulled on the oars, sliding back and forward on the seats, pumping legs and pulling arms.

On the bank, where it sloped to the edge forming the viewing green, Lacy was with some other girls, gathered to watch the boys in the shells. She sat on a blanket on the dewy grass with two friends, Charlotte Revine and Darlene Clemons. Charlotte was a bit older, twenty-one already. Lacy had known her since they were girls at prep, but Charlotte had been two years ahead. Their fathers knew each other from the school, both illustrious alumni, but Charlotte's father had fared badly in the crash. She had kept up pretenses but was actually working in a store part-time. Darlene was Lacy's age, just turned nineteen. She was Wilson's girlfriend. They had met at some community Daughters of the Revolution social event in Cranbury. She was more East Windsor, but they had gotten to know and accept her.

As the boats passed, Charlotte stood up from the blanket and shouted out to them, cupping her hand to her mouth.

"Come on, Donovan! Think of me between those legs! Stroke, baby, stroke!"

The other girls laughed, looking around, embarrassed. Charlotte had a wild streak.

"Charlotte!?" Darlene scolded.

Donovan looked over, his freckled pale face flushing a little red.

"Concentration, Donovan..." Wilson scolded, trying to keep his smile from breaking into a laugh. He looked over to the girls and waved. Darlene waved back and the boats kept rowing on.

"So, have you made up your mind, yet?" Darlene turned to Lacy.

"About what?"

Darlene gave Charlotte one of those "who's she kidding" looks.

"Aaron or Miki?" It was a question that was obvious to anyone who was paying attention.

"Why should I have to make up my mind?" Lacy shrugged. "I'm not an old maid. I have a whole life ahead of me. I'm a modern woman. Maybe I'll go into business or something."

"Liar," Charlotte scolded now. "You just want the candy from both dishes." She looked out to the strong male bodies pulling the oars. "And I don't blame you. If I had those two honey bees buzzing around me, I'd just take my coffee double sweet."

The other girls giggled in mild shock. Charlotte could be quite naughty. She looked along the shore for the other one.

"Where is Miki? I'd keep my eye on that one before someone steals him. Maybe me."

Lacy knew where Miki was. If she knew anything about him, it was that he lived by his schedule. It was Saturday morning.

Miki stood on the athletic field in white t-shirt and shorts, waiting with concentration, holding his javelin. He didn't care much for rowing. You were just one of a team, and when you crossed the finish line how did you know who won? He took his mark and paced forward, accelerating in three steps to the foot stop, arched and heaved, throwing his weight from the back foot into his shoulders.

The spear arced through the air with the tips wobbling a hair's breadth and jabbed into the grass.

Two coaching assistant markers ran out with a tape. The javelin was stuck in the ground several feet beyond the last mark. One of the markers held up a high sign with a grin.

He shouted back to Miki, "Good enough for a bronze!"

Miki shouted back, "Then, it is not good enough!"

He walked back toward a rack of javelins to take another, picturing in his mind the tips rock steady, envisioning the throw. He must keep the release from back to front on the perfect plane. Then, as he hefted the light shaft, his concentration was broken when he saw Lacy and Aaron walking together across the grass toward him.

"Hey, Miki..." Aaron called out across the field, stopping at the edge of the track's red clay. "Lacy and I are going over to Murphy's for an ice. You coming?"

Miki considered the javelin in his hand, picturing the steady tips.

"You go ahead," he said.

"All work and no play makes Michael a dull boy!" Aaron shouted, teasing.

Miki answered, impervious, calling back, "The Berlin Games are only a year away."

"Only a year?" Aaron winked at Lacy with a grin. "Suit yourself, buddy boy."

Aaron appreciated Miki's dedication. No one he knew had more intense focus, but Aaron believed you had to live a little, too. He gave a wave and slipped his arm around Lacy. They walked away as Miki carried the javelin back to the pit.

Lacy turned to look back to Miki concentrating, still holding Aaron's arm. She stopped at the track to watch him throw. They both watched the spear arc through the air, the tips rock steady in a smooth arc.

"He never lets up, does he?" Lacy mused.

"The machine," Aaron nodded.

Lacy thought about how different these two boys were, but still the same in some odd way.

"You have to admire that in someone. I mean, that's how people achieve something. Isn't it? That kind of drive. That kind of focus." She didn't mean it to be a criticism, but it was.

"I guess so." Aaron shrugged. "Me, I'd rather live a little. What happens, will happen."

It was not that Aaron wasn't focused that nettled her. It was more what he focused on, his casual attitude she knew hid a deeper drive. It was both what had attracted her to him and infuriated her at the same time, like the other parts of him that seemed in conflict. He could be kind and cutting, caring while refusing to ever be sentimental, intensely loyal to his friends and solitary at the same time. It was as if there was something out in the distance that only he could see, something that pulled him forward toward it, racing ahead of anyone close. But he wouldn't reveal himself, or couldn't.

Aaron's Buick roadster drove out on Pennington Road, winding through the thick and jumbled patches of trees interceded between by the little strips of farms carved out by the colonials, now mostly seeded with random grass. Lacy got a kick when he would shove the pedal to the floor when no other cars were in sight, flying around a blind curve where the road would rise and fall again, almost lifting her off the seat.

"Slow down!" she told him, clinging to the door handle, but she didn't really mean it. It was a just a moment's thrill before they would come to the crossing circle where Murphy's Fountain stood at the edge of the dirt lot where the road divided, between the route to Trenton in one direction and toward Pennsylvania and the Delaware Crossing in the other.

Aaron pulled his roadster into the lot with the rubber tires crunching on the loose gravel to park in front of the porch window. The little store and soda fountain had been at the crossroads for almost thirty years now. It was a popular stop along the road and ready hangout for restless college kids. There was probably even a roadside stand at this crossroads when George Washington's troops made the tactical retreat from Trenton in 1777, where General Mercer dealt the British a fleeting defeat at Princeton, getting the county around them named for himself.

Aaron and Lacy sat at a small table in the front of the store, at the window with a view of the passing road. Lacy had been thinking about something all the way since leaving Miki at the athletic field. She had been thinking about what Aaron said.

"Don't you have a goal, Aaron?" she asked. "Something you really want to do with your life."

"Do I really need one?" he answered, a little nettled. He hated defending himself to her. "With the old man's money, I'm pretty much set. I'll finish the degree, then I'll figure out what I'm gonna do." He had wrestled with ideas of what he might do with himself. His plan was for law school after undergrad, but he wasn't convinced that was his future. He didn't like to think about it that much, to tell the truth.

"Do you think you can just count on your dad's money? My father almost lost all of his. But he set goals and worked hard to get us back where we're okay. You can't count on that, anymore. There are people in bread lines, Aaron. I know, I've met them."

Aaron looked at her, thinking she was sweet and just a little naïve. Her father sat on the board of three companies, the majority stockholder in two of them, in coal and steel. The depression was all around them. Ok, maybe it was not the towers of inflated wealth of the twenties when profits from the post-war boom had built fortunes, which then collapsed again in the bust of the stock market, but they were much more than "okay".

"You're very noble and compassionate, Lacy. And that's wonderful. I love that about you." he told her, reassuringly. "I don't intend to be completely useless, like a lot of the upper crust gentry boy-oes in the eating clubs, with their lives all laid out for them. I mean, I want to make my mark. Do something special. Maybe I'll do an around-the-world flight or something."

"That's just a hobby, Aaron," she said, exasperated. "All you seem to have are hobbies. Nothing really ever seems to matter to you." But it was more than just his flippant attitude. "Am I just another hobby?"

He took her hands in his across the table.

"You are my life's work, Lacy. You're my goal. My dream." He kissed her and she closed her eyes and let herself sink into the feeling.

The other patrons at the fountain tables stared at the young couple kissing. A mother turned her child's curious face away from the sight. Aaron and Lacy finally noticed the staring eyes. They would move on to their favorite spot.

Aaron's roadster was parked on the road by the small stone bridge where it crossed the narrow stream of the Jacob's Creek which fed in a long winding stream to the Delaware.

Aaron and Lacy lay on a blanket in the tall grass near the stream edge where you couldn't see from the road, blocked by a thicket of Birch trees and Hackberry bushes. They kissed, deeply, sampling the sweet taste of each other, until the need turned to hands unbuttoning buttons. Aaron slipped his hand underneath Lacy's dress hem along her leg to her underwear, slipping his fingers into the band, starting to pull.

"Aaron, stop. Stop!" she said, trying to really mean it.

Aaron was on autopilot. He rolled on top of her, his fingers feeling inside her. She breathed gasps at the feeling and wanted him, but knew it was up to her. They were such an unlikely couple, so different, but there was something about him that filled her with a flush every moment they were not together.

She planted both hands on his shoulders and pushed, like peeling a burr seed from a cotton sweater. She got up from the blanket and shoved away, running down to the stream, pulling her clothes back together.

Aaron rolled on his back, looking up at the sky. Little puffy clouds were drifting over. He estimated they were about a thousand, six hundred feet. He could imagine them from above, looking down. After staring awhile he called to her without looking, while she straightened her bra.

"Are you alright?" he asked.

She finished rebuttoning her blouse, staring at the water in the stream, watching it carry little leaves through random swirls of current.

"You know I want to, Aaron. I really do. But I'm not like Charlotte."

Aaron smiled to himself, turning to look away so she wouldn't see his face. He knew she could read it from there. He had had Charlotte, and it was a pleasant memory. It came to him from time to time, but it was only the once.

"I wouldn't want you to be like Charlotte," he called over. "If I wanted that..." he rose on his arm looking over to her, "I'd be here with her. The Irish sure has his hands full there! Poor bastard."

"Quiet!" she scolded. Charlotte was her friend and she didn't want to think about how she might treat Donovan. She changed the subject.

"My parents have invited some people over for dinner on Thursday next. Do you want to come? They've asked Miki over."

Aaron stood up from the weedy grass and gathered the blanket, folding it in a tight wad of no particular order. He knew the meaning of the invitation.

"Well, if they've invited Miki, I guess I'd better be there."

Lacy came to him and brushed the errant grass from his shirt. "It's not a competition, Aaron."

"Isn't it?"

"Why do you say that? My dad wants to do business with Miki's father. It's natural he should want to get to know Miki."

"Natural? Is it?"

"Don't repeat what I say. Why do you do that?"

"Lacy, you know exactly what your father thinks of me. Your family. If you don't think this is a competition, and I'm the one with the handicap, someone hasn't been paying attention."

"Oh, Aaron," she said, exasperated. Not because he wasn't right, but because she didn't want to think about it. She hated being painted with the same brush as her parents.

"Well, it isn't up to them," she insisted, intending to be taken seriously, in control of her own destiny, but maybe just a little petulant. "If you think you need to win a prize, maybe it's me you have to impress."

She turned from him and marched up to the car at the roadside. Aaron stood by the creek, listening to the gurgles of the water as it flowed through the grass and pebbles, watching her. He tried to remind himself she was three years younger than he was. She was sweet and caring, but boy, she could turn on the attitude when she wanted.

Aaron drove in his roadster out toward Mt. Rose, following the curving road past the estates, counting the gates. He had been to the house once before and tried to remember the entrance. He slowed at the gated drive to the Dunbrough grounds. The gate was open and it looked like a few extra cars were parked on the paving stone drive in front of the Colonial style mansion.

Aaron pulled in and parked behind someone's Hudson. He hoped out and grabbed the bottle of wine and flowers from the seat.

The Dunbrough house was built well after the colonial days, in the boom of the 1880s when the Dunbroughs made their wealth from a modest collection of pioneer family homesteads in the Pennsylvania hills, with what they thought were worthless mineral rights. That was until Harris Dunbrough had an idea for a new coke production furnace in 1861, just in time for the Civil War's call for cannons. The family moved to Princeton when the first Dunbrough was admitted to the Ivy League college.

Aaron rang the door chime and waited while a series of bells echoed inside, like a church.

Irene Dunbrough opened the door herself, the maid must have been occupied with the guests. The pleasant smile, intended to greet a friend, fell from her face like a drawing shade when she saw it was Aaron with his flower bouquet in one hand and wine bottle resting in the crook of his arm. It was obvious that Lacy's mother was not pleased to see him.

"Hello, Aaron," she said politely, without opening the door any wider.

"Mrs. Dunbrough," he said, waiting a moment for further response. There was none. Irene's face was a desert. "Lacy invited me."

"Yes. So she informed me." She finally held the door open for him to enter. He offered the flowers to her. She didn't take them, her manner gracious but cool. "Very lovely," was all she would say.

The guests were gathered at the large table in the dining room. It was still afternoon, with the sunlight dappling through the trees across the lawn outside the French windows, but the chandelier was lit over the silver and crystal tableware. Miki sat next to Lacy while Aaron seemed the odd man out, his place apparently added between Lacy's father and the wife of one of the businessmen friends who was down visiting from New York. The table had been rather silent for several minutes when Mrs. Dunbrough turned to Miki. He had been particularly quiet, even while the guests had been trying not to stare at him, with his handsome blue eyes and square jaw.

"Michael, tell us how you started flying," Irene asked with encouragement.

"I joined a Glider Sports Club when I was eleven," Miki spoke easily in his clipped accent. He had learned English beginning at nine years old and perfected it in two years at boarding school in England. "My father was against it. He wanted me to become an engineer. To join the business, I'm sure. But manufacturing is not something which interests me a great deal." He paused to glance around the table with an apologetic nod, seasoned with a wry irony. "My pardons to the company."

"That's alright, son," said a guest, a man in his forties named Wilkerson, tapping his cigarette in the crystal ash dish, "my boy doesn't think much of his old man's business either. But after he's done sowing his oats, I know exactly where he'll be. How did you find your way up here to Old Nassau?"

Miki had told the story many times. What was he, a German of noble background, doing at an American Ivy League college?

"The whole of the Rhineland had been demilitarized since the war. Many huge numbers were out of work." He saw the pictures in his mind whenever he told the story. "I remember people begging along the road home from school. Many of our tenants could not pay the rents. I think my father invented some unnecessary work around the factory, since it was for all purposes closed. But when there were riots in Essen and Cologne, my father sent me here to finish school away from the troubles. Some of the family had come in the migration of the seventeen-hundred and forties."

"Before the Revolution?" asked one of the wives, as if that was an important detail.

"Yes," said Miki.

"It does seem unfair to keep these restrictive measures on your country, Baron." Wilkerson leaned forward to make his point. "People need jobs to keep them from getting out of hand. That really was the cause of the last troubles, wasn't it?

"I am happy to say I am ignorant of the reasons for the 'Great War'," said Miki demurring, "I am only personally aware of the result. I have not been back to Essen in two years, but there seems to be a concern about the Communists and the Jews."

"A concern?!" Anson Dunbrough spoke up finally, "I just had one of my labor guilds try to organize a strike last fall, passing out Communist literature." He had had little to say until the subject turned to what affected him the most. "I had to bring in the state guard to put a stop to it. The bastards even planted a bomb in the finishing mill."

"A free market has been the backbone of this country," another guest added helpfully, filling out the conversation in familiar territory. "But these socialist policies we're pursuing now, with that man in the White House... Alright, the TVA is generating some projects, but quotas on international trade to Germany, just to placate the British and French because they got their asses kicked without us. But this Hitler fella seems like he's got things moving again. We should be encouraging growth, but we won't even sell them gas for those magnificent dirigibles!"

Aaron listened to the conversation with a growing amusement. He couldn't help himself.

"Hey, Miki," he asked loudly. "I get it about the Communists, the end of civilization as we know it and everything, but what's the problem with Jews about?"

The guests at the table looked at Aaron like he'd just dropped his pants. Miki only smiled at Aaron, like a secret joke between them.

"I'm not sure. I think it is something about their penises," he said.

Miki and Aaron stared at each other, then broke into a raucous laughter. The guests were shocked and dumbfounded. Lacy hit Miki on the shoulder to quiet him, trying to make him behave, but couldn't help snickering herself.

"I'm sorry, Aaron," she said, but couldn't stop from laughing herself.

Irene Dunbrough turned to her guests, feeling the need to explain, "Aaron's mother is Jewish."

The guests all nodded solemnly, very understanding, as if they were acknowledging a deep confession.

"That's the real pity of it," Anson Dunbrough said with intended gravity, "in these tough times, the admission standards at the old school have declined, I'm afraid."

Aaron's laughter stopped. "Yep, they'll just let any mongrel through the door these days. What's happening to that ol' blue blood?" He met Lacy's father's glare with a steady gaze through a forced charming smile, then to the table at large, "See, my father is Catholic. One side blames me for killing Christ, but the other wants to slice my Johnson. I can't pick. But then, I'm Polish, so...you know, I don't get the joke."

The laughing all stopped.

Irene did her best to cut through the silence, "I think we'll serve dessert and coffee in the Great Room."

Aaron, Miki and Lacy sat on the back porch in the evening twilight, lounging on the iron filigree lawn chairs. The family's guests were inside, separated by the glass of the French doors. Miki and Aaron smoked cigars, occasionally unable to help a returning laugh at the exchange at the table.

Lacy was not as amused as they were. She paced between the chairs, stopping to glare at Aaron, crossing her arms and playing with the small childhood scar on her forearm with her finger tip. He could tell the habit when she was upset.

"Why do you have to bait him like that, Aaron?" she demanded. "He can't help that he's tied to some old outdated notion of the old alma mater."

"Oh, is that all it is?" Aaron didn't want to fight, but his blood was rising a bit. "Well, I'm damn glad to know it's not just me he thinks is slug worm immigrant pond scum, damn glad, right-eo! Excuse the hell out of me that my family line can't all be traced back to the Mayflower."

"God, Aaron, you can be so damn arrogant, sometimes! You blame them for the way they think, but maybe it's you who just can't accept who I am."

She hurried off, crying. Aaron sat up, worried. He called after her, "Lacy!" but she disappeared into the house, slamming the door for punctuation.

Miki just sat, calmly and smugly smoking his cigar, happy to be out of the line of fire.

"What did I say?" Aaron asked with a feigned shrug.

Miki casually rolled the cigar in his teeth. "The wrong thing, I think. But it's a second language for me. I am not as eloquent as you."

"So, tell me, smart ass, how come I'm bringing down the standards of the old school, while you, total and complete foreign bastard that you are, don't?"

"It's the title, of course. Baron von Steuven, son of the Count von Steuven. Meaningless in any practical sense, no longer official, a fading appendage from a day long behind us."

"You all think Hitler and that crowd are going to let you have your titles back, don't you?"

Miki shrugged. "He admires the Teutonic knights and Wagner's fat women in armor. It doesn't matter to me. That was all the Second Empire. In our Third Reich, rising from the ashes, my father is just a Promethean industrialist like your father, reborn with his concrete and bricks and buildings, and them..." He gestured inside with a toss of pointed cigar ash, "but I think it is the one symbol which American wealth, for all its power and pretense, cannot buy...and therefore still values. All those American daughters who ran off to marry the English for a few medals."

Aaron admired Miki's attempt to reason his own place in the world, but also thought, for all his pretended denial he was still a product of his history, and maybe a bit foolish. It was a dangerous dismissal.

"You think the new government is going to let your father keep his factories. I thought they were going to be nationalizing."

Miki thought about it, staring at the cigar ember burning down, rolling it in his fingers.

"They need him more than he needs them. Industry is driving the rebirth of the new Germany. And he is a von Steuven." He sat straight in his chair and held up his hand in a laconic heil salute. "He makes the pledge and the little Austrian corporal has the noble class beside him for the pictures. In a few years, it will be my father's class in charge again."

He glanced toward the door where Lacy went, "At least she doesn't care about titles and heritage, or any of that, which I find most charming in her. Very unlike many of the other girls I have met here. And it is perhaps fortunate for me, that I don't know what a Mayflower is, other than perhaps a Geranium."

Lacy stormed through the house from the grounds entry, wanting to avoid her parents and their guests who she knew would judge her every thought, but her mother spotted her hurrying to the stairs to go up to her room. Irene stepped into the hallway, leaving the guests occupied.

"Lacy..."

Lacy hesitated at the foot of the stair balustrade, trying to hide her eyes.

"Is everything alright?" her mother asked.

Lacy kept her face turned, tears welling.

"What's the matter? Is it that boy? Did he say something hurtful?"

Lacy finally looked at her mother, waiting for her to agree with her own prejudices. She looked around at the surroundings of the house, so proper and comfortable, and the guests, all carrying on about their privileged lives while all around them people were starving.

"Why couldn't I have been born in a Polish slum?!" she blurted and ran up the stairs, leaving her mother stunned and confused.

Lacy cried and was angry at herself for it. She lay on her bed in her room, surrounded by the totems of youth, a stuffed rabbit with floppy ears, pictures of movie heart throbs from Photoplay magazine, Clark Gable and Robert Young, but they were now alien things to her. A half-read volume of Nietzsche rested upturned on the night table.

She could hear the voices of Aaron and Miki outside in the yard, laughing together, drifting up, modulated by reflection from the pool surface, but it was Aaron she was thinking of. Why did he make himself so hard to love?

~~~

CHAPTER THREE

Murphy's

The steel scaffolding, like a cage, encased the lower floors of a midtown building under construction. It was what they called a "skyscraper", with the I-beams reaching toward the clouds where it ended like a broken bottle, forty-eight floors above the street, with girders raised by a hoist for the last six floors. A crane high above the ground hauled up huge buckets of concrete to pour the lower floors as the stages of work moved upward.

Heavy trucks with Miller Materials, Inc. painted on the sides backed through the fence gate, the axles weighted down with stone and bricks. Aaron stood next to a shorter, older man, with a trimmed moustache on a thick face under a hard hat and a tailored suit. Karel Miller was fifty-three and still spoke with a thick Polish accent, despite living in New York since he crossed from Gdansk when he was fourteen years old. He stood beside his son and gestured toward the top of the construction.

"From the earth to the sky. That is where we have come," he said with pride.

He tapped his finger on Aaron's shoulder with a hand scared by work, missing two fingers, lost in the vice of a falling pallet of paving stones.

"You, my boy, will rise higher still. I have lived my life for it. When your mother chooses your name, I know she was right. Aaron, the high one, who rises. I like this."

Aaron was uneasy, listening to his father's expectations as they walked through the construction site, picking through the stacked lumber and steel where men labored, covered with dirt and concrete dust. Air hoses and rivet guns hammered from the steel floors above. Aaron knew how lucky he was not to have to be one of them. And even they were luckier than the men who stood out on the street with no work. He tried to imagine himself in a two room flat in a lower eastside tenement with six brothers and sisters, and a laborer father with nothing to his name but the skill of his hands, rising to the man these dust covered workers now looked to, grateful for their employment.

Karel stopped to watch two workers swing the chute from the turning mill case of a concrete truck to fill a massive steel bucket with a ton and a half of fine aggregate mix. He turned to his son.

"When my father stepped from the boat and said his name, Miloszich, and the man at the table, he writes in his book 'Miller', I understand from that moment what is America. It does not matter from where you come or who you are, you can be anything." He dipped his hand into the bucket of wet concrete before being hoisted by the crane. "From the dust of the earth you can build cities. From the tenements of Five Points you can reach the stars. They can call you names and throw stones. It does not matter. Let them fall from your back. You are as good as they. Better. You show them."

He spotted another businessman on the site, Jeffers, the project owner and developer, also in a hard hat and Brooks Brothers, talking with his architect. Karel led Aaron across the site to meet them.

"Mr. Jeffers," he interrupted, introducing, "my son, Aaron."

Jeffers shook Karel's hand, then Aaron's. He looked at the college student, maybe measuring him.

"Is the old man teaching you the business?"

"I think he's trying to indoctrinate me." Aaron joked.

"No!" Karel said as if he was determining his own mind. "Stone and bricks are not for my boy. They only pay for the education. He will be more."

"Well, young man, come look me up when you've got your sheepskin. I'm sure the apple hasn't fallen far from the tree. Karel Miller's the smartest Polack I've ever had the pleasure to know."

Aaron managed an oblique smile, "Thanks."

Karel shook Jeffers hand again and walked away with Aaron. He slapped his son's back and looked up again toward the top of the building.

"It doesn't matter. Falls off the back. You show them."

They picked their way back through the busy site to the street where Karel's driver waited with the car.

"You come to the house at the beach on the weekend?" Karel asked.

"No, I have to catch the train back to the Junction. I have exams."

"Okay. Your mother will not be happy, but she understands. Work hard."

Aaron had lied. He didn't have exams for another six weeks. He was very uncomfortable in his own skin at home, between his father's expectations and his mother's questions about whether he was keeping up with his services. He couldn't tell her that he hadn't stepped a foot in a synagogue since entering Princeton.

As a Presbyterian school, they required attendance every Sunday at Chapel, and if you didn't attend you would have to file a formal dispensation that you were exercising your religion at another location. He had never told his mother that on the school application, on the blank line for 'religion", he had not written Jewish, nor even his father's church, Catholic, but had scratched a fiction, Episcopalian. His father was lapsed and not at all religious, perhaps which had allowed him to fall for a Jewish dressmaker's daughter from Krakow, but Aaron, perhaps in a too clever move by half thought he could escape by picking a faith where he could say he was attending, but the school wouldn't know. It wasn't that he didn't honor his mother's faith, but with his father's disinterest he had drifted into a state of neutrality. He thought he could avoid the question altogether, until fate served him the curve ball. On the one occasion he thought he'd better put in an appearance at the Trinity Church, in case he needed to have a good story, he had met Lacy. Now, he was trapped with a complex narrative he could barely keep straight.

The rowing sculls glided across the calm lake water. Charlotte and Darlene sat on a blanket on the grassy bank in their customary spot, but Lacy was not with them. Aaron could look over from the scull as he pulled his oar, to see that she was absent. It was the second practice she had missed and she would not come to the phone when he tried to call her.

It wasn't for two weeks until he spotted her with Charlotte and Darlene, taking their shortcut across the campus. He caught up to them at the arch of Foulke Hall.

"Lacy?!" he called out to her from the top of the steps. She stopped for an instant at hearing his voice, but kept walking. Aaron trotted down the steps, trying not to seem too eager.

"Lacy..." he called again. Finally she stopped with the other girls, turning back to face him, taking a deep breath. She had made a decision.

"Are you trying to punish me, or something?" he asked, trying to keep any anger out of his voice.

"No. I just have things to do. I have my own life, Aaron. The world doesn't revolve around you."

He didn't want to respond, afraid he might make it worse. The silence was heavy.

Charlotte helpfully interrupted, "She's applying to Smith, our thoroughly modern Lacy."

"Smith?!" Aaron reacted in surprise, flavored with a hint of amused derision. "Not satisfied with being a snob, you want to be a radical snob?"

She had mentioned going on to school, but it seemed as much about escape from home and her life of bourgeois privilege as anything else. He had meant it to be an acknowledgment of her more noble goals, but it didn't come out that way. It now just seemed to be an escape from him.

Lacy clearly seethed at the remark, glaring at him in dead silence a moment, and then spun on her heel to walk away.

"Lacy, it was a joke!"

She stopped a moment, but didn't look back, answering him with what she intended as maturity. They were adults now, after all.

"I'm starting to find your jokes quite tedious, Mr. Miller." She stole brief a look at him, thinking it might be her last, then hurried away.

"Lacy!" he called after her again, but it was hopeless. He just stood on the walk, repeating with a snide imitation, "Quite tedious, Mr. Miller."

Charlotte and Darlene just observed him patiently. They had been party to Lacy's conflicted ramblings for two weeks.

"She's nineteen next week." Charlotte commented helpfully. "It's the sophisticated stage. I find your jokes quite hilarious, myself, Mr. Miller." Charlotte was obviously still attracted to him. They had had the one intimate occasion, but she did not feel the weight of permanence in regard to sex which filled Lacy's traditional romantic mind. She was much more practical, or at least she thought so.

"What's the matter with Lacy?" It was Donovan's voice as he trotted down the steps to them.

Charlotte stepped back from Aaron and slipped her arm through Donovan's.

"Much too complex for the simple male mind, dear," she said as she pulled him a little closer, not wanting him to lose the train of thought of their relationship. "C'mon, buy me some ice cream. Or a diamond. I'm not sure what I'm in the mood for."

Donovan allowed himself to be pulled along in the direction of the corner drug store on Stockton Street where they often met off-campus. Darlene tagged along with them, but Aaron held back, watching Charlotte with Donovan, wondering if he knew.

"Coming?" Charlotte called back, an inviting smile, but a signal that their secret was safe.

"Go ahead," Aaron called back.

"Suit yourself." Charlotte winked and continued on, pulling Donovan with her, completely under her control.

Aaron raced his Buick along the Pennington road at top speed. He pushed the pedal to the floor, burning out his frustration with the air and gasoline mixture being pulled into the eight cylinders. He enjoyed the wind in his hair. It wasn't flying, but close, as the trees whipped past in a blur of green and bright specks of sunlight. The car floated with a lurch as it lifted over the rises and then bottomed again on the grade. On the floor by his feet, three empty beer bottles rolled with a clinking clank from one side to the other with each bend.

As the car raced past Murphy's soda shop, Aaron's blurry vision could make out two familiar forms visible at the table by the window. He stabbed for the brake pedal. His foot missed it the first time, but then found it. The roadster's brakes smoked as the car skidded to a near stop and snapped in a spinning turn in the middle of the pavement.

Miki and Lacy looked up from their conversation at the sound of squealing rubber. They looked out on the road to see Aaron's Buick roaring back on the road and careening into the parking area, skidding to a stop in the gravel. One of the beer bottles tumbled out of the door as Aaron pushed it open with his foot and stepped out of the driver's seat.

Miki stood up from the table as Aaron pushed in the door. Miki was ready for a fight, but Aaron just grinned that big sloppy little boy smile he could muster as if nothing is wrong.

"Hi. I was just passing by and thought I'd stop for a cool one."

Lacy was calm. "It looks like you've had a couple already. We're kind of in the middle of something, Aaron."

"So I could see. Mind if I join?"

Lacy thought about the other customers, some families with children. She wanted to be honest with him.

"Come outside for a minute." She started for the door, but Aaron didn't move.

"We're not a team anymore?" Aaron just stood, staring at them. Lacy pushed past him and went outside, swinging open the screen door with a creek of the spring hinges. Aaron still held Miki's eyes in an intense glare that was half question and half challenge. Finally, he shoved out the squeaking door to where Lacy waited on the walk by the window, nervously playing her finger on her arm.

"Is there something you want to tell me that's not fit for the kids? Cuss me out?" he asked with an edge of sarcasm meant to blunt the coming blow. "Come on, Lace, here I am. Go ahead and tell me what an arrogant, unfocused, near-do-well slum rat I am."

"Aaron..." She wanted not to tell him at all, but it was a big bright road sign that couldn't be gotten around, "Miki has asked me to marry him."

Aaron stood frozen to the spot. He looked through the window to Miki, still inside, standing by the table looking out at him, with no revealing expression. Suddenly, Aaron turned and started for the door to go inside.

Lacy grabbed him. "Aaron, don't!"

He stopped again and spun back. His legs were wobbly, but his mind focusing from the cob webs for a crystal moment.

"So, what did you say?"

"I haven't said anything, yet. I'm as surprised as you are."

He tried to calculate permutations of the future in his mind, choices to be made, decisions, but they were just a bit foggy.

"Is that what you want? You want to get married?"

"I want someone to love me for who I am. All that I am."

She said it as honestly and forthright as she could manage. She had never been the sort of girl who imagined princes and bouquets. Her visions had been more of being something in the world, but when it came to it she wanted to be loved.

"Well, if getting married means all that to you. I'll marry you." He blurted it, really meaning it, but as if the idea had just appeared from nowhere.

"Wow, Aaron, that's the most romantic proposal I've heard in a long time."

"What? In the last hour? Jesus, this has got to be the most romantic spot in the world!" He gestured around the porch walk with its dime candy machine and mechanical rocking horse with rusting paint.

"Aaron, please. Don't get upset. Don't make a scene. I'm going to tell him I'll think about it." She hated finding herself in this moment. She loved Aaron. She believed he cared about her, but he could be maddening sometimes, and everything else.

Aaron stared at her another second, taking in her features as if studying a map, the blue eyes with flecks of iridescent green, the nose bridge just a little too wide, the little scar which cut a tiny gap into the golden stands of a her left eyebrow, the imperfection of perfection, he thought. Then, he threw open the squeaking door, going inside.

The screen door slammed with a bang behind him as Aaron stepped just inside the door, looking across at Miki, challenging, ready to fight, but feeling the eyes of the mothers and children all staring at him. Finally, he turned again without a word, and stormed out.

Lacy came back inside to Miki. She didn't know what to say. She didn't really know what she felt at that moment. She didn't want to hurt either of them. Maybe she didn't have to decide at all. She could put it off and go on to school.

Miki didn't say anything either, as they both watched together out the window as Aaron jumped back into his roadster and fishtailed out of the lot.

Aaron drove like a madman to the airstrip at Lawrenceville. His Buick tore across the grass runway, cutting in front of a Stearman biplane accelerating to takeoff. The Stearman pulled hard up into the air, just missing the car, almost stalling as the pilot shook his fist at the wild driver.

Aaron skidded to a stop in front of one of the corrugated metal hangar sheds. He pushed open the door of the Buick and almost fell out to the ground. He caught himself and leaned against the door to drain the last of the beer from a bottle, tossing it into the back seat with the empties, clinking with them like a gathered row of soldiers ready for inspection.

Staggering to the hangar, he slid back the door, revealing his racing Ryan inside. He didn't know exactly what he was going to do, but knew he needed to make a point, and he was sure that whatever it was would come to him.

The old town of Princeton was rather quiet on Sunday afternoons. The shops were mostly closed, but people strolled along Nassau Street after church and students wandered in small clumps. The sound of a roaring engine was heard above, growing louder, pitching higher.

Pedestrians looked up, searching for the sound. They had never actually seen an airplane over the town. They occasionally flew along the river between Trenton and Philadelphia and followed the main highway of Route 1, but not over the school.

The silver of the Ryan's aluminum glinted in the sun, piercing the hanging clouds. It suddenly dove strait out of the sky as if it would crash, then pulled out of the dive to level and roared right down Nassau Street, its wheels only ten feet off the ground just missing cars and rising to hop over telephone wires.

The Princetonians out for a quiet stroll ran for cover behind trees and into doorways, coming out again in shocked wonder as the plane rose again into the sky, up and up, and then rolled on its back, over again as if it would fall, but rolled once again into a dive.

The rugby team was practicing on Bedford Field, next to the new stadium, as the Ryan appeared from the sky roaring into a dive across the field, the wheels just inches from the grass as if it might land. The players scattered from the screaming missile and hugged the ground as the plane zoomed past, its wings wobbling on the edge of control.

Miki had driven Lacy back home, with few words between them. She had only told him she needed to think about his proposal, but didn't want to say anything else that she couldn't take back. All the ride home, she just kept seeing in her mind the look in Aaron's eyes, standing on that porch.

Miki's Nash pulled just into the drive beyond the gate. Lacy wanted to walk to the house. She needed to think. Miki insisted on stepping out and walking part of the way. He wanted to reassure her that his offer was more than just the practical arguments for making it. Then, before he could say anything, walking up the driveway, they heard the sound of the Ryan engine.

Aaron flew just beneath the strata of low clouds, feeling like he could reach his hand out of the cockpit and scoop the misty moisture droplets. He wasn't sure if he could pick the Dunbrough house out from the others. From above they all looked alike, boxes on expanses of green lawn cut from the surrounding thick trees, with winding drives. Then, he had spotted Miki's Nash on the curve of Brooks Bend. His vision was sharp enough to pick out the two-tone colors of the fender trim and the side vents in the hood from five hundred feet, curving along the road, appearing briefly through the tree canopy. If only his mind were as clear as his vision. He wasn't sure what he had come for, it was in a fog. He was drunk and shouldn't be flying, he knew that. Lacy! That was it. He had come out to see Lacy, but he would have to get lower to see her better. He pushed the stick.

Miki searched the sky for the sound as the engine pitched, telltale of the plane arcing into a dive. He spotted it, a silver spec against the clouds, growing larger as it headed toward them.

"Oh, God, it's Aaron!" Lacy could see it, too.

Miki pushed Lacy back behind the car, and stepped into the middle of the drive, standing out so Aaron could see him.

Aaron could pick out Miki in the drive, in the open space between the trees. He thought he should say hello to his friend. Former friend, anyway. He aimed the stick straight for him. He dove closer and closer, with the earth rushing to meet the nose of the plane, the prop blur flashing between him and his target. The trees and cars grew from toy dots to real life as they rushed toward him. He pulled back just over the gate.

The plane leveled over the drive, the tilting wingtips just missing the overhanging branches, heading straight for the Nash and Miki standing in front of it, then zoomed just over Miki's head and pulled up with a roar of the engine. The plane just missed the roof of the house, rising back up into the sky.

Lacy stepped out from behind the car, glaring furiously. He could be so maddening sometimes.

"I'll kill him!" she said, watching the plane rising away, getting smaller as it gained altitude.

"If he doesn't kill himself," Miki said, and walked out further into the road clearing to watch his friend. He was worried. He knew Aaron was good and lucky, but luck can only last so long if you tempt it. Lacy came with him and they watched as the plane banked over into a turn, circling around for another pass.

Aaron held the stick over, feeling the gravity in the turn, his eyes fixed on the trees and drives below, keeping his target in sight as his fixed point. He found the house across the open green field lined with trees. His vision seemed to blur for a moment. He blinked and wiped his eyes with his free hand, trying to focus. His eyes were moist and he didn't know why. He wasn't wearing goggles. He had forgotten them. He looked around the cockpit to find them as the plane nosed over. He was sure that's why his eyes were wet, the wind. He blinked again, trying to focus. He would find his goggles in a minute. Just now he needed to concentrate as the trees were rushing toward him. What was he doing? He couldn't quite remember. Was he landing? He laughed. He wasn't quite sure where he was. Maybe he was supposed to land.

Lacy and Miki watched the plane dive around, swooping low over the trees and heading straight for them again. Then the plane wobbled an instant, dropping too low before it cleared the trees at the edge of the field across the road. The right wing hit a tree branch. The wing sheered away, ripped by the force.

The plane smashed into the ground, cartwheeling, throwing up earth and grass, mixed with metal in a maelstrom of havoc, with the sickening sound of crunching and folding aluminum.

Lacy and Miki could only watch helpless as Aaron's machine, once a definable shape, tumbled and rolled across the grassy field, snapping into twisted wreckage, until it finally came to rest in a cloud of dirt.

Lacy ran across the field. Miki ran after her, trying at first to keep her back from whatever they might find, but then racing ahead to get to the wreckage.

Surrounded by barely identifiable debris, they frantically searched around where the cockpit used to be.

"Aaron! Oh, God, Aaron!" Lacy called out as she pulled at bits of metal, cutting her hands. She didn't care, but only looked desperately for some sign.

Miki searched the wreckage, calculating in his mind where the force of the strike would have carried the fuselage and its occupant. What angle was the machine falling and how fast it was traveling would determine the crash debris pattern. He thought again to pull Lacy away before she found body parts.

It was then, a few yards away, a dirt covered form rose from the grass. It was Aaron. He tried to sit up, but he fell back to the grass. The earth still seemed to be moving to him and he was numb.

Lacy saw him first. She gasped in shock and relief and ran toward him. Miki followed right behind. When they got to him, Aaron was lying on the grass looking up at the sky. He seemed to be in one piece, except for some blood from a small cut on his forehead and covered in globs of dirt.

As they stood over him, he could see Lacy's concerned face leaning over and Miki standing behind her. For some reason he thought it was funny and he giggled.

"I fall down, go boom!"

Lacy could just stare at him a moment, grateful he was alive and obviously not so badly hurt, but she was angry, too.

"Goddamn you, Aaron!" She thought of all the things that made her mad about him and it seemed an appropriate time to tell him.

"You arrogant, selfish, reckless, uncaring son-of-a-bitch! You scared me to death! You son-of-a-bitch!" She kicked him in the side, just to see if he was listening. Aaron just giggled again and winced in pain at the same time.

"Ow!"

Miki pulled Lacy away, before she could do real damage. Aaron could have a spine injury or internal wounds. She tried to kick at him again, just in half effort, then, stepped away, crying. She couldn't look at him any longer. She turned away and walked across the field, sobbing.

Miki knelt by Aaron. His legs were moving. He tried to sit up again, but grimaced in pain, and lay back again. Miki felt his left side. Aaron winced.

"A broken rib, I think. Hopefully it hasn't punctured anything," he said, reassuring, mostly himself.

Aaron looked at his friend, grateful for his concern. He still couldn't remember if he was trying to land, and where his goggles had got to. He smiled, then asked in his half-conscious still drunken delirium about what was important, "Hey, Mick? How's my plane?"

~~~

CHAPTER FOUR

Luigi's

Donovan, Wilson and Anderson waited in the hall outside the Academic Standards office of Nassau Hall. Aaron had been inside with the review board for over an hour. They joked in gallows jest if he might have any skin left when they were done flaying him.

The door finally opened and Aaron pushed out, carefully closing it behind himself, not for any particular deference for the door, but for the bandages underneath his shirt wound tight to hold his rib in place. Any quick movement would send a sharp stab of pain from his hip to his shoulder, but he thought himself lucky, given the alternative.

"Well?" Donovan asked expectantly, hoping for the best.

"I'm expelled." The interrogation had gone as badly as they had feared, but the result was not cataclysmic. "For the semester. I can reapply next year."

"That's a bit rough," Donovan was sympathetic, but still a bit annoyed. "They couldn't cut you some slack? We all stood up for you."

"They had a letter from the Alumni Association. Lacy's dad, I don't doubt, and his buddies." Aaron tried to hold back his anger and his gloom.

"Crap!" cussed Wilson, "just because you buzzed the athletic field?! Davis drove across the grass last year trying to spin 'I love you, Sheila' in donuts. They didn't expel him! The Olympic trials are a month away. Maybe you can appeal. We'll get a petition."

"What's the use," Aaron said with a futile gloom. It was more than expulsion on his mind. "Forget the Olympics, Wilson. You're better off without me. Or haven't you heard, they don't want any Jews in Berlin."

He stormed off down the hall, leaving them behind.

Wilson looked confused. "What is he talking about?"

"Jesus, Wilson. Get your head out of your ass! Read a goddamn newspaper once in a while." Donovan also stalked off after Aaron, leaving Wilson and Anderson bewildered.

Charlotte was waiting by the arch steps as Aaron and Donovan appeared. She could see the mood on their faces.

"What's the matter?" she asked.

Donovan couldn't help but let a little of his own anger out, "Old 'Brick' here, finally got himself thrown out of school."

"Why? For dive-bombing the Rugby Team?" Charlotte said, trying to add some salve. "They could use a little shaking up. Actually, I think they should make it part of the game. It would get a few tushes in the stands, anyway."

"Really, for lowering the admission standards of the old alma mater. They found out about my mother's Jewish background."

"That's hooey! They let the Irish in." Charlotte joked, and nudged Donovan.

"Thanks a lot," he grunted, running his fingers through his red mat of hair, "I didn't know it showed." He turned serious, "Can they really be that snickety about it? There are Jews at school. It's not a restriction."

"They made a big case out of it. Said I lied on my application about my religion. Because it's my mother, that makes me Jewish. It doesn't really matter what I choose. If I reapply, I have to change it."

"Bastards. You're right, then," Donovan nodded, "it was Lacy's dad who wrote the letter. They're the ones who knew, right?"

"Is that so bad?" Charlotte asked, trying to be helpful. "You're just going to the Trinity to be close to Lacy. And well...you pretty much put the scotch on that yourself."

"It's not that," Aaron was solemn. He didn't really care about religion that much. His was in the clouds. But it mattered to others. "If I apply to the school as a Jew, I'm on the rowing team as a Jew."

"Oh." Charlotte got it. "Berlin. Do you really think they're going to restrict who participates? I've been hearing a lot of people saying we should boycott."

"Yeah, maybe we wouldn't qualify anyway," Aaron shrugged, but that was not all. "If I graduate as a Jew, that's who I am, forever."

Donovan stared at him, "Well, that does it then. You're screwed. You'll have to be a lawyer!"

Charlotte chimed, mischievously, breaking the gloom, "C'mon, let's go over to the Nassau Club, get drunk and piss all over the old school ties!"

Aaron laughed. He enjoyed her streak of irreverence for all things proper. "You're a wild child, Charlotte. Are you sure you're not a man under all that tulle?"

"I don't know," she smirked. "Why don't you ask bashful 'Red'."

Donovan looked uncomfortable whenever Charlotte got close to talking about sex.

Aaron let him off the hook. "Want to go score a beer, Red?"

"I have Glee Club rehearsal." He suddenly moved to escape, starting to walk away.

Charlotte called after him. She couldn't help teasing, "Be careful, honey. You never know when your voice might change."

Donovan glanced back at the remark, but trudged on his way, staring at the sidewalk.

"What was that about?" Aaron asked.

Charlotte slipped her arm through his, whispering hushed as if a secret, "Didn't you know...the fighting Irish of Old Nassau is still a virgin."

Aaron looked at her in shock. Could that be possible? He had been dating Charlotte for over a year.

"Now, that's a surprise. How could anybody stay virginal with you nearby?"

Charlotte smiled at the compliment, then a sigh, "It's not for want of effort on my part. It's that good solid Catholic upbringing. He's saving himself. Maybe for the second coming, I'm sure." She whispered, pulling him closer in confession, "The first one came and went in about thirty seconds! During the warmup phase, he never quite made it to official sin. If he ever does get up the nerve to propose, I can tell you it's going to be a long marriage but a very short honeymoon."

Aaron laughed, but was worried for Donovan with her. "Do you want to marry him?"

She was honest and direct. She didn't think she fooled Aaron at all.

"It's 1935. I'm almost twenty-two. A girl needs a future."

The Glee Club had gone out to dinner together after rehearsal. They always went to a little restaurant across the bridge on Washington Road run by an Italian family from New York, Luigi's. It was their regular place so they wouldn't run into the usual crowd at the eating club. They could take up several booths in the back to share the large plates of noodles with tomato sauce and what they called "stinky bread", with garlic and cheese on it, and could talk as loud as they wanted. It was Donovan, Wilson and Anderson, of course, almost inseparable, Miki with Lacy, and Wilson's girlfriend Darlene. Charlotte had told Donovan she would meet him there. Aaron said he could drive her, but they never showed up.

They had come out the back door together into the parking lot, heading for their cars when they heard it. It was a sort of groaning sound, coming from the dark, toward the back of the lot.

Wilson was the first to notice it. "What's that?"

The others were laughing at some joke at Anderson's expense, but stopped to listen. They couldn't tell if it was an animal or a person.

"Is someone hurt?" Lacy asked with her natural concern.

They walked toward the sound, coming from a car parked under a tree at the edge of the lot, away from the bare bulb glare of the lamp pole. It was a Buick roadster, with the top down. It was moving a bit, rocking on its springs.

"Isn't that Aaron's car?" Donovan asked, the first to recognize it, but too late.

They all walked up to the car as the groaning turned more clearly into a mixture of breathy feminine moans and masculine grunts. They stood there, like a human

Petrified Forest as they could see the couple spread across the back seat, the girl's dark hair crushed against the opposite door top. Aaron was screwing Charlotte, humping away with great fervor as she clawed her fingers into his back. His bare buttocks was between her legs spread out over the backs of the front seats.

Lacy stared in pained shock. The others watched the two of them go at it, totally oblivious to the gathered audience. No one said anything for the longest time, until Anderson stepped to get a better angle on the scene.

"So, that's what it looks like. Wow, I think I'm getting wood!"

Suddenly, with a growl of rage, Donovan dove over the door into the car, taking the two rutters by surprise. He started slugging wildly, crying and growling, all at the same time. He was hitting Aaron. Hitting Charlotte. Just swinging away at whatever target he could hit.

"Donovan! Jesus!" Wilson shouted.

Aaron tried to defend himself from the wild flying Irish fists and to block the blows aimed at Charlotte.

"Donovan! Shit!" Aaron shouted as he tried to shield Charlotte. "Leave her out of it!"

Wilson, Anderson, and Miki tried to pull Donovan off of them. Darlene even reached in to help, but the Irish was in a blind fury. They managed to hold his arms back and finally dragged him out of the car.

Lacy just stared at Aaron, trying to pull up his pants, and Charlotte, her nose bleeding, trying to cover herself, pulling her skirt back down over her legs. Lacy turned, crying, and just ran.

"Lacy?!" Aaron called out to her, trying to get out of the car. "Lacy...dammit!"

As he struggled to get out of the car to go after her, Miki pushed him back into the front seat. The German just met Aaron with cold blue eyes. He wasn't as angry as he was disappointed and maybe just a little satisfied. He knew deep down that Aaron had managed now to settle any doubt Lacy still had.

"Crash and burn, my friend," he said.

"Friend? You damn son-of-a-bitch!" Aaron was angry. He was mostly nothing but angry. He struggled to get out of the seat, ready to fight, to hell with his ribs. They ached from rutting in the back seat of a car, anyway. Wilson and Anderson helped to hold him back, trapping his balled fists with their arms. They held him until he calmed a little.

"Haven't you done enough damage, Aaron?" Wilson asked with judging disappointment in his voice. Wilson was the most forgiving of all of them, the voice of calm reason among the raging testosterone.

Aaron fell limp, stopping his fighting against them, almost helpless now. "I love her!" He was crying, a helpless boy. "I love her."

Miki looked to Charlotte in the back seat, hiding her face in the upholstery, crying and shoving off the guys trying to help her.

"So, it is plain for anyone to see."

"You're a damn thief, Miki." Aaron was calmer now, cold. The boys released him and he stood up, facing Miki, favoring his aching side.

"It is up to her to choose, Aaron. It is not you or me, now. It's up to her."

He turned and walked away to follow Lacy who was at the far end of the lot at his Nash, sunk on the side fender, crying.

Aaron tried to go after him, but the others held him back, pushing him firmly against the door of the car. He finally fell back into the seat, holding his hands over his face.

"Fuck!"

Lacy cried in her bedroom, curled in a ball on her canopied bed. Why was this so hard, she thought. Aaron could be such an ass. She thought it, but would never say it out loud. Her father opened the door. He never knocked. She thought about telling him to leave her alone, but she wouldn't say that, either.

He sat on the bed beside her and stroked a hand on her side, trying to comfort. It was like she was nine again. He could be an ass, too, but he could also be a steady certainty in a world of confusion. She didn't often agree with her father, but she was in a mood to listen. She wanted the thoughts in her mind to just stop.

"It's just as well you learned the lesson now, rather than a life of pain." Anson Dunbrough counseled with the voice of assured confidence. "This is a time you will be grateful for later. It's the character of their breed. If I've ever learned anything in this world, darling, it's to stay to your own kind." Lacy hugged him. She was vulnerable, lost, nine again. "Do you understand that now?"

Lacy nodded, drawing in her tears. She had a reason now for her rage, an object to focus on to stop all the questions.

Irene Dunbrough appeared at the bedroom door, looking in on her husband and daughter. Anson met her eyes as if all was well.

"Good. Now, we should think about your future."

Aaron stood in the drive in front of the Dunbrough house. It had been three weeks since Luigi's. She had not answered his phone calls. Whoever would pick up the receiver, her mother, the maid, her father, the response had been the same. She couldn't come to the phone. She was busy. Washing her hair. He had even staked out services at the Trinity, but she did not come. She would know he could find her there.

He looked up to the second floor windows with the curtains drawn. They had moved a bit when he first called out. He knew she was there.

"Lacy? Lacy! Come on...!" He called out.

Finally, the front door latch clicked and he started to the portico expectantly. It was Irene who stepped part way through the door, but holding it close. Aaron stopped with one foot on the portico step.

"She doesn't want to see you, Aaron. I'm sorry." Irene was calm and cold.

"Like hell you are," Aaron said. He thought about pushing her aside and charging into the house, and up the stairs. Instead, he walked back out to the drive, standing where Lacy could see him, and shouted at the windows.

"Lacy!!"

Lacy just sat on the floor near the window, crying as she listened to Aaron's voice calling to her in futility. She wanted to run out to him. She wanted tell him she was sorry, tell him she loved him, but it couldn't be. She wanted to tell him he was an asshole, but that she forgave him. She wanted him to go away, because it hurt.

~~~

CHAPTER FIVE

Lakehurst

The summer of 1936 had begun with the usual passing thunderstorm. The quavering flashes and rumbling booms of angry sky gods had passed the night before, but the twenty-first day of June dawned with a cloud-pocked blue sky. The runway field at Lawrenceville was beginning to dry out, but it didn't matter so much to Aaron, he wouldn't be flying.

He was in his rented hangar, working on his shattered plane. He had opted against sending it back to the Ryan factory in California and had decided to reconstruct it himself. He was not in school for the past four months and couldn't return until the fall semester, so he had the time. Perhaps it was a sort of penance, putting his life back together and taking stock, covered in grease and wing dope. It was nearly finished, a Phoenix reborn from shattered pieces.

Outside the hangar, he heard the roaring rattle of Jack Mason's Stearman engine. He took a pause to wipe his hands on a rag and take a sip from his Coca-Cola bottle, going flat on the workbench. He stepped out of the hangar to watch his fellow pilot go through his maneuvers. Mason rented one of the hangar sheds down the line. He didn't race, but performed at some of the aerial show gatherings where Aaron had begun his racing.

The Stearman made a loop high above the airfield. It rolled flat over the top and dove for the ground, but began to spin as if out of control like it was going to crash, circling around and around in tightening twists. Then, at the last minute, it pulled out of the dive with a power roar and leveled just over the muddy, puddle wet grass, rising again into the sky. Aaron thought to himself that the maneuver had been off by a turn, a little sloppy still, but thought the student pilot was making progress.

Mason had been in the Lafayette Escadrille in the war, one of the Americans who had volunteered to fly with the French, who named themselves for the marquis who had come to the aid of a fledgling America in the Revolution, and saw themselves as returning the favor. He had shot down one of the Von Richtofen's Flying Circus over Verdun, taking on an Albatross in his little underpowered Nieuport, earning a Cross de Guerre. Now, he was giving flying lessons. Aaron had traded the daredevil pilot for lessons himself when he was first learning to fly and had been regaled with the tales of the cadre of young Americans who had gone over to encourage a reluctant country back home to get engaged in the fight.

A Ford coupé turned into the field gate from the road and drove along the taxi strip. Aaron recognized Wilson's car as it splashed in the puddles, driving too fast, in some damn hurry. The car pulled up to a stop by Aaron's hangar and Wilson jumped out. He seemed overly excited. He was holding a white paper card in his hand.

"Aaron..." he called as he came, walking fast. "Aaron, are you going?" he asked rather importantly.

"Going where?" Aaron asked, as if not having the slightest idea what he was talking about. But he did know.

Wilson handed him the card. Aaron knew what it was. He had gotten one in his mail box. It was a wedding invitation. He started to hand it back. He didn't open the envelope when it came in the mail and had thrown it away, and wasn't going to read it now.

"No, I'm not going to the wedding," he said with the certain finality of putting a troubled memory behind him.

"Well, of course not." Wilson nodded, but with a secret knowledge of something remarkable. "Neither am I. The wedding's in Germany! Or almost in Germany... Read the damn card!"

Aaron took it back again and read it. He looked up again to Wilson, meeting his expectant gaze with surprise.

"The Hindenburg?"

"They're taking the damn dirigible to Frankfurt," Wilson explained excitedly. He had talked to Lacy and she told him the whole plan. "The Captain is going to marry them over the English Channel somewhere! So they can toast in French champagne!"

The Stearman's engine roared behind them, then, cut out to silence. The plane touched down, landing, and rolled to a stop a few hangars over, the prop fluttering to a stop. The pilot hopped out and pulled off his leather pilot's cap. It was Donovan. He stared over to Aaron and Wilson, but stayed distant. He rarely spoke to Aaron, anymore. They saw each other at the field, but were hardly friends. He turned away to post flight check around the plane.

"Does Donovan know?" Aaron asked Wilson.

"I don't know. Lacy and Charlotte are...well, you know. But if you got one, he must have. I just got it, myself. It's tomorrow...4 pm!"

Aaron handed the invitation back to Wilson, "Better tell him, if he doesn't know."

"You going to go? To see them off?" Wilson asked again, letting the question hang in the air. Aaron didn't answer. Wilson understood, and trotted over to the other hangar to Donovan.

Aaron slid back under his plane to finish up tensing the strut wires.

The sky was clear with a layer of high cirrus clouds over Lakehurst Naval Station. A landing crew stood around in the open field in blue Navy coveralls and a dozen or so Packards and Cadillacs were parked near the departure area.

The massive dirigible hangar was large enough to swallow a small city. Two of the giant air whales could be housed side by side inside of it, but so large they would poke their tales out through the great doors. The Hindenburg had been assigned to share the facility with the American naval dirigibles, but the bay for the German Zeppelin was vacant now, open like an empty maw.

Aaron's Buick, followed by Wilson's Ford, bounced across the concrete joints of the runway to pull up to the passenger lounge. Aaron hopped out of the roadster along with Anderson. Wilson, Darlene, Donovan, and Charlotte had all crammed into the Ford for the forty mile drive to the New Jersey coast. Charlotte and Donovan were still together. He had forgiven her, or at least said he did, but the Irish carry things deeply.

They all paused together to look toward the mooring post rising up into the sky from the open field, held by guy wires. It was really quite wondrous.

The flight would not be departing until the next day, but the arrival of the great Zeppelin on its third Atlantic crossing was an event. With all the press who would be covering the departure, the Dunbroughs had thought to invite friends and family for a sendoff party on the arrival. Max Schmeling would be on the flight. The veteran German boxer had just defeated Joe Louis in a shocking upset, knocking the American boxing sensation down twice for the first time in his career and the crowds would be insane.

As they pushed through the glass doors into the waiting lounge, crowded with well-wishers, Aaron could see Miki and Lacy surrounded by the Dunbroughs and their friends, the well-dressed business sort.

There were some young people he recognized from the Trinity Episcopal Church he no longer set foot in and a few prim girls and their parents he didn't recognize, but guessed they were her chums from school at St Mary's Hall. Lacy was dressed in a smart traveling suit of midnight blue with orange piping, her hair in a tight pulled-back sophisticated knot, rather than the flowing fall of blond he liked. He thought how much Miki's creature she was now.

Lacy brightened when she spotted them coming in and waved them over. They gathered around her. Miki shook hands with Donovan, Wilson and Anderson. Lacy hugged Darlene. She hugged Charlotte, too.

"I'm glad you all came. The ship is late. Today of all days," she said, allowing just a touch of nervousness to show through.

"If you need a Maid of Honor, buy me a ticket!" Darlene said, looking around at the lounge with large grainy photographs on the walls of the Zeppelins in the sky and views of cities below. "This is so exciting!"

"I'm really happy for you, Lacy." Charlotte embraced Lacy again, as if old friendship had wiped away any recrimination. She looked between Lacy and Miki, very sharp in his black gabardine waist coat and black tie.

"Wow, getting married in a balloon! That's something," Charlotte said with smirk, unable to help a needle at Donovan, "Jerry wants to have our wedding in a church. Now, there's something to remember..."

Wilson slapped Miki on the back, feeling the expensive material. "Thanks for the short notice, old man. Escaping the hounds?"

They had known for a year that Lacy had accepted Miki's proposal. The announcement of the engagement had appeared in all the society columns in New York and Philadelphia. The date for a wedding had been the subject of unintended secrecy, so when the invitations came it was a surprise for them all.

"My father asked me to come home," Miki said with a rather serious tone that seemed to suggest there was more that he didn't want to talk about, "things are changing."

"I'll say." Donovan chirped. "Factories are back to work. Does your dad need a hand to run things?"

"Something like that," was all Miki would say.

Aaron stepped over. They just stared at each other for a moment. Then, Aaron held out his hand. Miki took it in a firm grip.

"One lucky bastard," Aaron grinned. "Old friends shouldn't be enemies."

"Perhaps we'll see you in Berlin?" Miki didn't say it, but he had already been offered a place on the German Olympic team.

Aaron glanced to Wilson and the others. "Not going."

"There's a still a lot of chatter about boycotting the games," Donovan said with an unspoken glance at Aaron. "You know...the Jewish thing. Up in New York they're picketing the German Consulate, since the vote to go."

"I think it is all quite stupid, this idea," Miki offered curtly. "Jews should compete like everyone. But it's a government policy. I don't concern myself." He was cool, as if he would rather not discuss it.

"Well, it doesn't matter much," Aaron said with a feigned casualness. "The boys here screwed up the regionals."

"We couldn't get Aaron reinstated in time," Donovan still seemed to have a burr under his skin. "That dumb stunt he pulled last semester..."

"Go ahead. Blame everything on me."

"Forget it," Donovan said cooly, trying to end it.

There was a sudden palpable buzz of excitement from the gathered well-wishers. A bell rang somewhere and they started to push out the door to the field.

"Here it comes!" Darlene exclaimed with a thrill. And the college friends filed out with the others to see.

In the distance, out of the gray overcast sky, the bulbous whale form of the Hindenburg appeared. It was making its turn toward the field about a half a mile out. They all were drawn in increasing awe across the concrete field as the monster dirigible grew larger and larger, the hum of its propeller engines growing louder. The great nose seemed to push wispy fumes of cloud moisture along the sweep of its sides. As it drew closer, people were visible at the windows along the ribs. As it turned in a gentle decent, the Swastika on the white circle was visible on the expanse of its tail plane.

Aaron stepped up next to Lacy as she gazed up at the sky, thinking about her future.

"It's amazing, isn't it? It's so huge." She looked over and realized it was Aaron next to her, "Oh, Aaron..." She smiled with just a little ill ease. "Thanks for coming. I was afraid you wouldn't want to."

"And miss my last chance to see you happy?" he said. And he meant it. "Are you happy?"

She smiled, warmed that he cared and started to cry a little. She hugged him.

"Yes."

"Then, that's all that matters. What more could I ask."

"And a little scared. It's all going to be so different."

"I can't even imagine..." He looked again at the airship as it dropped lower over the field and the mooring lines dropped out to the ground. The landing crew ran out to grab them. "But Miki'll take care of you. That I know. He's a good guy."

Lacy looked at him. She was happy he seemed to be taking it well. It had been a hard choice and the last thing she had wanted was to hurt him. Even now, she felt a pain of doubt, if she had listened to the wrong voices. But it was too late. Tomorrow her world would be entirely different.

The landing crew pulled on the mooring lines, easing the nose of the giant ship toward the giant mooring post. Lacy started to walk out toward it, fascinated.

Aaron watched her walk toward the amazing sight, as if looking at her for the last time. He noticed a little shimmer of static crackling along the skin of the ship from the nose mooring cone.

"Lacy..." He came out to her, taking her by the arm and pulling her back, "Why don't you wait until it's tied up?"

They stood back together as the landing crew walked the craft to the mooring post. It took a couple of attempts before the nose mooring ball slipped into the bell housing and the clamps closed around it.

Safely moored, the crew tied the lines, and the mooring post gantry rolled slowly toward the hangar for the great ship to dock and unload its passengers.

When the gangway steps to the passenger gondola lowered to the ground, richly dressed passengers began to disembark, including two men in Nazi military officer uniforms. They saluted with a smart heil, extended their arms with fingers tight in a twenty degree angle from their wrists.

"They look just like the newsreels." Lacy turned to Aaron, "My God, I'm shaking. Nerves, I guess."

Miki came over to them. He seemed focused on the business before them, as was more usual now. He acknowledged Aaron, but without any real sign of warmth.

"My dear, we have to sort the luggage."

Lacy took a last look at Aaron, with a nervous smile. "Well, here we go. Take care of yourself, Aaron. And don't crash that stupid plane of yours again, or I'll never forgive you."

She walked away with Miki toward the luggage carts, leaving Aaron with the huge gray curvature of the

Hindenburg dangling above. After a moment, Donovan joined him.

"Well... The loser buys the beer." He didn't get any response from Aaron. Maybe he didn't hear. "Hey, loser, you'll never guess what Miki did."

"What?"

Donovan couldn't contain a secret smile as he held up a small padlock key.

"What is that?" Aaron asked, genuinely unaware. He couldn't think why Donovan should be grinning like a child who had broken into a secret jar of cookies.

"Eat my exhaust, buddy boy."

Then, Aaron realized it was the key to Miki's hangar.

As the planes raced around the pylons in the 1936 National Air Races in Los Angeles, in the limited trials, Aaron's Ryan seemed to be outdistancing the rest of the pack. He was now racing in the pro class. The new belt-pumped carburetor supercharger he had added was giving him another fifty horses and allowed him to hold twenty miles-per-hour top speed increase in the turns. It was a prototype for a model a small manufacturer in Nyack was trying to sell to the military. He had gotten it from a friend of his father's as a proving test for a new single wing fighter the Army was developing.

"Miller holds a solid lead in his silver bullet," the loudspeaker echoed across the crowd. "Mitchell in the Mobil seven in second, and Donovan in last year's second place finisher GeeBee Three falls from third to fourth as he's passed by the Stinson."

Aaron flew the Ryan through its paces, around a pylon, down the stretch, banking around another pylon with ease and precision. He was better than last year, but something was gone for him. He kept looking over his shoulder to see Miki, but he wasn't there.

Donovan, flying Miki's now three year old GeeBee, manhandled the unruly plane through the course, flinging into the turns, going wide, almost losing it. The control stick was heavy and since taking it over, he could only wonder how the German had kept it under control. It flew like a rock with wings. He was passed by another plane, then getting back on course, he powered ahead. He was desperate to catch Aaron, but the reconfigured Ryan was a half lap ahead and pulling away. Aaron had put something in the plane after he rebuilt it, but had said he couldn't tell Donovan what it was.

Aaron's Ryan kept up the smooth pace, slicing through the back markers with ease. His father didn't come to the race, but the executives from the Continental Engine Company were there to watch Aaron's performance. They had not allowed him to publicly announce the sponsorship. If their carburetion gas supercharger didn't work, they didn't want to have to deal with negative publicity or the ridicule from rival Cummins, since the Army plane design from Curtiss-Wright was still a secret.

"Miller seems to have no competition with the absence of Von Steuven from the field," the loudspeaker announced, unaware that it was not Miki's absence, but a pressure valve pump that now propelled Aaron a full lap ahead of the field.

Aaron's plane roared over the waving checkered flag.

Aaron was hoisted onto the stand by the cheering crowd, but the sound of adoration seemed to fade in his mind to a white noise. He looked around at the crowd surging toward the stands. The faces seemed to meld together into a meaningless mass of humanity. The trophy prize, handshakes and slaps on the back seemed far away as the photo bulbs flashed.

The movie theater was half empty. Aaron sat next to a girl he had met at the Beth El Synagogue of Burlington. Over the winter he couldn't avoid going home and his mother knew a friend who said she knew a girl who lived just down the road from Princeton. It was forty-five minutes down the road. He was trying to remember her name. Donovan sat with Charlotte in the row behind them, and Wilson was with Darlene.

They had come to watch William Powel and Myrna Loy in a new comedy, but as the lights dimmed, a Movietone newsreel flickered on the screen. The high contrast black and white image panned around the huge Albert Speer designed Berlin Olympic Stadium of cheering crowds and Adolf Hitler at the imperial style podium, opening the games. The news voice droned on about how many attended and the athletes competing. It was so alien and far away, until Leni Riefenstahl's camera focused on Miki in his white shorts with emblazoned Nazi Swastika patch, poised at the javelin pit. He launched forward and flung his spear. The crowd cheered as it arced through the air. The camera found Lacy in the stands. She rose, shouting encouragement for him, her voice silent in the edited stock sounds of the crowd, the image choppy and stuttering. The javelin jabbed down to earth, inches behind the farthest mark. The markers ran out to measure. Miki turned away not even wanting to watch the mark, knowing it wasn't good enough.

The newsreel voice spoke over the footage in a mocking tone, "America competes in Berlin as the German Reich puts on an impressive show." Images flashed of a foot race with an athlete flying ahead of the pack in the 200 meters and launching off the board into the long jump sand, his darker skin in high contrast black and white. "But Hitler's dreams of superiority are dashed when American Jesse Owens beats the best the Nazi leader's Third Reich has to offer as the Germans fail to win a single gold medal in the track events."

The newsreel cut to a shot of Miki, "The Baron Michael von Steuven, heir to one of the Aryan nation's industrial dynasties can only manage a silver medal in the javelin as his American socialite bride does her best to cheer him on..."

The camera focused on Lacy in the stands, cheering, then, her reaction sinking, cut to a shot of a practice throw where Miki stumbled on the toe board, obviously not his silver medal effort. The voice tone was snide, "Looks like this 'master race' needs a little practice..."

Then, the voice turned serious as the fast moving newsreel cut to images of tanks and goose-stepping German soldiers moving across a bridge to cheering locals. "While in the Baron's homeland, German Troops and Armored Divisions cross the bridges over the Rhine River into the Ruhr Valley, as the Nazi leader remilitarizes the Rhineland, reclaiming the buffer zone established by the Versailles Armistice Treaty of 1918."

A title graphic burst on the screen to the blare of trumpets, "Spain: Civil War!"

Images flashed of fighting in the streets of a city. "In Madrid, Nationalist forces led by Generalissimo Francisco Franco mounted an intensive counter attack against Republican fighters in the heart of the nation's largest city. Franco is being supplied by Nazi Germany and Mussolini's Fascist Italy, while both neighboring France's new government of the Popular Front of Léon Blum and Britain's Stanley Baldwin, have pledged neutrality."

They couldn't remember much of the movie when they went all went out together afterward. Seeing Miki at the Olympics, where they might have been, was all they could talk about. Lacy had been writing to Wilson all along, as they had been pen pals since they were kids.

She had posted a letter from Frankfurt-on-Main when the airship arrived, telling of the wedding performed by the head of the Deutsche Zeppelin Transport Company who was captain on the flight. He was a Dr. Eckner, who apparently didn't care for the Nazi regime very much since they had nationalized the company he built. Miki had been enjoying conversations on the sixty-one hour flight with Max Schmeling, talking about his fight with Joe Louis and boxing in general, while smoking cigars in the smoking lounge. Lacy thought it was rather dangerous with all that explosive hydrogen gas in the bags all around them, but had been assured it was perfectly safe if they kept in the lounge. There was a Lord Donegall on the trip, Edward Arthur Chichester, the 6th Marquis, who spent most of his time traveling as a journalist, writing about sports. He was an avid aviation enthusiast and interviewed Miki, before pointing out his castle near Belfast as they flew over the dockyards where the Titanic had been assembled. There were three American Navy officers on board, a Rear Admiral named Greenslade and two lieutenants. They were going over for an inspection of German shipbuilding in Hamburg and some proposed meetings with the Reichsmarine Admiralty. The top naval commander, Grand Admiral Raeder, had written a history of the war and Greenslade was eager to discuss a few points where they disagreed.

Lacy said she spent much of her time with a Mademoiselle Goudard, who was the daughter of a French industrial engineer, traveling with her father and a woman who Lacy was quite fascinated with, named Lecler. She was a foreign correspondent on a trip for the New Yorker Magazine to write about women in Germany. It was her second visit. She had gone in 1934 and traveled personally with Herr Hitler. She had written about how German ladies viewed him like a matinee idol, the ultimate German bachelor, and was curious how they viewed him after nearly four years in power. She had also visited the work camps and one camp in particular near a village close to Munich called Dachau she thought was troubling. There was also a professor of architecture from Princeton on board who had filmed the trip with his 16-millimeter camera. He promised they might get a copy and wanted Wilson to get in touch with him.

Lacy had also written from Essen when they had settled into a house Miki's father owned, apparently an old family second house Lacy thought was a bit of a fixer-upper. From her description, it sounded like it was rather large, as she had commented it only had three full time servants to manage it and the grounds. It was in the middle of the industrial zone along the Ruhr River.

She had written again after traveling with Miki to Berlin for the trials and gushed over Miki's success. Her opinion of the German architectural style, evident in massive building projects all around the city, was not to the positive. "Square, heavy and cold" she wrote, with emblems and signs on everything, taking any charm from the capital. The nearby city of Düsseldorf with its riverside park and old town of gingerbread houses she thought was much more appealing. She had promised to write after the Olympics.

Aaron tried to listen to all the news about Miki and Lacy's new life with equanimity and good wishes, but found another emotion rising, which he tried to fight. He tried to remember his date's name through it all and it finally came back to him, Helen, just in time to take her home. He had to drive her all the way back to Burlington. They stopped a few blocks from her house on a dark street near a park. He fucked her in the back seat, then, dropped her off. On the drive back to Princeton, he didn't think he would be making any trips to Burlington again.

~~~

CHAPTER SIX

Essen

The smell was acrid and a thin haze of smoke filled the whole building, despite its massive size. The assembly lines seemed to stretch into the distance underneath the roof of angled wire-infused glass which covered the two football fields' long factory building. Lacy stood with Miki and her father-in-law on the steel rail balcony, watching steel track wheels for Panzer tanks move along the assembly line. It was one of five assembly buildings of the Von Steuven Works. The pounding ring of stamping machines was near deafening, even through the soft rubber earplugs. In the rear of the building a river of hot molten steel poured from a giant crucible bucket into die forms, shooting sparks of orange molten manganese.

"The contract with your father's mills has made this possible," Otto von Steuven told Lacy. He spoke English very well from two years he spent in England at Cambridge University before finishing his education at Heidelberg. "But it is Herr Hitler's plan to make Germany self-sufficient with materials from the East."

"Where in the East?" Lacy asked.

He leaned against the steel rail, looking over his works. "Silesia, the Sudeten, Moravia were divided from Germany after the war."

"Aren't those part of Poland and Czechoslovakia?" Lacy had studied up on geography and German history when it had become clear to her that Miki intended to take her home with him. "How will he do that?"

He glanced to Miki with a feigned disinterest. "For that answer, I think you need to ask Herr Hitler."

When she first met him, Lacy had thought Otto Lustig Graf Von Steuven was very similar to her own father. Physically he was very different, of course. He stood shorter than Miki and was balding in the back of his rather round head. He had a thin mustache over his upper lip. It was turning gray and made a bit uneven from the scar he had gotten from a rapier tip during a fencing duel as a student at Heidelberg. He walked with a slight limp from an old wound he had gotten in the war. It was not from fighting in the trenches at the front but from a piece of steel from an exploding test shell at his proving ground. He was similar in temperament, quiet much of the time, until he thought he had something important to say, and similar in a self-assurance that came from his family position and in his love of making things and making money.

He had not come to meet them at the hangar in Frankfurt but had sent a car and a driver. He had made the excuse that his factories were running overtime and he was at the beck and call of generals and ministry officials, day and night. It was one of the reasons he had insisted Miki give up his school for a year and come home, but Miki didn't want to tell him he had no interest in running factories.

As they stepped outside to take the car to the house, Lacy marveled at the red brick factories which stretched across the valley like crowded tenements with belching smokestacks, crisscrossed with silvery streaks of railroad tracks. Next over to the Von Steuven works were Krupp, and beyond that, the IG Fabrik.

A buzzing roar above them caught their attention and they looked up as three Heinkel 51 biplanes with Luftwaffe cross markings flew over, heading toward the airfield at Mulheim. Miki thought they were like lumbering kites. Was this the aircraft of a new Luftwaffe? For all the talk of the rebirth of German industry and rumbling international complaints about armaments, he thought the Nazi air advance was pathetic.

The Schloss Kester stood at a crossroads near a bridge on a raised hillside of manicured grounds overlooking the Ruhr River, six miles from the factories of the Von Steuven Works and five miles in the opposite direction to the town of Mulheim. The little village around it with the same name was a collection of shops and a few lanes of houses, most of which had been there for over two hundred years. Schloss was the German word for palace and the house had actually once been a knight's castle, with a first mention of it from 1292. It was what was called a Wasserburg, a water castle, and had once been surrounded by a moat, all gone now. The manor house as it presently stood was built in 1646 in a classic Renaissance style, but with some later Baroque additions in the roof. Only the one stone tower now incorporated as a staircase in the southwest corner, the basement vault foundations, and a low, thick, ivy covered stone wall were left from the original medieval fortifications. It had been taken over during the Napoleonic conquest of the Ruhr Valley in 1804 and an entire wing had been demolished, where now was a garage and servants quarters above. Several cars were parked on the gravel courtyard.

A dinner party was in progress with Lacy and Miki hosting a collection of business types and young upper class. An Army General Major and a Luftwaffe Oberst (Colonel) from Mulheim had also come. Lacy enjoyed her role as hostess, supervising servants and flitting like a butterfly between conversation groups, laughing appropriately at stiff German humor. Her German was practical enough. She had been diligently studying the language since her first introduction to Miki in New Jersey and had been speaking for almost three years now.

When she had first arrived at the house her father-in-law had given them, she had thought it was an old, drafty place with a sort of musty smell. The seventeen rooms on two floors with an open-beamed attic space and stone vault crypt below were at first intimidating, but over four months they had managed to make it what she thought was a worthy home. Much of the musty smell was gone when they had ripped up the ancient carpet and replaced the rotting wood floor through the first level. They kept much of the furniture, but reupholstered some of the more grand pieces. She had found some art for sale from a museum in Düsseldorf. The Nazi cultural ministry had ordered it replaced by what they considered more appropriately moral idealism, but rather than allowing the old works to be destroyed, the curators had offered it to a local art seller. The grand hall, foyer and library were now home to a Venus by Verrochio, a Tintoretto, two Van Eyck's and a nude countess by Jean Clouet.

The guests were seated around the long table in the dining room bristling with silver and crystal. Several of the pieces had been wedding gifts and much of the rest were family heirlooms. An extra girl from town had been taken on to help with the serving, Berta. The permanent servants were not enough for entertaining, with one groundskeeper who maintained the property, a housekeeper, and a cook. Lacy had found the girl through the local butcher in the village. She was only sixteen, and her parents operated a small brauhaus inn. She had ambitions to go to hotel school, which Lacy thought was admirable, and working in large manor house would be good for her resume.

A young woman leaned over to Lacy to make conversation. She was the wife of one of the army officers.

"How have you taken to your new home in Germany, Frau von Steuven? It must be quite different for you?"

"Not so much." Lacy explained, "I grew up in a quiet university town, but this industrial area is not unlike the northern part of my home state. And I struggle with the language, of course."

"I believe you're managing quite well." The young lady smiled, complimenting.

One of the business executives, who had been trying for much of the evening to decide whether to bring up what had been on his mind, finally caught the eye of the Wehrmacht General Major who was directly across from him.

"These production requirements from Berlin are becoming very difficult to manage, with no increases in finances," he said, leading by degrees to his point. "Does the War Ministry expect us to finance rearmament from our own pockets, Herr General?"

The Brigadeführer turned to the question with a stolid patience. His assignment to inspect production in the Ruhr had inured him to these types of comments, but he committed the questioner's face to his memory. He would ask his name again later to write it down.

"A certain loyalty to the needs of a Greater Germany is what the ministry and the Reichsführer expect, Mein Herr. We have enemies all around us who wish to strangle us. Is it too small a thing to ask that all sectors of society contribute what part is their duty?"

Miki chimed in, his disdain for politics very near the surface.

"Whatever one might say about the Nazis, they seem uncultured bullies...at least people are working again instead of begging."

The general turned to Miki. He had come to the dinner invitation thinking he would be socializing with the father, but a little disappointed that the Geshäftsführer had not come.

"Will we soon see you in a uniform, young von Steuven? An Olympic medal, while admirable, has only a place on the shelf."

"Von Steuven has a factory which calls his attention, I suspect," the businessman suggested helpfully, thinking he had a bead on the young man's mind, and perhaps hoping to ingratiate himself with the son.

Miki just smiled with a private amusement at those who saw his future in their past, then a glance to Lacy.

"Gentlemen, at the moment I have a beautiful wife who requires my preoccupation." He raised a glass of champagne, and they raised a toast to Lacy, who feigned embarrassment.

The Luftwaffe Colonel with the stub of a cigar in his mouth underneath a thick mustache which partially covered an old burn scar he had received in the Battle of Lorraine, leaned on an elbow. He had been quiet for much of the dinner, but had been taking a measure of Miki through most of it. Eduard Ritter von Schleich had been credited with thirty-five kills in the war, and had been called "the Black Knight" for his black painted airplane and family heritage. He had been in charge of flight reserve training after the war, and the Hitler Youth aerial programs before the formation of the new Luftwaffe in 1935, and now had been called back as chief of fighter training in Munich. He had been very keen to meet Miki when he heard of his returning to Germany.

"And your flying," he asked with a patient concern, as one used to the temperaments of young men eager for adventure, "you have put aside that preoccupation? We have all followed your sport victories in America."

"I'm afraid, Herr Oberst, with all due respect for your records in the last war, the old technology I see holds little interest for me. These biplanes might just as well be gliders." The colonel nodded with a shrug, but rolled the cigar in his mouth as if chewing on a secret.

As the guests were leaving, paying their respects to the host and hostess as the young maid gathered their coats against an early autumn rain outside, Von Schleich lingered to casually look at a large display cabinet in the foyer which reached to the height of a man. Behind the plate glass on three shelves were Miki's flying and sports trophies. The Silver Olympic medal hung over a photograph of Miki throwing his Javelin. There were photographs of Miki with his GeeBee and earlier planes in Germany. One photograph in particular of Miki shaking hands with Doolittle seemed to hold his interest. He waited for the others to leave. Finally, he bowed to Lacy with an old world gallantry which seemed to be missing from many of the business class of Germans she had been encountering.

"A most enjoyable evening, Baroness,"

Lacy seemed to be taken a little by surprise by the title. "Thank you, Oberst von Schleich, very kind, but I'm not really a baroness."

"No, but I think of it as a courtesy." He was of the same class as they and even though he had been a farmer for a time after the battle glories of the war, still liked to remember the world of his youth. He kissed her hand with a wry reference to the trophy case, "and I can't help but acknowledge a most beautiful addition to the collection."

He started to go, but stopped and turned to Miki, as if an afterthought. "Miki, since you have some free time, perhaps you would come for a visit to the south. I would like to show you something."

"Of course," Miki said courteously, not knowing what the colonel had in his mind. "Where is your command? I'll take the train down next week." He assumed it was somewhere near Munich.

"I'll send a car," said the colonel with a hint of secretive seriousness. "It is a little out of the way."

The drive from Essen took the better part of a day, including two sections of the new high speed motor roads. The driver of the Mercedes staff car, a young corporal named Kunsdorff, tried to empress Miki, the champion flyer and German Olympic hero, with the speed he could achieve on the straight stretch between Frankfurt and Darmstadt, pushing the needle to 160 kilometers per hour, pressing the 8-cylinder motor to its limit. Miki was impressed, but it wasn't quite the same as flying around pylons at ten feet. He was intrigued that the new engine was supercharged by a similar pump design to some that had been appearing in racing planes.

They arrived at the former Lufthansa airfield at Schliessheim near Munich at just after fifteen hundred in the afternoon. They had made the trip in just under nine hours, including a stop for a roast pork lunch near the Mercedes Daimler-Benz factory at Stuttgart. The station was not marked with military designations, and still retained the appearance of a civilian airfield. A few training biplanes were parked at the distant edge of the field, but much of the activity seemed to be around a collection of hangars which appeared to be newly constructed. The car stopped at the guarded gate, where a soldier carefully checked over the driver's orders and Miki's identity papers. He saluted smartly with the outstretched "Heil Hitler". He waited for Miki to return the salute, but Miki was still not used to this formality. He wasn't in the military and in Berlin the formal salute had seemed mostly for ceremonies in the presence of party officials, for public parades and eager schoolboys.

Corporal Kunsdorff turned to look back to his passenger to see what the problem was. From his consternated gaze, Miki finally thought it would be better to appease, and raised his hand in the laconic manner he had first noted some of the officers on the Hindenburg flight make. The guard seemed satisfied at last and signaled for the gate barrier to be raised.

Kunsdorff drove across the field to the hangars where another staff car was parked, and Miki recognized Colonel von Schleich leaning against it. He was smoking a cigar, with his cane laid aside on the fender. Kunsdorff had telephoned ahead from Ulm to tell his office when they would arrive. Miki got out of the car, stretching his legs after the long ride. Von Schleich greeted him with a handshake instead of a salute.

"Did you have a good drive?" Von Schleich asked with a slight hint of a smile.

"I've never seen so much of Germany in one day. A lot of factories," Miki answered, "people seem to be back to work. This is good."

"I doubt you will see so much from ground level in the future." Von Schleich seemed to be hinting at something.

Miki looked around at the old trainers at the edge of the runway. "So, this is the mighty Luftwaffe of Greater Germany?" he joked.

"A part of it. My small part, for the time being," Von Schleich answered, saying a good deal less than Miki thought he could.

"Where are all the soldier barracks? It still looks like Lufthansa operates here."

Von Schleich gestured around the field with his cigar. "It attracts less attention. There are some things we are doing we are not ready to tell the world. Come."

He picked up his cane from the fender and walked to the one of the unmarked hangars. A guard was on duty and upon a nod from the colonel, flipped a switch which rang a bell somewhere inside the hangar. An electric motor growled and the corrugated door of the building which hung from a sliding rail, slowly slid back enough to allow them to enter, then stopped.

Miki stepped from the light of day into the hangar. As his eyes adjusted to the dim light which cut through the crack of the hangar door, he was overtaken by a certain awe and delight.

Resting, staggered wing to wing on the hangar floor, were two matched aeroplanes. They were sleek like a shark with single wings jutting from under the angular pilot's canopy. They looked as if they were designed for racing, but the barrels of two machine guns jutted just out of the top of the cowling, and in the middle of the propeller spinner, a hole inside a casing intended for another weapon.

Miki walked around the front of the first plane, touching the wing aluminum and looking under the fuselage like a boy at Christmas, noting the air intake for the supercharger under the engine housing.

"What is it?" he asked.

Von Schleich watched the young baron with some satisfaction as he seemed to take in every feature of the machine with fascination. This was certainly what he had intended, for he knew many young men like Miki, but few as talented.

"It is a Bayerische Flugzeugwerke 109."

Miki continued around the plane, feeling the curve of the large three blade propeller.

"Who is the designer?"

"Messerschmitt. Willy Messerschmitt. It is based on his Taifun sports plane."

Miki nodded, "Yes, the one they presented at the Olympics. I did not see it fly. But this is...much different." He marveled at the eight engine exhaust vents sweeping from under the cowling. A canvas tarp was laid over part of the nose, to just behind the pilot's cockpit window along the side.

"How fast does it go?"

Von Schleich stepped around next to Miki, taking the cigar from his mouth, a sly grin.

"We don't know, yet. The prototypes achieved a top speed of 420 kilometers, but that was with a different motor. We borrowed Rolls-Royce engines from the British for the tests. These are the first production models. They have a new Mercedes-Benz inverted twelve cylinder, the 600. We are building them as fast as we can. And we are waiting for a new higher horsepower plant from Junkers...and new weapons."

He stepped away to the middle of the hangar, his voice echoing on the metal walls and roof as Miki continued to examine the plane.

"We need pilots, Miki. We need skilled pilots, to put them through their paces. Berlin has signed an agreement with the Spanish Nationalists to aid in their struggle against the Socialists. Volunteers are leaving daily to fight. They will need planes. Spain will be our testing ground."

Miki looked up to the cockpit, drawn by an aching need.

"Is it ready to fly?"

"I was beginning to wonder when you would ask." Von Schleich gestured toward an airman in a Luftwaffe Flight Sergeant's uniform, waiting by the door of the hangar. "Oberfeldwebel Schluss will familiarize you with the controls."

Miki climbed onto the wing. The flight sergeant reached past him to open the canopy.

"I should warn you, the cockpit is tight and the controls are unforgiving, like a woman," Von Schleich grinned, "but in the air, you will feel as if you were born there."

Miki climbed into the cockpit, sliding down into the hard seat behind the stick. Flight Sergeant Schluss showed him the controls and explained the gauges. It was all familiar, yet quite different and new to Miki, filling him with a thrill he hadn't felt since climbing the aluminum steps into the belly of the Zeppelin.

He looked out the side of the cockpit to Von Schleich, watching him from the hangar floor.

"Tell me, Herr Oberst," he asked with a barely contained curiosity, "what if I had come all the way here and not have been interested in your new machine?"

Von Schleich nodded to Schluss who stepped across the wing root to the canvas tarp draped over the cowling. He pulled it away, revealing underneath, the markings of the nose of the plane, and just below the exhaust vents, the painted emblem of a Javelin, like a thunderbolt in the hand of Zeus.

Von Schleich grinned mischievously, "You know, Miki...the thought never occurred to me."

~~~

CHAPTER SEVEN

Spain

A plane fell from the clear October sky, out of a loop, pulling out and leveling for a landing on the newly laid strip of asphalt at Lawrenceville. Aaron's Ryan settled just over the threshold and the wheels touched down for a short stop and rollout. Aaron taxied toward his hangar where his roadster was parked with a pretty girl in crinoline sitting on the fender, watching him. He had met her on the second week of the new semester. Her name was Elizabeth. She wasn't Jewish, but like many of the girls he had dated, she was impressed with his flying records and his money. And she screwed like a rabbit. It was a distraction.

As he got out of the cockpit he also saw Wilson waiting for him. He waved a letter as Aaron stepped off the wing.

"I got a letter from Lacy!" Wilson shouted, ignoring Elizabeth, as Aaron's friends had all learned not to get too familiar with his string of girlfriends. Though, they all thought Elizabeth was one of the best of the lot.

"Oh yeah?" Aaron asked, with feigned disinterest as he checked around the plane for his post flight. "What does it say?"

Wilson looked at Elizabeth, wondering now whether they should be having this conversation in front of her, but what the hell, he thought.

"Miki's going to Spain."

Aaron looked up from his plane, interested now, "With the Condors?"

"Lacy's not very happy about it." Wilson held out the letter.

"Who's Lacy?" Elizabeth asked.

Without answering, Aaron took the letter to read with curiosity. In it, Lacy wrote of the three months Miki had not been home, except for a weekend every three weeks. He was flying again. He had been flying off to someplace she couldn't say in a letter, for three weeks away and then home with her for two days. He had joined the Luftwaffe. The letter seemed careful, as if she expected it to be monitored. This was confirmed by a thick black ink painted over some of the words and a red stamp on the envelope with the Nazi eagle and a tape which had resealed it with the word 'Geöffnet', meaning 'opened'. There seemed to be a lot of "I can't say exactly" sort of phrases, but he knew her well enough he could read between the lines and picture the scene in his head.

"Spain?" Lacy couldn't believe it. How could he just stand there in the middle of their bedroom and announce he was leaving. There had been no discussion.

Miki was wearing his crisp gray Luftwaffe 1st Lieutenant's uniform, pulling clothes from a chest of drawers as Lacy stood by the window which looked out on the manor woods which had turned to the golds and browns of coming winter in the Ruhr.

"My God, Miki, I hardly see you anymore. You come home for two days, you won't tell me anything about what they're having you do in this secret air program you've been working on, and now you tell me you're going to Spain?!"

"It is my assignment," Miki said in that even controlled manner of his, Aaron conjured so clearly in his mind.

"I thought they were volunteers." Lacy said, with Aaron adding a little zinger he couldn't help, "What are you supposed to do there, kill gypsies?

Miki would just turn from his packing, "It is my duty, Lacy."

"Duty? To whom?" Lacy would be proper in her language. But would she be speaking to Miki in German now, or in English, when they were together alone? Aaron wondered about that, but he could clearly hear her attitude, and it made him smile just a little as she would be giving a piece of her mind to Miki, poor bastard.

"The Nationalists?" she would demand. "Franco? Who are they, but the next gang of thugs to come along?!"

"My duty to Germany."

"I don't understand you, Miki! You're changing."

In the letter she said he was changing and she didn't understand him anymore. She didn't really write the next part, but Aaron could hear it all as if he was standing there, listening.

"You never seemed to care much about all this before. What's happening to you? I thought you didn't like the Nazis."

"Lacy, I am to fly. That's all that matters."

"Don't I matter, Miki?"

Miki would step over to her, wrapping an arm around her as she turned away to the window, starting to cry.

"I'm here alone all day, managing this house with no one to talk to except the servants, who never seem to understand what I'm saying even in perfectly correct

German. I go into town to the market and hear them whispering behind my back, 'Amerikanisher Frau'."

"It will only be for a few months." He would turn her around, and take her face in his hands.

"You see, I am in love with my beautiful Amerikanisher Frau." He would kiss her and she would be comforted.

"It will be better. Von Schleich is forming a division near Paderborn, thirty miles away. Until then, you must be strong for me. When you are at the market, tell them proudly that you are 'the Baroness von Steuven' and you must have the very best cut of meat!"

Lacy would laugh, amused at his very male view. "Of all the things I thought I might do or be, over-demanding house frau was not at the top of my list. But if that is what you need me to be, that's what I'll be, my husband."

She would kiss him, forgiving him, unlike the forgiveness she had denied Aaron. He held the letter in his hands, picturing the kiss, and didn't realize it made his face red.

"I guess the 'Baroness' got what she wanted. What does she expect him to do, stay home and water the Petunias?" Aaron handed the letter back.

Wilson noticed the mood in Aaron's eyes.

"Who's Lacy?" Elizabeth asked again, totally lost, and getting a little annoyed that it was probably something she should know.

Aaron grabbed her and pulled her off the car fender. He pulled her close against him and kissed her in a lip-locking clench. "Someone who moved away," was all he said, trying to put it out of his mind.

It was in June of 1937. The lights had dimmed in the theater. Aaron was in the back row, tongue sucking on a pretty girl in blue and polka dots. It wasn't Elizabeth. She had lasted about a month and there had been two more through that semester after her. Donovan was three rows down with Charlotte. They had learned not to sit too close but to leave a little space. Aaron's hands were out of sight, somewhere they weren't supposed to be, as the girl giggled and moaned softly.

Charlotte nudged Donovan with a sharp elbow. He sat straight and held out the popcorn, trying to cover his lap with his arm. How Aaron got away with it, he didn't know. It was like some sort of magic trick.

He leaned over close to Charlotte to whisper, "What's her name again?"

Charlotte shrugged. She had stopped trying to learn them.

The soft moaning from the back row kept getting louder and it seemed like Aaron was going to have this girl right there in the theater, until the blaring theme of the newsreel started. Grainy black and white footage flickered on the screen of Spanish soldiers fighting at the edge of a town with armed rebels, dodging behind farmhouses in the midst of olive groves.

"Franco's Nationalists mount an offensive near Bilbao, steadily advancing, with air cover provided by German and Italian volunteers. The Republicans' borrowed Russian and French biplanes are no match for the Condor Squadron's new killing machine, the Messerschmitt."

On the screen was aerial footage of the sleek Bf109s attacking a flight of Polikarpov biplanes.

Donovan watched, totally fascinated, but Aaron behind him was still totally involved with the girl.

"Here are some of the Condors relaxing between missions," the Movietone voice droned.

Donovan suddenly reached back to Aaron, calling in a loud whisper to get his attention, "Hey! Hey, Aaron! Look!"

Aaron looked up from the girl's neck and froze. He stared now, completely forgetting her.

On the screen was footage of a Bf109 at rest on the ground with four pilots in baggy Nationalist Volunteer uniforms, laughing and smoking cigarettes in casual camaraderie. Miki was in the middle.

"Isn't that Miki? The second one from the left..." Donovan asked.

The screen reel cut to a Messerschmitt arcing over into a dive. Clearly on the nose was the Javelin emblem.

"With the most feared bird of prey of them all, the Javelin..." said the voice.

In another angle from the ground in the scratchy black and white, the Messerschmitt swooped from the sunny sky to pounce on a Polikarpov, machine guns spitting fire. The biplane fluttered into a swirling dive, smoking, as the 109 swooped past, banking away.

Aaron was now totally transfixed by the images on the screen. The girl in the polka dot dress pouted.

"Aaron! Aaron, honey! Who cares about that? Let's smooch!"

She grabbed at him, to pull him away from the screen. The newsreel went on to other segments: Neville Chamberlain becoming Prime Minister of England and the Duke of Windsor, the former king Edward VIII, now abdicated, marrying the American divorcee, Wallis

Simpson; Franklin Roosevelt starting traffic on the brand new Golden Gate Bridge across San Francisco Bay with the flip of a signal switch in Washington. Aaron ignored it all, going back to fooling with the girl through most of the movie. Beatrice! That was it. He finally remembered, her name was Beatrice!

~~~

CHAPTER EIGHT

Kristallnacht

Lacy turned the big Mercedes saloon car at the corner by the little old church at the center of the village. She drove along the curving country road past the small brick houses and workers apartments on the road in the direction from the manor to Essen. The car reminded her a bit of the Packard back home, but the motor was quieter and it steered with more ease. Workers, in pale blue dirty overalls, walking home from the factories after their night shifts, looked up at the big car as it passed. They seemed to Lacy to have hard life faces, from long hours in the smell and heat. One walk through the Von Steuven works had been enough for her and she had not visited since, except to the offices inside the gate to take papers for Miki and chat with the secretaries.

In the back seat of the car were some packages she was posting home to her mother, and some letters, including another to Wilson. It was a little annoying she had to drive all the way to Essen, but the Haupt Post was the only one for miles which would accept international mail. It was Wednesday and she was hoping the nice postal clerk would be on duty, Karolina. The other one she had run-ins with before was a nightmare, and always looked at her like she had come to Germany to roast and eat the children. One of her packages, she had ripped open in front of her and refused to send it without an approval stamp from the Reichspost-Inspektor, but the wrapping was so damaged she had to take it home and start over. And it was just a sweater.

Lacy had learned to be careful with her letters. Her mother had said that one of them arrived with so much black ink all over it they couldn't understand what it was even about. She thought it was odd that the letters that came to her from America were also opened, but not marked up with ink, even when some of them said things she'd rather not know.

Wilson had been keeping her up to date on a string of girls Aaron had been dating. She had been happy to hear that Aaron had been reinstated at the university and was doing well, but his aimless love life of conquests she could have readily accepted being censored out. He had won his race in Los Angeles in 1936, but did not fly his plane in the last two years. He had promised his father he would concentrate on his school work and had graduated with Donovan. Wilson still had a year to go at the school. Aaron had been accepted at Columbia Law School in New York and Donovan was going to Rutgers. Wilson had commented it might be good for them to be at different schools. They were still friends, but something always seemed strained and competitive between them. Donovan and Charlotte had finally gotten married after his graduation, but she was staying in Princeton with her parents while he went back and forth to New Brunswick.

It was getting toward dusk as Lacy came out of the post office. It got darker earlier in November here than it did back in New Jersey. She had been correct that Karolina was on duty, and they had had a pleasant conversation about Karolina's daughter, Katrina, being promoted to group leader in the Bund Deutscher Mädel, the Girls Hitler Youth League. The group had been founded by a former postal worker and Katrina had joined a year before it had become compulsory. Karolina was very proud of her. She was to form the local unit of the new Belief and Beauty cultural section, to guide girls to become proper Aryan wives and mothers. Lacy could appreciate Karolina's pride in her daughter's accomplishment, but felt a twinge of distaste at the emphasis of this new branch of Nazi indoctrination.

Lacy had kept much of her opinions about the Nazi movement, into which she had been imported, to herself. She would hear the housekeeper talk about how Herr Hitler was making the country strong again, and nod her head. In the village, when she visited the beverage shop to try to correct the sparkling water deliveries, they would tell her how proud she must be to have a husband who was such an example to them all. They had all seen the posters of him with his Javelin, in his crisp white Olympic athletic shorts, his shock of blond hair, and blue eyes the color of the sky turned up and focused on the blood Swastika flag waving in the clouds. It was so inspiring, and they saw in him the purity of their race. The dinner parties with some of the managers from the factory, where the conversation sounded so much like those dinner parties of her parents, except in German, had been almost uncomfortable to sit through.

She had met them all. In Berlin, at the Party reception to celebrate the German team, she and Miki had been paraded before the Party leaders in a handshake line, then treated to champagne and caviar with them all milling about, the lower officials trying to sidle as close to Hitler as they could before he would turn from them like a weather vane in a changing wind. The Führer had pretended to be kind to her, as if she was a long lost daughter, for about long enough to sneeze, then he would wipe that floppy unruly hair of his and turn away. He had seemed to snub Miki altogether and all the athletes, oddly, since they were the guests of honor. He was apparently upset that Jesse Owens, the "Schwartze" had beaten them to the gold in the early events. The Germans had done better in the field events, but Miki's silver medal was apparently a disappointment. Lacy would have liked to meet Mr. Owens and congratulate the Americans, but she had been kept away from them on some excuse, until they had left.

Herr Speer, who had designed the stadium, and was in the process of transforming Berlin into the new imperial Rome on the Spee River, she thought was rather nice as a person. She didn't care much for his architecture and had told him so, in pleasant terms. She had had a long discussion about architecture with Professor Labatut from Princeton who had been taking movies on the Hindenburg, and it was fresh in her mind when she spoke to Speer. She thought for some reason her opinion might be useful to him, from a fresh point of view. He had a casual manner and didn't really seem to complain when she realized he probably could have, as soon as it had come out of her mouth. He actually answered her critique about the coldness of it with an argument of his intent to build a sense of confidence. She didn't agree with him, but appreciated that he took it as a discussion. He even offered to take her and Miki on a building site tour. She said she would like that, but they never did.

Dr. Goebbels, she could do entirely without. A hard little rat-faced man. He had insisted that Miss Riefenstahl film her over and over in the stands, as if she were cheering for Miki, when she was actually staring at some filming assistant who was eating a sausage at the time. Goebbels gave the staged footage to the newsreels. Riefenstahl had refused at first to use it in her Olympia film, but he made her cut it into a later version. He had also personally supervised the photographing of Miki for the propaganda posters. There Miki was, the symbol of his Aryan ideals, and he treated him in person like he was a piece of gum on his shoe. She believed the Propaganda Minister was actually jealous of her husband's noble family, even though he went on and on about Teutonic knights, and of course the Jews this and the Jews that. She had found out later it was Goebbels who had kept her from meeting Owens and the American team. His wife, Magda, she thought was so unlike him, and wondered how they got along at all, especially after Leni Riefenstahl had confided in Lacy, in one of her rants when she would swear like a sailor, that Goebbles was cheating on his wife with an actress friend of hers.

Lacy stepped out of the post office into Hachestrasse and the door was locked behind her. It would be dark by the time she got back to Kester, but she thought she should stop at the stationary shop on Lindenallee. The postal paper was so perfunctory, and all of it was infused with the Nazi watermark that she felt like she was working for the Propaganda Ministry whenever she used it. It was fine, and even preferable for corresponding with government offices on Miki's behalf, but not so pleasant for writing personal notes. As she walked toward her car, suddenly there was shouting from the streets ahead and people running.

Lacy hesitated on the sidewalk. She didn't know what was happening. A loud crashing sound came from the next cross street. She stepped to look around the corner of the building at the end of the block, when suddenly a group of young men wearing brown shirts and Swastika bands on their arms ran past her. There were four of them and one seemed to have a flame coming from his hand.

Lacy looked around the corner and was amazed at the sight. The four Hitler Youth boys ran up to a synagogue, with its stone Star of David already covered in graffiti. The boy threw the bottle with the flaming rag crashing through the window as the boys shouted, "Juden! Juden!" The windows exploded out in a shower of glass and flame. Lacy cringed and covered herself. Her forehead was cut by a piece of glass. The brown shirt boys ran up the street. More were coming out from everywhere. They grabbed up stones, bicycles, chairs, anything they could find and smashed them into the windows of any shops marked by the yellow painted stars or scrawled with the damning "Juden" in poster paint.

Lacy watched in shock as the quiet city at sunset was turned into a riot. Another shop, a few doors down from where she stood, exploded in flames. An old woman and a boy ran out from the shop into the street. Their clothes were burning. The Hitler Youth boys just pelted them with rocks and shouted their Juden taunt at them. The burning boy just kept running, down a side street, screaming, until he was out of sight, but the old woman, maybe sixty years old, fell to the ground. One of the brown shirt boys stepped up to stand over her, uncaring of her cries. He unzipped his fly and urinated on her, which almost put the flames out. Then he ran off with the others, laughing, until they too disappeared around the corner.

Lacy ran to help the old woman, taking off her coat and throwing it over her. She tamped out the last of the flame which was burning from the gasoil spilled on her from the bottle. The coat was warm under her hands as she wrapped it around the woman, who looked up at her with terrified eyes and only mouthed the words, "Why? Why?"

Lacy looked around for help. Up the street, she saw a policeman. He just seemed to be standing, as if he had nothing at all to do as the sounds of smashing glass and shouts of terror came from all around. Lacy waved to him and he came toward her. He had a curiously cocked head look as if he was more curious than anything else.

"Help! She's hurt!" Lacy shouted urgently. "There was a child...!" She pointed down the street where the boy had disappeared, but the policeman leaned against a wall with his arms folded. He just gazed at her and the old woman with that curious look.

"What is the matter with you?!" Lacy shouted. She couldn't understand why he was just waiting there. He didn't say anything. He did nothing.

Fires were burning all over the city, with the streets strewn with glass, smashed furniture and store goods, but otherwise deserted as Lacy walked back to her Mercedes car. A Jewish man, maybe a relative, had come to her with the old woman and had taken her away with him. Lacy had offered to take her to a hospital, but the man said no and the woman was too frightened. Lacy had wanted to do more, but she realized she didn't know where there was a hospital that would take a Jewish patient.

As she approached her car, parked at a rather careless odd angle on the curb between two buildings, she was thinking that with every new anti-Jewish law that had been passed and then, the painting of businesses and houses with the Juden star, she had never really said anything to anyone of consequence. Except for writing home about it, and once, or maybe twice, complaining how ugly the graffiti made the streets look, and that one of her favorite fabric stores had closed when Herr Kimmel and his family moved away, she had done nothing about it.

With all the complaining of others about how terrible the Jews were and inane talk about international conspiracies of banks, she had more money than most of the Jews she knew, and had found them to be kind and fair in her dealings with them. She knew important people, and she wondered if there was some department she should have contacted with at least one voice of protest. Maybe it was that she didn't want to make a problem for Miki, with his troublesome American wife. She knew she was being watched. It had been almost a year since she first noticed that little funny Volkswagen people's car parked on the road outside the gate with the man in a black leather coat reading the newspaper, and those two clicks she sometimes heard on the phone line when she called anywhere outside the local exchange. Maybe she should have complained anyway, she scolded herself, but then the sounds and smell of a burning city around her told her that it was too late for that. She could only help now in the way which had come upon her unexpectedly.

As she walked calmly to her car, she looked to see the street was empty and no one was watching. When she was certain it was clear, she gestured with her hand partially hidden by her purse toward the dark shadowed space between the two buildings. Two figures hurried from shadows. Lacy opened the rear car door and they climbed into the back, keeping low. A teenage boy was already lying on the floor below the seat, and the man and the girl lay down on top of him, below the windows.

Lacy got into the front seat and slid under the big steering wheel. She calmly took her keys from her purse, slid the key into the slot, turning it to the on position, and pressed the starter with her foot. The engine rumbled to life and with a clash of the gear shift, Lacy drove away. She looked in the mirrors all the way to Hohenzollernstraße, but no one seemed to be following her, or paying any notice at all.

After Lacy had brought the first three to the house, and was certain she had not been seen, she turned around and drove back to Essen. The brown shirt youth hooligans had moved on to other neighborhoods in the outer districts and had left their carnage to the fire brigades who carefully watered down the stores next to the burning Jewish ones to keep the city from being inundated. Lacy drove around the streets near the post office in what she was sure was a futile effort, but she couldn't live with herself if she didn't at least try to find the old woman.

After twenty minutes of circling around and thinking it was probably hopeless, the boy she remembered suddenly came running out into the headlights of the big car. They had recognized the lady who had tried to help and took a chance.

When Lacy had brought them to her cellar, she had driven off again, this time to Mulheim where the Kimmels had had their store before they were forced to leave. She had met a neighbor friend of Herr Kimmel she thought could help, if she could convince him.

The door to the darkened cellar at the top of a short flight of wooden stairs opened and Lacy turned on the light switch. The dim electric light bulb glowed on the old stones of the medieval foundations of the manor. Another flight of steps turned deeper under the Gothic arch to an uneven flagstone floor where stacks of wine cabinets filled the space. A thin dust covered the bottles laid on their sides in the cases, sorted by variety. Lacy led an older man down the stairs into the cellar. He was stooped by the years, but still energetic. His clothes were crisp and well-tailored and he carried a leather bag in his hand.

Huddled in the cellar, in an alcove behind the wine cases, were six people. The man from Essen with his nine-year-old daughter and teenage son were waiting there. The old woman who had been attacked in her milliner shop and pissed on by the boys was sitting on a wooden case of Chateau Latour Bordeaux wine with her frightened grandson, and a woman who was a neighbor was dabbing her burns with water. They all looked up nervously when the light had come on, but eased when they saw it was the 'Baroness'.

"This man is a doctor. Herr Neuenstein. He is from Mulheim," Lacy assured them. "I'll get some food and blankets." She turned to go back up the stairs, but the woman who was tending to the old lady stopped her with a shaking voice.

"Madame..."

Lacy looked back to the woman's face, her eyes telling of loss, fright, and confusion.

"What are we to do?" she asked.

Lacy didn't have a good answer. She hadn't planned any of this. It was as complete a surprise to her as it was a shock to them. She thought she should learn their names, but hadn't really had time to think of that until now that they were all looking at her with a hope and expectation she was sure she didn't deserve.

"You can stay here for a day or so. Maybe it will pass by then," she told them, trying to smile with a reassurance she didn't really feel that much herself.

"It will not pass," said the man, stroking the hair of his young daughter to calm her. He seemed tired. "I should have left with my brother last year. But, 'no', I said, 'it will pass'." He looked at the others with a sad acceptance of inevitability. "It will get worse."

The sound of a pounding on the front door came from upstairs. The door chimes rang and the pounding resumed. They all held still, looking with frightened eyes to one another, and to Lacy.

Lacy was hesitant. She had called the housekeeper from Essen to tell her that she and her husband could have the night off and she could go out for the evening. Perhaps they had come back. But the housekeeper wouldn't need to knock on the door. Even if she had left her key, she knew the way through the back door of the pantry. Then, it occurred to Lacy that maybe the housekeeper had become suspicious of being given this particular night off and had told someone, or worse, had waited and seen her coming and going.

The knocking was still urgent as Lacy tried not to hurry from the hall through the grand foyer. She stopped a moment to gather her composure, dreading what might be on the other side of that door. For a moment she convinced herself that it was a tradesman who had not been paid for something, coming to settle a bill. That would explain the urgency, wouldn't it? Maybe she could just let them think she wasn't home, but they obviously were not going away. She took a breath and turned the electric light switch for the outside. Then, she reached for the door latch of the large carved door and opened it.

Outside, on the portico steps in the light of the lamp were two men in leather coats. One of them, she recognized as the man who sometimes read the newspaper in the little car by the gate. She didn't know the other. Her heart beat faster as she tried to remain still, and smile.

"Yes?" she said, as befitting of her position as she could manage, remembering that tone her mother always seemed to have when she answered the door to Aaron, or any sort of tradesman she didn't know.

The Gestapo agent that she didn't recognize thrust his badge identification forward toward her. She could just read the name, Stenhoffer, under the red ink eagle Reichs Stamp before he quickly slapped the leather case closed. He was obviously the senior officer.

"Secret Police," he said, as if that phrase were as natural as a salesman announcing his brand of wares, "Frau von Steuven?"

"Yes. What can I do for you?"

"We have been informed that you were in Essen this evening."

Lacy tried to maintain her composure, as if the visit was a total mystery. "Yes. I went to the post."

Agent Stenhoffer didn't bother with any invitation but stepped through the doorway past her. The other Gestapo agent followed behind him as if tethered by an invisible rope. They stood together for a moment in the middle of the foyer, looking around, taking in the museum art on the walls, as if wondering what price it might fetch when the house was seized. Lacy wondered if she would be sent to the camp near Munich that correspondent on the Hindenburg, Paula Lecler, had told her about, Dachau. Or was there another one closer by, now?

"May we come in?" Stenhoffer asked, as if he was not already standing with his calf boots on her Persian carpet. Lacy glanced outside the door she was still holding open. There were two cars parked in the courtyard drive, the little folks' car and a black Mercedes. Two more agents, these in the gray and black uniform of the Ordnungspolizei, were waiting in the second car. She closed the door, but didn't answer the obvious rhetorical. She just waited for him to get to it.

"You are aware there has been some looting?" Stenhoffer slid his identity wallet into his coat pocket with a cool, measured manner of certainty. Then, he took time to take off his gloves, as if to stretch out the torment. "A few trouble makers."

"Yes. I saw some boys," Lacy said evenly, "the Brown Shirts."

Stenhoffer fixed her with a look of momentary surprise, as if it was a joke, then a total lack of humor.

"That, Frau von Steuven, is not what we are discussing."

112

"Then, what are we discussing?" Lacy asked.

"You are alone in the house?"

"I gave the housekeeper the evening off. She and her husband went out, I believe." She watched the agent carefully, but he seemed to register nothing at the mention of Frau Lindl. Maybe she was not the reason he was there. "The maid is at her sister's in Mettmann for the week. She's ill. Her sister is. My husband is in Spain."

The second agent turned from his interest in looking at the display case of Miki's trophies. "That is not correct," he said, as if catching her in a lie.

"He volunteered," Lacy answered, turning to him, unable to hold back her pique at the sense of accusation. "He was to be gone for a few months. It's been almost a year and a half. He's a Lieutenant with the Condor Squadron. You must know." She knew they had a full file on both her and Miki. They had been listening to their phone conversations and reading all her letters.

Stenhoffer answered her with a cool detachment as if she should know the obvious, "Captain von Steuven is in Berlin."

"Berlin?" This was news to Lacy. She hadn't spoken to Miki in three weeks. She had been worried something might have happened to him in his plane, but he had told her he would be in a rear area for a few days. He would sometimes go for two to three weeks without calling her.

Stenhoffer reached back into his coat for the opposite inner pocket from his I.D. to pull out a notebook. He opened it with a crisp snap, and flipped a few pages, licking his finger with each one, to stab it and slide it over to the next. He found the page he wanted.

"Hauptmann Von Steuven arrived from Vitoria two weeks ago. He is to receive the Spanish Cross."

Lacy was shocked. She had no idea Miki was back in Germany and he had apparently lied to her when he called last. "Then, you know more about my husband than I do."

Stenhoffer didn't seem to care whether she knew where her husband was or not. He finally got to his business.

"We are looking for a man from Mulheim. A bookkeeper by trade, suspected of passport forgery. His name is Steinmetz. A Jew. He is the ringleader of an illegal political organization."

Lacy held steady. She could answer that truthfully, at least. "I don't know any Steinmetz." She relaxed just a little, maybe they were on the wrong track. She even allowed herself a little wit, "And I don't know many Jews. I'm Episcopalian."

Stenhoffer looked a little confused a moment. He checked his notes, flipping the pages quickly with his wet finger, finally finding a page.

"You are Lutheran? Are you not?"

Lacy felt an ease. Between her family, Aaron, Miki, and the university, she had had many discussions of religion in her life. The Gestapo could pull out her fingernails and she could run rings around them.

"My husband is Lutheran," she explained patiently. "You don't have Episcopal churches here, so it was easier to attend with him. I do miss the communion sacrament. I thought of converting to Catholic, but your Lutheran churches do have all that lovely Baroque art. That's a pleasant substitution."

Stenhoffer seemed suddenly completely at a loss. He pulled a fountain pen from his pocket to write a note, but seemed uncertain how to categorize it, scribbling quickly in detail.

Lacy felt such a sudden flush of relief and superiority in the face of this officious toad, she allowed herself an added bit of sarcasm, "I don't really have any experience of what sort of art they have in synagogues, and I probably will never have a chance to find out, now."

He looked up sharply at her and she quickly regretted it as soon as it slipped from her lips. She should not tease the devil.

"Look, it's late and I'd like to go to bed," she said with finality. "Or do you intend to arrest me?"

The Gestapo agent looked to his partner, then, snapped his notebook closed. He walked to the door, stopping to turn back.

"If you see someone nearby, or anyone comes to your door who you do not know, you will inform us immediately."

The second agent handed her a card with a phone number and simple address of the administration office in Essen. They opened the door themselves and went out.

Lacy watched a moment as they got into their cars. A light snow had started to fall, the first of November. It had dusted the tops of the vehicles and the paving stones of the courtyard with a fine white powder. The sky had been a high gray all day and a cold snap had drifted across the river. Lacy had been thinking that it might snow and it was coming down now. She watched as the cars drove away, blending into the dark by the gate and away down the road until the motors faded. She closed the door and leaned against it to catch her breath.

Waiting for her heart to stop pounding, Lacy looked around at the house, just taking in familiar objects, so far from her parents' home back in New Jersey, where all she had to worry about with the police was whether she would have to stay in her room for two days. There was that time when she was twelve, when she and her friend Maisie had ridden their bikes down the street with a stick, smashing all the driveway lamps. Someone had reported them and a Princeton police officer showed up at her door and made them sweep it all up, a mile and a half of broken glass.

She thought about that. Broken glass. All those windows with the graffitied stars, shattered on the pavement, and the flames. Who would sweep it all up? Would she drive into the city tomorrow and it would all be gone, as if it never happened? Like the incident on Bismarckstaße in Mulheim three months ago?

Then, she thought about the six people in her cellar. Where would they go? They couldn't stay there for long. Her housekeeper, Lindl, was such a fanatic. She and her husband both had joined the party in 1933, before it was popular in the north. She had a portrait of Hitler in the living room of her cottage, the ridiculously romanticized one with him clothed as an armored knight carrying the blood banner flag. She even had the personal oath framed in a sampler, even though she was neither a soldier, nor a civil servant. "I swear that I shall be obedient and faithful to the Führer of the German Reich and people, Adolf Hitler, and abide by all the laws conscientiously, so help me God." Lacy thought she was rather like those women Miss Lecler had written about who idolized him as a bachelor stud horse of national glory. Lacy didn't blame her so much for that, as her husband, Herr Lindl, the groundskeeper, might cause any woman to fantasize a little, but Lacy would have picked a film star. Or Aaron. She did still fantasize about Aaron. Once or twice, maybe, when she was angry with Miki, and he was off on his training. Or in Spain. Okay, it was more than once or twice.

She tried to stop thinking about Aaron. But it was that smarmy Gestapo agent at the door who had gotten her thinking about her mother. Her mother and her father who had pushed her to marry Miki. It was her choice, at least she thought it was. She was so angry at Aaron, and frightened for him. She had cried like the world was ending when he stood outside her window that afternoon, calling her name. But she believed her father when he told her Miki would be right for her. He could take care of her and be steady for her. That Aaron was not the stuff of her world.

It wasn't that Miki wasn't good to her. He was steady, and kind, and reliable. He protected her when the complaints came about her American loyalties. He had interceded with his parents when they judged her. God, the arguments she had with his mother over the art and the drapery. But Miki would step between them and tell Margarethe Gräffin von Steuven that he loved his wife's taste, even though when she had shown him her selections he had expressed no opinion whatever, other than a shrug and smile of his blue eyes. There was something cold about Miki, now that she knew him so closely. Some place in his heart that she couldn't reach, and wasn't sure if anyone could.

Steinmetz. An accountant. The name kept coming to her. She had told the truth to agent Stenhoffer that the name didn't mean anything to her, but she now started to

remember that Herr Kimmel had said something about
an accountant he knew who had helped him get an
Ausfahrt Visa for his cousin who didn't have the correct
papers, when they had all decided to leave Germany. It
was a year ago, now. Kimmel's thirteen year old son had
gotten into a fight with some Hitler Youth boys who were
waiting outside the private Jewish school his father had
enrolled him in after he was forced out of the public state
school, and he was beaten quite badly. Lacy had shopped
at Herr Kimmel's for her drapes material and wall cloth.
He had especially imported some beautiful hand-loomed
damask from Moravia, where he had some distant
family. All the German shops only had that machine-
made utility cloth, certified to be touched only by Aryan
hands. It was so odd, that Magda Goebbels headed the
National Fashion Institute, but she couldn't get her
husband to approve more than sixteen colors and twenty-
two pattern designs. Maybe if she had agreed to let him
screw his actress mistress in exchange, Germany could
have had a proper fashion industry, but then uniforms
only came in gray, brown and black.

The Kimmels had closed their shop in October of
1937 and had left to go to Holland where Herr Kimmel
had some more family who had settled in Rotterdam back
in 1928, when the wave of anti-Semitism first raised to a
high pitch in the election campaigns of the National
Socialists. Everyone had said they didn't really mean
what they were saying. Hitler was going make the
country strong again. The Jews didn't really conspire to
fix the Versailles Treaty so that ordinary Germans would
be crushed by the loans from the money lenders for
reparations, but Joachim Kimmel's uncle Rudi said, "just
watch, they will believe, they will come for us", and he

packed his house, his wife and three children, and left. It took almost ten years before Joachim finally decided his uncle was not a lunatic, but the most prophetic man he might ever know.

If the Gestapo was already looking for Steinmetz, Lacy thought, trying to reason out a plan, he certainly wouldn't be at an office looking over accounting books. How could she find him, she wondered. Maybe he was in her basement. She had never asked their names. But they had all come from Essen, and Stenhoffer had said he was from Mulheim. Then, she thought about Dr. Neuenstein, down in her cellar. He was from Mulheim. Surely he would know a Jewish accountant named Steinmetz. But would he admit it? If there was some secret organization supplying exit papers and documents, forged documents, would he know about it? And would he trust her enough to tell her?

She decided to ask him outright. But first she needed to get them some food. There was some bread and apple tart still in the pantry. Maybe some beer or sparkling water for the kids. They could drink all the wine they wanted, but the bottles might be counted missing if Herr Lindl made an inventory for his wife. Lacy didn't drink very much wine when Miki was gone, so it would be noticed. They might think she was having an affair with someone, though certainly not Herr Lindl, who had the look of a hairy-backed balding bulldog, not the stuff of romantic fantasies. Wine wasn't very good for thirst, anyway.

She headed toward the kitchen, glad the snow hadn't started falling earlier, or else Stenhoffer would have found a dozen footprints in the courtyard in a messy trail between her purple saloon Mercedes and the front door.

That's how someone had seen her in Essen. They knew the car. Everyone knew the von Steuven car. She thought she would never take it again for her trips to the city. She could get the gray Opel out of the garage. It couldn't fit very many people at a time, but would draw less notice. She could just say the Mercedes was too big and heavy for her to steer.

It was all starting to settle in her mind what she had to do and she felt a calmness of purpose she hadn't felt since that afternoon, watching the boys in the planes over Cleveland Field. And then, she thought about Miki. He had never lied to her before.

~~~

CHAPTER NINE

Tentelgasse

Frau Lindl was fulfilling her morning routine, dusting the great hall and quietly tisk-tisking to herself over the awful obscene art that the mistress had hung on the walls. If the cultural ministry thought it unworthy to be in a museum, then it had no business being openly displayed in a respectable home. She wasn't quite sure what was wrong with it. The naked human body was acceptable in other forms. The leader had encouraged all Germans to be healthy in body and spirit, but these images of cherubs and saints were not of the lean and toned Aryan form reaching for achievement that was the appropriate taste. And there were some of those ugly modern ones, with sharp angles and people who didn't look like people at all. She had often wondered if she should report them, but was worried she could get into trouble herself, and Karl had scolded her that she should not make trouble.

The mistress had told her that Baron Michael had returned to Germany and might be coming home soon, but didn't seem to know when, or if it was certain. She preferred it when he was home. He looked so handsome in his uniform. It was his natural place. He was what was best about Germany, a symbol for them all. She was proud to work in his house. The mistress, well, she was a foreigner, and everyone knew what Herr Hitler said about foreigners. No wonder she wasn't being informed about the movements of a Reich hero. Lindl thought she should check on the wine stocks, as the Baron liked it so, and all should be ready.

She tried to open the door to the wine cellars. The knob turned in her hand but the door wouldn't budge. It was locked, which she thought was odd. The cellar door was never locked. She wondered if Karl had broken something and was hiding it. He had started to get clumsy since he turned fifty. Something in his hands had made them shake. He had once dropped a lamp and was so embarrassed to admit it he had swept all the bulb pieces under the throw carpet. It crunched when anyone stepped on it. She reached for the ring of keys in her pocket on the thin chain which tied them to a belt loop on her smock. But as she sorted through them to find the key, the door rattled from inside. Was it Karl still locked inside, she wondered, but the door opened and Madame von Steuven came out.

Lacy closed the door quickly, startled by her housekeeper just outside of it. Had she been listening? She searched Lindl's face for a clue to what she had heard or knew, but the woman seemed a blank.

"The door was locked, Madame," Lindl said, almost as if a protest.

"Yes. And I'd like to keep it that way." Lacy held out her hand. "May I have your key, please, Hilda?"

Frau Lindl felt a little insulted. Did the mistress not trust her with the wine stocks? Did she actually think she would steal? Maybe Karl had broken something. Maybe he dropped a full case of expensive French wine and had hidden it. Of course the mistress would blame her. Maybe Karl had said something stupid about the art.

Lindl found the cellar key and took it off her ring. She handed it over to Lacy, as if she'd been demoted.

"Have I not been satisfactory, Madame?" she asked.

"Not at all. I'd just like to have a private area. If that's alright?"

Lindl didn't think the mistress needed to be sharp with her. If Karl had broken something, he would just have to explain it.

"Is anything missing, Madame?"

Lacy thought it was an odd question, but at least Hilda Lindl didn't seem to have a clue that something had been added to the contents of the cellar rather than removed.

"No, Hilda. There is nothing missing. Thank you."

Lindl nodded, then walked away down the hall, acting a bit like a scolded dog, Lacy thought. For a woman with a well-paid job in a fine house, a cottage of her own to live in and an aging husband who might otherwise be put out to pension with his advancing palsy, she might be more grateful. But she had other concerns on her mind.

She would have to be careful with Lindl. She could fire her with Karl's health as an excuse, but a sudden change might arouse suspicion, and Lindl would certainly run straight to the Cultural Ministry to make a stink about the art she was always clucking about. Lindl apparently didn't think Lacy knew about her opinions, but the housekeeper would make some comment about it to nearly any tradesman who came to the house. And if the Gestapo hadn't already returned to catalog it and crate it off, the art was the least of her concerns. Miki's father was supplying half the Panzer parts for the armor build up, the sixth richest man in the Reich, and Miki was a decorated hero, a symbol of the nation. Did her housekeeper think the ministry would be bothered about their art collection? But what was in her basement and the venture she was about to undertake, was a different matter entirely.

Dr. Neuenstein had been at first reluctant to admit anything, but after some frank admissions from Lacy about what she intended to do with the information, which could send her to a work camp if he were to reveal it, he opened up. He did know Steinmetz, an accountant who had turned over his ledger pens for the tools of a document forger. Steinmetz had been in the army in the war, in the documentation service, and knew all the means of registry. After the Enabling Act was established in 1933, he had joined a loose group of Jewish veterans who had taken up commercial trades and made their skills available to dissidents and those who wanted to leave the county, but didn't have the means to fulfill all the necessary requirements or were under suspicion. And Kimmel did more than just utilize Steinmetz' skills for his cousin and his own escape. He had made arrangements to spread the network though his connections in the milliner's trade. Jewish businesses were closing and under surveillance, but Kimmel had brought in gentile friends who wanted to help.

Lacy had asked Dr. Neuenstein if he knew the state secret police were searching for Steinmetz. His answer both shocked her and excited her in some deep way.

"If they knew any more than Steinmetz, I would not be here. I would be under arrest," he had told her.

Neuenstein was deeply involved with Steinmetz and the organization. They had heard that a family they helped was stopped at the Dutch border. One of the children apparently said something to raise suspicion. That family had only dealt directly with Steinmetz, so couldn't have revealed anyone else, as they had a system where any one member only had contact with one other member by name. If a member was compromised they would have to make one arrest at a time and the chain might have time to protect itself. No one had been arrested, so they must only know of Steinmetz, who may have managed to escape before being questioned.

Lacy parked the Opel on Tentelgasse in Essen. It was a quiet little side street only a few blocks from the incidents she had witnessed a few weeks ago on what was now being called "Kristallnacht" in the international press. Many of her neighbors didn't see much international press, only the approved reporting in the Frankfurter Zeitung, or whatever Dr. Goebbles wanted to put in his Racial Observer, and the caricatures of evil Jews and lampooned international figures in Der Stürmer. Lacy still received her subscription of Vogue Paris to keep up with fashion and the London Sunday Times, which arrived only intermittently now, sometimes looking like it had been run over by a truck, with black ink on the tread. And her mother still sent her copies of the Princeton Packet, at least when her mother could circle the wedding announcements of her friends from school.

The city was back to normal, as Lacy had expected, though many of the shops that were destroyed had been boarded up. She walked down the little street under the now barren Linden trees to Hagan. She was looking for an address Dr. Neuenstein had given her. She hadn't written it down, but had memorized it in case she were stopped, and hoped she got it right. How many tailor shops could there be on the street? As it turned out there were three! God forbid she would walk into some random shop and tell the wrong person who she was and what she was up to. But the number above the door of the second shop, Lublin's, seemed right and everything else fit. She took a breath and stepped through the door.

The bell tinkled and the tailor behind the counter looked up expectantly. The counter was covered with cloth bolts of gray-striped and plain blue suit material. The tailor, she guessed to be about forty years old. He was thin and wore round unrimmed spectacles. On the wall behind him where hung photographic portraits, side by side of the Pope and the Fürher. He looked at her with at first a hopeful expectation. She was obviously a well-heeled lady who would spend good money, but her purpose would soon change him.

"Guten Tag, meine gnadige Frau," he greeted her pleasantly.

"The leaves of the Linden are green," she said without waiting for preamble.

The smile dropped from his face for a moment, but he tried to regain it again.

"Yes, Madame, and the Rhine is golden. What may I help you with?"

The words were from a popular Aryan anthem song. If someone questioned the odd phase, they could just say they were commenting on the trees outside. Lacy did not ask the tailor's name. She might assume it was Lublin, but she could answer truthfully, if questioned, that she did not know who he was. He might have been an employee. Maybe Lublin had passed down the shop. He did not ask her name either, though undoubtedly he

126

might recognize her as a famous person. It was a thin façade.

"I would like a suit. In green. For my husband. I have the measurements." Lacy said, fighting the twitching nerve in her stomach, and nervously teasing the little scar on her arm. She placed a small piece of paper on the counter with some numbers written on it in pencil which could be read as inches and sizes. The tailor glanced to the window of the shop, looking out onto the street. It seemed clear. He rested his hand on the paper and slid it off the counter, slipping it into his vest pocket. Then, he gestured toward a curtain which separated the front of the shop from the work area. Lacy could see a sewing machine and cutting table beyond it.

"If you would like to step into the back, please, Madame. We are out of green at the moment, but perhaps I could show you something you might prefer."

Lacy followed him into the back. He took one more glance to the street, then, slid the curtain closed behind them.

Lacy stepped out the door of the tailor shop. The bell tinkled as she pulled the door closed behind her. She looked at the small gold watch she had pinned as a pendant to her suit jacket. It was Swiss, a present from Miki, from one of his training missions. Eleven twenty-one. She had spent about forty minutes inside the shop. Not so much as to arouse any concern, she thought. She was carrying a bolt of rolled cloth under her arm, a plain blue-gray. As she turned from the door, she nearly bumped into someone.

"Pardon me," she said, politely distracted, but froze when she looked up from her gloves. It was the policeman from the night of broken glass, the one who did nothing as the old woman screamed. He stood on the sidewalk, arms crossed, looking at her.

"Good afternoon," she said, wondering if he had been watching her all along. Maybe he was following her. Is he the one who reported to the Gestapo that she had been in Essen? He was regular Ordnungspolizei, and not the security police. From the look of him, he'd probably been a policeman before the Nazis and the new system. He would only have changed uniforms and now reported to an SS Officer above him.

He said nothing and Lacy did not remind him of their previous encounter. Lacy tipped her head to him by way of a nod befitting her class and walked past him. The policeman watched her for a moment but made no sign if he even remembered her. She started to turn onto Tentelgasse, but then instead, decided to cross the corner and continue down the main boulevard. She would walk around the block, pausing to look in windows as if shopping. She thought she would have to be careful about too many trips to the tailor, or be careful to check if this policeman was around before she went in. Maybe she would really have the tailor make a suit, which she could take back, so she could complain about the fitting. But then, would they find this strange, when her husband wasn't home?

She was thinking this as she pulled into the drive of the house and realized that was probably going to be the easy part. A military staff car was parked in the courtyard, by the door.

Lacy opened the front door to find Miki standing in the foyer of the grand hall, his back turned, talking to two Luftwaffe officers, showing them his trophy award case. He turned at the sound of the door. Medals dangled from the front of his uniform, and the gold Spanish Cross with swords and diamonds between the patée cross was pinned to his pocket, just below the flap. The other two fliers also had crosses, but more simple, in bronze.

"There you are. We were looking all over," Miki said, with a smile.

Lacy found herself just staring a moment. She was happy that he was home, but so much had been happening, and it was a surprise.

"Miki?!" was all she could get out.

"Who else?" he said with a cheerful smirk and held out his arms for her. Lacy wasn't sure what to do. She was holding the bolt of cloth from the tailor shop and what it contained, hidden, rolled inside. She carefully laid the cloth on a side table, making sure it wouldn't roll open, then she hurried to him, hugging him.

"You're home. I was told you were in Berlin."

"Yes. We were taken to meet the Führer."

"Hitler?"

Miki grinned, amused at the question. "He's the only one I know of. Unless Feldmarschall Göring has other plans." He looked to the other officers and they chuckled with him.

"I'm just surprised you didn't tell me."

"My orders came quickly. We were stationed at Chemnitz, near the Czechoslovakia border. But it turns out we had nothing to do."

He shrugged with an amused smile, hiding behind it the secret maneuvers Hitler had made in advance of his threats of war if the Sudetenland of German speaking Czechoslovakia was not given to Germany. British Prime

Minister Neville Chamberlain and French Premier Edouard Daladier had signed the Munich Pact with Hitler and Mussolini, so Chamberlain had declared "peace in our time". The European powers had capitulated without a shot fired and the country had celebrated the great victory and prowess of their leader.

"I didn't think you would care for all that. All the uniforms, everyone a general. You didn't enjoy it the last time we were there. God, the politics! I'm glad to be home."

Lacy was glad, too. There had been parades in Essen, Duisburg and Düsseldorf. Lacy had given Frau Lindl and Karl three days off to march in the Duisburg parade with their Nazi party chapter, but all the city had turned out to cheer and wave the flags.

"You're right. I wouldn't have cared for it. But you might have asked me. At least you're safe." She kissed him.

He introduced the others. "This is Oberlieutnant Kellmann and Lieutnant Frische. They were my wingmen in Spain."

The two young officers, each about twenty, bowed and took Lacy's hand gallantly. Lacy thought they both looked very young next to Miki. He was only twenty-three now but seemed much older somehow than when she had last seen him.

"You owe Kellmann here a bottle of wine." He slapped the First Lieutenant on the shoulder. "He saved your husband's butt more than once and I have promised him..."

"Wine?" Lacy asked nervously.

"Yes. Some of that Latour we have been saving," he said, not noticing her unease. "Unless you have become a drinker while I have been gone. And a very thick cut of Ruhr valley beef. Kellmann is from the Alps of Bavaria where the cows all have two legs shorter than the others and are only good for cheese."

They all laughed as Kellmann punched his shoulder in good-natured camaraderie. Lacy tried to hide her nerves.

"Of course. I'll send to the market. The icebox is a little bit bare. But, we'll have a wonderful welcome home dinner."

Miki noticed the bolt of cloth on the table. He stepped over to look at it. Lacy hurried to it and picked it up, tucking it under her arm.

"Have you been taking up sewing while I've been away?"

"I just thought the guest room needed some new curtains." She nodded to the officers, "I guess I must be clairvoyant. I'll just put this away. There's some brandy in the den."

As she trotted up the stairs with the cloth, Frisch looked to Miki, confused, "Den?"

"Amerikanisher Frau..." Miki joked and the others laughed as they walked into the salon.

Lacy closed the bedroom door, listening at it a moment. Then she went to the bed and laid down the bolt of cloth. She unrolled it a couple of folds until the documents inside where uncovered, forged financial documents and identity papers.

She grabbed them up and looked around quickly. She went to the dresser in her closet and laid them underneath a pile of sweaters in a drawer. She would have to think of a better hiding hole, but just now she had a more urgent problem.

Lacy opened the cellar door and stepped through. She turned the lock behind her and switched on the light. There was no one in sight as she went down the steps into the racks of wines.

"We hear voices and boots." It was Dr. Neuenstein in the shadows, in the space behind the shelves.

"My husband is home, with some Luftwaffe officers."

The others hiding with him looked at each other, worried. There were three of them now.

"I have the documents for Herr Bernstein, Lisa and Wilhelm. Train tickets to Antwerp for you. You must go. Frau Shimmel will go to her sister in Poland."

"How will we get out of the house now, with soldiers?" young Lisa asked.

Lacy held up the wine bottles. "They're working on brandy, now. The wine and schnapps should do the trick."

The moonlight cut through the windows into the bedroom. Lacy lay naked in the bed, with Miki's arm draped across her body. His face was half-buried in a pillow, snoring. The sex had been welcome. It had been a long time now, feeling his weight on top of her and his hands, and inside. She felt more like a wife, now, but her mind was divided. She had discovered a scar on his hip she hadn't noticed before. He passed it off as nothing to be worried about. It wasn't a bullet but a hot piece of engine metal that had burst through the cockpit seat. The wound had healed, but what bothered her was that his plane had gone down. He had crash landed in a field. And he hadn't told her. And there were people in her basement.

Lacy gently lifted his arm and slipped out of the bed. She stepped over the discarded night slip on the floor and padded to the dresser. She tried to quietly slide the drawer open, but it sounded like a freight train in the dark. She looked over to Miki. He was dead out. He must have been very tired from his long trip and all the sycophancy.

Miki and his pilot friends had been full of the boisterous energy of young men through three hours of dinner, drinking and cigars, comrades in arms. Lacy had listened to tales of aerial maneuvers and Spanish dancing. Miki promised to show her some steps, but what had lingered in her mind was the discussion of dark-eyed girls and a dog they shot from their planes. They claimed it was mad, but how could you tell from a thousand feet and two hundred miles-per-hour? But it apparently made for a good moving target for a bet between them. Miki had won the bet, tearing the animal into pieces with the 7.9 millimeter machine guns. Lacy learned of the intricate mechanism that allowed the bullet to pass through the propeller blades without hitting them. She also learned that to kill a Polikarpov, you had to come down from a high altitude and shoot the pilot from above. Just putting holes in its wings wouldn't bother the Russian made biplane at all, as it was very sturdily made and could dance around a straight flying Messerschmitt at low altitude, but watching the pilot's head explode from a rapid burst made for a very short fight.

Lacy dug the papers from under the clothes, and took a sweater and a skirt from the drawer. She slipped quietly out of the room.

Miki coughed in the pillow. He woke up and rolled over on the bed. The thick and soft feather duvet mattress was such a difference from the hard and thin military wadding cot mattresses he had spent the last nineteen months sleeping on. The hotel in Berlin had not really been much better. The Adlon was one of the best the city had to offer, but Miki thought that while their bedding coverings were indeed first rate, the frames might as well have been laundry wash boards. He reached his arm over for Lacy, but she wasn't there.

If he had arisen at that moment to look out the window, he could have seen Lacy in a coat with four other figures creeping across the moonlit grounds, into the woods.

Lacy led the group through the trees, until they came to a slope looking out over the factories of Essen across the river. The lights were still burning on round-the-clock shifts.

"You'll have to go from here on foot before the sun comes up. Doctor, you go to Duisburg station. Herr Bernstein, you, Lisa and Wilhelm go on to Krefeld. Catch the morning worker's train."

Dr. Neuenstein was reluctant to go. He had no close family and his practice had been closed, but he felt a responsibility to the network and the effort. Lacy had insisted that he must go now. She would take over. Steinmetz had not been seen, and maybe he was gone, but if he were arrested he could name Neuenstein, and that was dangerous for them all.

He held her hands for a long moment, then, looked into her eyes. "Why are you doing this, Baroness? I'm grateful... We are grateful, but it is dangerous for you."

Lacy tried to ease him with a joke. "How dangerous can it be? I'm the wife of a war hero." It was not a very

134

good joke. Hiding them in her house could send her to a work camp. Passing forged documents and assisting wanted conspirators to cross the border could just as easily lead to the alley behind the state administration office and a quick bullet in the head.

"And besides...how can I not?" she said simply. "And I'm not a baroness, we don't have titles anymore."

The doctor smiled warmly, admiring her nerve. "It's just a courtesy," he said.

The doctor and the others nodded their thanks. Lisa wrapped her arms around Lacy to say goodbye, as if departing an older sister. Then, they headed off together down the slope to the river through the trees. Lacy watched them for a few moments, then, turned back toward the house. The lamp was on in the bedroom window.

Lacy slipped back through the pantry door and closed it as silently as she could. It was old wood and didn't fit the frame as well as it could. She padded through the kitchen to the hall, thinking to go up the back stair. She listened to see if anyone was stirring, but it was quiet. The fliers must be dead asleep in the bedrooms above. She crept across the hallway toward the stairs.

"Where did you go?"

Lacy jumped a little, startled. She turned to find Miki standing in the doorway to the darkened dining room, in just his pants.

"You scared me."

"Scared you?" Miki seemed, not suspicious really, but mystified.

"It's been so long since anyone else has been in the house," Lacy said. She wondered how much he had seen, or how long he'd been waiting.

"I woke up and you were gone. What were you doing outside?" He was looking at her bare feet, covered with wet leaves.

"Oh... The moon is beautiful out. I went for a walk. You were snoring so loudly, I couldn't sleep."

Miki thought about it a moment, puzzled. Then, he smiled.

"I was snoring?"

"Loud. Like the engine of the plane you used to fly, racing Aaron."

"Aaron? That was long ago. It seems so." He thought about it. He had thought about Aaron a lot when he was diving from the clouds over Madrid. "I was snoring? You could have awoken me. Tell me to be quiet."

He stepped from the doorway to her, touching her face with his hand, reaching into the opening of the overcoat she had put on with his other hand to cup her breast beneath. She was not wearing the clothes she had taken from the drawer. The sweater was on Lisa, on her way to Krefeld.

"You could have told me to make love to you again," Miki said, soft as a whisper.

Lacy said nothing for a moment. Then, she shrugged the overcoat off her shoulders onto the floor at her feet.

"Make love to me again."

Miki grabbed her up and laid her down on the coat on the floor, spreading her legs, on top of her on the polished Elm floor boards.

In the cellar croft, three people were still huddled among the wines and stored furniture, still waiting for

136

their papers. They sat in the dark, listening to the sounds of love-making and thumping on the floor above them.

Miki was home for just five days. He and the fliers toured the factories and hunted in the field hides in the wooded thickets along the river slope. They had eaten fresh shot game, drank brandy and finished off two cases of Latour. Lacy had to make the excuse that she was keeping an ordered account of the cellar to keep Miki from going down below.

Kellmann and Frische had found plenty of local girls to admire their uniforms and medals. Lacy was sure they had both had Berta, the serving girl who had wanted to go to hotel school, who had since decided it was now her duty to have an Aryan baby for the future of the Fatherland. It didn't really matter which the father might be. And Miki made love to Lacy every night.

On the fifth day, Miki and his two wingmen stood at the door in their uniforms, crisp and pressed. Lacy had made the excuse of taking their uniforms to Essen for cleaning, so that she could make a visit to the tailor shop. She would take the three in the basement out as soon as he and his friends had gone.

Lacy was torn. She didn't want Miki to go, but his being home had been a week of constant fear of his discovering her secret. He could have demanded to go into the cellar or ask why the door was locked, or wondered why the pantry seemed to always be empty when it should have had leftovers of their sumptuous meals. But he didn't, and now he was leaving again. She would be alone. She didn't know for how long. Miki had said they were stationing his Jäger Group in eastern

Prussia near Poland. The newsreels had been showing the vicious attacks by the Poles on the German speaking peoples there and it all looked so horrible. Lacy had been as affected by the brutal assaults on innocent Germans as everybody else, and had thought Hitler's threats were justified.

But as she had watched the burning farms and slaughtered animals, there had been something about the lamenting wail of one German-Polish mother over the bodies of her dead children, and how they were angled so perfectly in the frame. The mother's tears and the children caught in the light. It oddly had made her think of that film assistant eating his sausage that Lacy had watched as Miss Riefenstahl made her cheer over and over again for Miki in the Berlin stadium stands. More emotion, more emotion, Leni had kept telling her.

~~~

CHAPTER TEN

Princeton Lawyers

The newsreels which played before the screwball comedies had been filled for weeks with images of Stuka dive bombers and burning buildings, Panzer tanks of the Wehrmacht rolling across the Polish border and the new German word that all Americans would now know how to pronounce, "Blitzkrieg".

Hitler had annexed Austria and marched his storm troopers from the ceded Sudetenland to occupy the rest of Czechoslovakia, Bohemia and Moravia. Italy had invaded and annexed Albania. World leaders had wrung their hands, but hoped they would be satisfied, but with the invasion of Poland, Britain and France had declared war with Germany. The winter of 1939 was cold and especially snowy in New Jersey and New York, much more than the usual passing storm and black ice which would turn to slush in two days. War news from Europe had calmed, but news from Japan and China had taken its place. The war discussions had now been about whether America should arm the British and the French.

The Dunbroughs and the Wilsons hosted an event in Princeton and had invited Charles Lindbergh to speak. The aviator had said that he didn't view Germany, Britain and France as implacable foes but as parts of a common fraternal order. He was skeptical of the moral righteousness of the British and French, and more concerned about the Oriental hordes which posed a greater threat to the fabric of Western Civilization.

Irene Dunbrough had stood up and spoke of her own daughter and her husband as part of the decent people of Germany who wanted peace, but that her country had needed to respond to the dangers around it. Lacy had been careful in her letters now to never mention the word "Jew", nor had she told her mother of Miki's increasing victories. She no longer said where Miki was stationed, nor of his movements, as she had known they would have been blacked out. She had only spoken mostly of fabrics for decorating the house and having suits tailored for Miki. But on April 9th of 1940, the German war machine invaded Denmark and Norway, and President Roosevelt had gone on his Sunday broadcast to argue that the isolationist fantasy of the nation "as a safe oasis in a world dominated by fascist terror" was for the overwhelming majority of Americans, not a dream but a "nightmare" of a people without freedom.

None of this seemed to be on the minds of the recent law graduates of the class of 1940 who had gathered at the Nassau Club, dancing the new "Jitterbug" to the swing beat of "In The Mood" as Glenn Miller led his band from the bandstand.

A banner across the dining room declared "Congratulations Princeton Lawyers of 1940!" This was a long standing joke of tradition. Princeton University did not have a law school, but every year the Princeton graduates who completed their law degrees at Yale or Harvard, Columbia or Rutgers, returned to celebrate with their fellow Princetonians.

The private Nassau Club had been founded by Woodrow Wilson and fifteen others of the university faculty in 1889. Much of the world had been shaped by the men who drank and smoked cigars under its roof. Wilson had conceived the idea of the League of Nations from his discussions in the parlor. The league had very definitely failed and the ballroom was now filled with new lawyers ready for their chance to conquer and shape the world.

Wilson, who liked to refer to the former president as "Cousin Woodrow", though he was actually a third cousin, twice removed, from a different branch of the family, was there. Darlene was there, too, but with her new husband. Donovan and Charlotte were still together, or at least, reunited. The commute from Princeton to Rutgers had been too hard and Donovan had moved to a fraternity house on the campus. He had promised to marry Charlotte after graduation, but this was his first week back and they had been arguing. Aaron was there, alone. He had actually graduated from Columbia four months before, and had been taking interviews with firms who did business with his dad's company and the builders he supplied. This was his first night back in Princeton in nearly two years, and he was glad to see the familiar faces of his friends. Anderson was actually still only halfway through grad school, but they had invited him anyway.

"Some band they got to play." It was Anderson. They had all gathered near the punch bowl, four penguins in tuxedoes, while their dates were all off somewhere, wherever women seemed to go to talk about the men.

"Yeah. The dean's old law firm does all the contracts for RCA." Donovan whispered as if it might get back to someone.

"Out into the real world now, fellas." Wilson was the first to brag of his good fortune. "I got an offer from Lincoln, Clevens."

Donovan smiled a secret smirk, knowing he had him beat. "Dickens, Taylor. And Knight & Melvany. But the only question is, do I want Wall Street or Midtown?"

"You pig! What about you Aaron?" Wilson turned to Aaron, who didn't answer for a moment, watching the dancing. "Come on, Aaron, did you get an offer? I know you interviewed at Melvany."

"Hughes, Hubbard." Aaron said with a seeming casual disinterest. The others' jaws dropped.

"Hubbard?!"

Finally. Aaron broke into a grin. "Associate. 23rd floor corner office at One Wall Street. Starting 15 thou a year."

"Jesus!" Wilson almost snorted his punch. "You wanna buy me a car?!"

"My dad's company bills half-a-mil a year there, so I guess they want to give some of it back."

Charlotte and Darlene came back from the powder room with another girl, Kelly Dickens, Anderson's date. Charlotte looked at them all in a row.

"Surrounded by handsome lawyers. A girl could cry." She slipped her arm into Donovan's. "Now, if only one of them would dance with his wife."

Donovan was in a cool mood. He was always shy about public affection. "Maybe the next one."

"Barrel of monkeys," Charlotte pouted. Then, she reached her hand out to Aaron. "Wanna show him how it's done?"

Aaron had none of Donovan's inhibitions, one of his many faults. He took Charlotte's hand and they swung out onto the dance floor. Wilson followed with Darlene and Anderson with his date, leaving Donovan by the punch bowl.

Aaron had learned the swing and jive moves in the nightclubs of New York and swung Charlotte like a hepcat. Charlotte whispered in his ear as he swung her past him, bringing her in close, then, spinning her away

"Something's missing from this picture."

Aaron answered on the next beat when he brought her close again. "What is that?"

"Aaron's latest squeeze baby." The conversation carried on in this rhythmic yo-yo for a several bars.

"A guy gets bored."

Charlotte laughed, "Or tuckered out." She swung out and back again, close in his ear with a husky breath, "That's alright, honey, lay back and have a cigarette."

Donovan watched Aaron swing Charlotte, spinning into his arm, sliding through his legs. His mood grew darker with each move. He had never been able to get the image of Aaron's bare ass thrusting between Charlotte's legs folded in crinoline in the back seat of a Buick, and here he was watching her slide between his legs on the parquet floor. They had only said their vows a week ago. He had chased Aaron around the pylons, always behind, and now Aaron had called on his father's relationships in the city to get a 23rd floor office! A rage boiled from some secret place.

Suddenly, Donovan charged across the dance floor. He shoved Aaron, sending him sprawling on the floor. He grabbed Charlotte's hand and pulled her away from the other dancing couples, who stopped there gyrations as the band held up in mid-beat. Donovan pulled Charlotte out into the foyer.

143

Aaron picked himself up, brushing down his tux, calling after Donovan, "Cut in, anytime."

He shrugged it off and went back to join the others. He felt bad about screwing Charlotte in that parking lot. It had been the mistake of his life. It was not a choice he could adequately explain, even to himself, other than seeing Lacy and Miki together in the old soda shop in his mind whenever he thought about it. He was glad she and Donovan had finally gotten married. It might settle Charlotte down a little.

Glenn Miller held his baton a moment for the room to settle. He was used to these sorts of things in his shows, not on the big stages, but in some of the boisterous jazz clubs with young hipsters swilling too much beer. It was the tuxedoes and old school atmosphere of the Nassau Club that made this one a little out of the ordinary. He thought maybe a mood piece to bring it down a little and signaled the down beat for "Moonlight Serenade", but before the first note, somebody shouted from the back of the hall.

"Hey! Hey!" It was one of the grads who had been listening to a Philco radio. "Listen!" He cranked the volume nob so the NBC Red Network crackled through the room. It was not the usual voice from New York, but an unfamiliar British sounding voice.

"German armored divisions are advancing at a rapid pace across the Belgian plain. Sources in Brussels and Amsterdam are reporting heavy air assaults that began at sunrise this morning..."

The grads in the celebrations all stopped, hushed, to listen to the news of war taking over Europe.

"In London, newly seated Prime Minister Winston Churchill has ordered immediate Royal Airforce support

144

of French and British forces mobilizing from Dieppe to Valenciennes..."

The more familiar voice from the New York studio broke in. "You have been listening to BBC Radio International News. We will interrupt our broadcast with further updates..." The radio returned to a music broadcast of Eddie Duchin.

The Princetonians just looked at each other, sobered. Someone shouted. "Well, at least there's four thousand miles of ocean between us and the Krauts!"

Sensing the need for distraction, Glenn Miller pointed his baton to Gene Krupa. The lighting engineer turned the main lights down and keyed the spotlight. Krupa pounded a long staccato roll groove on his snare. The crowd turned as Krupa began to wail on his drums.

Aaron listened a moment, losing himself in the beat. Suddenly, he hopped onto the bandstand. Glenn and the band looked surprised. Aaron stepped up right beside Krupa, picking up a pair of his spare sticks. Aaron had played some in the New York clubs with Cab Callaway. He started to drum with Krupa, right with him, both of them turning loose. Aaron's old classmates cheered him on.

"Go, Brick!" they shouted.

The news of war faded in the pounding beat of toms and high hats, but the beat and drums of war didn't fade. The news reports soon told of a half-million British and French troops trapped on the beaches of Dunkirk under blistering air attacks from the German Luftwaffe. And there was talk of a coming invasion of Britain. It was June 4 of 1940.

Winston Churchill had made a speech to Parliament that was broadcast around the world, "We shall fight in

France, we shall fight on the seas and oceans, we shall fight with growing confidence and growing strength in the air, we shall defend our island, whatever the cost may be. We shall fight on the beaches, we shall fight on the landing grounds, we shall fight in the fields and in the streets, we shall fight in the hills; we shall never surrender."

Four young newly-minted lawyers did not accept their offers. The law firms of Melvany and Hubbard would have to find others. It was on a Thursday morning that Aaron was standing on the platform at Princeton Junction waiting for the train to go back to New York that it came to him. He would not go to New York. He would pack a bag and go to Canada. He had read that the British Royal Air Force was calling for training of Commonwealth pilots. A call had gone out to able-bodied men with flight experience. He would not make the trip alone.

A column of British troops slogged their trucks and gun wagons through the muck from recent rains on the road to Bruges, trying to reach the departure point at Dunkirk Harbor. Haggard and exhausted, they carried their field-bandaged wounded on horse carts. They had been cut off by the Wehrmacht Panzer divisions which had rolled through the Ardennes, right past the forts of the Maginot Line intended to hold off a German invasion. The forts had been built in defense of an infantry war in the principle of the last war, with trenches and barbed wire, but near useless against a fast moving armor assault and air attack.

The whining roar of two German Messerschmitt 109s caught their ears. They tried to scatter from the road, trying to make it to the trees. Many did, but the wounded on the carts and the trucks could not be moved to cover. The column was spread out on the open road for near half-a-mile.

Miki was in the attack lead. Kellmann was slightly behind and above him as his wingman. Miki was in total concentration as he pushed the stick forward, with the ground rushing toward his canopy windshield matching his mental count. Settling low across the trees, he lined up with the road, his wingtip in the corner of his eye in measured distance from the tree line to his right. The last of the column came into his cross-hairs, human figures running and scrambling in the mud.

The forefinger of his gloved hand gripping the stick extended to caress the fire button. He held just a second's pause, then pressed.

The twin 7.92 millimeter MG17 machine guns on the cowling and one 20 millimeter cannon in each wing flashed fire. Streams of lead and explosive cannon shells shot ahead of the racing plane, every seventh bullet a magnesium tracer, streaming toward the column like a string of party lights.

The cannon shells smashed into the trucks and wagons, and faster traveling bullets from the machine guns tore through the soldiers in a traveling path of destruction, spitting pieces of metal, cloth, and glass. An ammunition wagon exploded in a ball of rising flame and smoke.

The bullets spit into the mud, and ripped through the slow moving wounded and soldiers trying to take cover under the vehicles, spitting blood and bits of bone and flesh.

The two 109's roared low just over the trucks, following the path of mechanized carnage, flying right through the exploding munitions wagon and bits of debris, then arcing up into the sky. The British soldiers staggered from the trees to try to help the rest of the wounded. They looked up and could see the Javelin in a fist painted on the yellow nose of one of the planes.

Miki looked over his shoulder to the column falling away. He glanced to Kellmann on his wing, then, pointed back over his shoulder. They would make another run. He pushed his stick over to the left, rolling in a half-turn.

As the British soldiers dragged their wounded comrades toward the trees, the two 109s banked, arcing around, diving for another run.

Then, the troops heard another roar. In a flash, two British Spitfires shot low over the trees and across the road. The Soldiers cheered as the Spits pulled up in tandem toward the 109s.

Miki saw the Spitfires and nodded to Kellmann. He broke off the dive and pulled back hard on the stick, climbing for altitude. He glanced over to Kellmann, right with him, and raised his gloved hand in a signal. They had been fighting, killing, and ruling the skies for almost two years in Spain and Poland. The pilots of the British planes had likely never been in combat before. They trained and practiced, but had never met a German pilot in the air, and certainly none like Miki.

The two 109s in unison rolled over in a half-eight to a dive, dropping past the climbing Spits. The Spitfires were caught off guard, their wings wobbling in the pilots' confusion as the Messerschmitt hunters smoothly split from their dive and out of the loop, climbing just behind them.

148

Kellmann's machine guns fired. Bullets tore into the lagging Spitfire, ripping metal up the side and smashing into the engine cowling. Smoke billowed from the Spitfire's exhausts. It lost altitude and slid off toward the trees, engine hacking.

Miki's 109 arced into a perfect line behind the lead Spitfire, racing up on his tail. Miki lined up his gunsight on the tail of the Spitfire, flipping his firing switch to the cannons alone. He would only need a short burst for this pilot. The Spitfire rolled into a dive, trying to escape. Miki rolled right behind him, his gunsight almost never leaving the target.

The soldiers below watched the skies, as the Spitfire's pilot tried desperate maneuvers, banking, rolling, diving, but the Javelin never left his tail. He seemed to know where the opposing pilot was going before he did.

Miki's crystal eyes never left his prey, controlling the plane like a machine, like he was part of the mechanism, as he concentrated on his target, a desperate inexperienced young pilot no match to his cool control.

Miki held his finger off the trigger for a few seconds before he knew he would end the dogfight with a kill. He sang the old college fight song he always sang in the cockpit before a kill, "Fight for Old Nas-sau, fight for our ivy halls... Fight for Old Nas-sau, Princeton stand..."

His left hand shoved the throttle forward for an extra burst of power and he closed on the Spit. So close, it seemed like his propeller was going to chop through the tail. Miki's right hand extended his finger to the firing trigger.

"...proud and tall..."

The 20 mm cannon shells flashed from the gun pods and exploded into the Spit's fuselage. A second burst cut through the left tail wing. The Spitfire snap-rolled over into an inverted dive, straight for the trees below. In a screaming whine, the British plane augered into the woods, breaking into pieces and exploding in a ball of flame on a hillside.

As Miki's 109 pulled up, back into the sky, the British soldiers stared stunned at the rising fireball in the distance. Their saviors were both dead and they were left defenseless. They only had a moment before the two 109s arced around, joining again in a precision crossing turn and lined up for another strafing run.

The clouds over Canada hung gray, low and thick. A chill breeze was blowing off Lake Superior. It was mid-June at Fort William, Ontario, but snow patches still lay on the ground. Temporary tent cabin housing had been hastily built off the edge of the airport grounds and a wire fence erected around it. Lining the edge of the packed clay runway was a row of biplane trainer airplanes, mostly DeHavilland Tiger Moths and a few Stearmans.

A group of young men who had answered the call from the Commonwealth Air Training Plan stood in a line at a registration table for their documentation and assignments. Most of them were pimple-faced seventeen, eighteen and nineteen year old Canadians. A few were Brits who had been living in Canada. Most had never flown before and were being assigned to ground class and simulator training before sitting in an actual airplane. Out on the field, another group of fifteen recruits were gathered around an instructor by one of the planes.

Aaron, Donovan and Wilson were in the line of new applicants waiting to step up to the administrator's desk, inside the open flap of one of the tent field offices. They had driven up together in Aaron's car and hadn't bothered with a hotel, or even to change. The administrator in command, a British colonel, was standing behind the corporal at the registry book, looking over his shoulder. He didn't bother to look up.

"Name and home address?"

"Aaron Miller. Box 7, Route 31, Plainfield, New Jersey."

The colonel now looked up and saw the three of them in their Ivy League casual clothes. He glanced over to Aaron's car with its New Jersey license plate.

"Americans?" It was mostly a rhetorical question.

"We're here to volunteer to fly with the Royal Air Force," Aaron said simply, as if it were that simple.

The colonel looked at their clothes, their faces. "Come for a bit of a lark, then? Have we?"

"We've come to fight." Donovan was a little insulted.

"Right. I suppose you all think this will be a great sport." The colonel stepped around the table, looking them up and down. "Bit of flyin' about in an aeroplane. Come home heroes, then? Tell the chums and the ladies all about it?"

Donovan and Wilson were a little uncomfortable at the grilling. Aaron wasn't. He knew their skills were needed.

"Yes, sir. That's exactly it," he said.

"Well then, you can't just walk onto an air field and jump in a bloody craft. You'll have to spend four weeks in flight ground school and a simulator. I suppose that's not the thrill you were thinking of, is it?"

"Not my idea of a thrill," Aaron said with a slight smirk, "no, sir. We all have flight experience."

Wilson stepped forward, thinking he could help. "Do you know who this is, Colonel?"

"No, I don't believe I do. Do you damn well know who I am?"

"This is Aaron Miller. Two time National Champion," Wilson bragged.

The Colonel looked Aaron over, with a smirk, "Champion of what?"

Aaron eased Wilson back before it got worse. "Why don't you let us prove our skills. Then, you can decide where you want us to go."

"Right, then. Sign your names. Go and see the instructor, Flight Sergeant Rokings. He'll be the one to determine if you're qualified." The Colonel sensed something in Aaron and the young men with him that they might not be joking. "If you're wanted, you'll have to give up your citizenship and take an oath to His Majesty, King George the Sixth."

"We're prepared for that," Aaron answered for them, "and looking forward to meeting him."

The colonel eyed him with less than full appreciation for his cheek.

A crowd of young trainees were gathered around the Chief Flight Instructor, at one of the Tiger Moths, as he droned on in a strident-pitched Sussex accent. The class was fresh from simulator training but had yet to fly and Sergeant Rokings was one who believed every step was a baby step, if they wanted to live to be old men.

"An aeroplane does not operate like your car." He strode back and forth, tapping a pointed stick on his hand, as if he might spank them with it. "An aeroplane operates on the principle of aero-dynamics. The wheel, or stick, does not turn the wheels, the pedals do not apply the brakes, and the propeller does not pull your aeroplane up into the sky!"

The trainees listened in rapt attention, totally raw recruits. A few were anxious to get past the basics. They had spent two weeks in a classroom with paper airplanes and didn't need to know what a stick was.

"If you wish to survive your experience with flight," Rokings went on with his usual introduction, "you will come to know the elegant principle of 'the co-efficient of lift'".

He pointed at the end of the wing with his pointer. "This is the aileron. It is attached to your stick. To turn or bank your aeroplane, the aileron changes the co-efficient of lift so that part of the air pressure holds you in the sky and the other part pushes you to the side. Now, we'll learn a few important items that may save your lives..."

He walked stiffly to the nose of the plane. "...the parts of an aeroplane!" He walked around the craft, pointing with great importance to each part with his pointer, "Spinner... propeller... engine... wing... aileron... undercarriage..."

Aaron had had enough and pushed out of the crowd. He climbed up on the lower wing and lifted his leg into the open cockpit.

"And what in the holy name of all the bleeding saints do you suppose you're doing?!" Sergeant Rokings barked, red in the face.

"Flying, sir," Aaron answered, settling into the cockpit seat. He had flown a DeHavilland. He didn't think it was a great airplane, a bit underpowered but reliable enough.

"Oh! Flying! Had a few lessons, then, have we?" Rokings had lots of experience with these types before, babies who thought they were toddlers. "Think we're a bit ahead of the others? Well, then you've got another think coming!"

Donovan stepped past the instructor to the engine crank. Aaron switched on the magneto and Donovan turned the crank.

"Here, now...!" The flight instructor could do nothing at this point.

The pistons turned over and smoke belched from the exhausts as the engine chuffed and roared to life. Sergeant Rokings was about to climb onto the wing to pull Aaron out, but Aaron gunned it and the Moth rolled out onto the field. The incensed instructor ran after, waving his pointer.

"Here! Hey! You...!" Finally, he gave up as the plane rolled out onto the clay runway. "Alright, then. Kill yourself and it shan't be on my head! I will tell you that right now!"

The biplane lifted off the ground into the sky, and rising past 130 feet, Aaron threw it into a climbing half-roll. The recruits gasped as the plane flipped to perpendicular, losing altitude, its wingtips nearly brushing the line of planes at the end of the runway, then, rolled out again level, rising into the sky.

After gaining altitude, Aaron banked around, diving low across the field just past the statue-still instructor, pulled into a loop, then a falling leaf spin to pull out just over the heads of the amazed trainees watching the aerobatic display.

The plane landed and rolled back to the parking spot. Aaron hopped out and stood before the instructor.

"Qualified? Sir?"

Rokings walked around Aaron for a long time, not saying anything, just tapping his pointer. Finally he could barely suppress a smile.

"You could have killed yourself, y'know. And destroyed one of His Majesty's aeroplanes. We need aeroplanes, as well as pilots."

"I guess I would have had to pay for it, sir."

"I ain't no 'sir'. Do I look like a toff to you? You'll address me as Flight Sergeant."

"Yes, Flight Sergeant."

The instructor turned to Donovan, standing back, "You've had a bit of practice, too, I suppose?" Donovan nodded confidently. He'd put a lot of practice into the Stearman at Lawrenceville. This was his first DeHavilland, but he was sure he could manage it. Rokings looked to Wilson. Wilson smiled, but with rather less confidence.

"Right, then! Give us show."

Donovan climbed into the cockpit and took the plane up into the air for a short series of turns and rolls, less audacious than Aaron, but adding the Immelman he'd worked on, the maneuver named after a German ace in the last war, diving into a loop but rolling out to level at the top altitude as an escape. He finished with a diving turn out to a landing. When he had rolled the plane back to the line and climbed out, Sergeant Rokings turned to Wilson.

Wilson hesitated. He glanced to Aaron and Donovan, nervous, but trying to hide it. He wondered if he should just admit that he had only had a few hours in the

Stearman at Lawrenceville. They had trained for two days before leaving, but he had not even soloed.

The other recruits were all looking at him with expectation. Gathering himself, he walked to the plane and started to climb up. Aaron stepped over to crank the engine. He bent close to Wilson as he stepped onto the wing root.

"Just the basics. Alright? Get it off the ground and back down again."

Aaron stood back with the instructor and Donovan as Wilson started the engine and taxied out to the runway. The engine revved and the plane rolled, gaining speed, weaving a little.

Halfway down the runway the engine suddenly roared as Wilson pulled on the stick too soon, trying to pull up too steep. The plane rose a moment, then lost lift and sunk back to the clay. Its wheels hit hard and the plane slammed, nose down. The forward momentum carried the tail up and it flipped over onto its back. The plane rested in the middle of the runway with Wilson hanging from the straps.

The instructor turned to Aaron with a cocked eyebrow. The colonel strode out from the administration tent where he'd been watching along with the rest of the camp. Wilson unfastened his belt and slid out of the cockpit into the ground.

Aaron looked to the silent colonel and the stone-faced flight sergeant.

"If we go, he goes."

~~~

CHAPTER ELEVEN

Night Bombs

Lacy carried a tailored suit back to her Mercedes saloon car parked on Hagen. It was pointless to try to hide her visits as she had become a regular customer of the shop. The tailor had made a number of suits for her now. She was the rich wife of the aristocrat war hero, so it was easier to hide in plain sight. She even took care to write in her letters home about them, knowing they would be read and reported. Luckily, no one ever bothered to notice that the suits she bought and incessantly demanded perfection in the sleeve seams and cuffs would not fit her husband. If they had examined them they might have noticed the slight stiffness in the lining below the shoulders where the documents were carefully sewn inside.

The big Mercedes drove down the road from town back to Kester. The little Volkswagen had stopped following her three months ago as she made it a point to take the same route to the city, stopping in at the factory office on the way to Essen. She rarely had any real business at the Von Steuven works, and hated the smell, but stopped in to talk to the secretaries and bring gifts and ginger Lebkuchen cake she had her cook make for them. She had made it a boring routine.

At the intersection in front of the old church, a 37 millimeter anti-aircraft flak gun was now placed on the corner, surrounded by sand bags and manned by helmeted soldiers of the Luftwaffe. Lacy had learned the new German word of Flugabwehrkanone with her neighbors as the defense weapon would now be a present part of their lives. They had taken up the position since the first night flight of RAF bombers had dropped leaflets and the bombing of the ports of Kiel and Wilhemshaven six weeks before.

The leaflets were in German and had warned that the British would be coming. Her neighbors and friends had all seemed to believe that they could launch a war on the rest of the world and stay comfortable in their homes, untouched. Frau Lindl had gushed with pride when the Führer had conquered Poland in a week, then France, Denmark and Norway had surrendered in less than six weeks. Hitler had brought them all the glory he had promised and seemed a genius. He had promised to make a greater Germany, and it was true. They were the masters. Now, Dortmund and Düsseldorf had been bombed, and Hamburg. The bombs would soon stop, they believed, when Britain was defeated. Hitler had promised.

Lacy waved to the boys at the gun emplacement. They were still sharing the ginger cake she had left them on her way to Essen. Their commanding Hauptmann had complained once that she should not be indulging them, but they always looked so bored, watching the skies and waiting. She had placated the captain with a bottle of wine and an invitation to the house to meet Miki. He had been a fan of "the Javelin" since the Olympics, and even more enamored of his war victories, now up to sixteen. Only Werner Mölders with whom Miki had served in Spain had more.

Miki was stationed at the new Luftwaffe training base at Geseke near Paderborn. It was only forty minutes away. He was lecturing new pilots on tactics from his experiences in Spain, Poland, Rotterdam and Belgium, but he complained that the High Command was sending all the best candidates to bomber school. He had kept his close Jagdgeschwader fighter group with him and Command had allowed him to keep the ones he thought had promise.

Lacy arrived to find the house filled with young Luftwaffe pilots and a collection of local girls. The boisterous young men lounged around, boots on the furniture, drinking and smoking cigars. Two young officers were with girls in the corners of the salon. They had completed two weeks of formation tactics and Miki was allowing a celebration. They were being reassigned to forward bases on the French coast in two days' time where they would be escorting bombers over the English coast to destroy the British air capability. The fast, twin engine Messerschmitt 110 fighter-bombers and Stukas had been striking the coastal defenses and harbors since the second week of July, but now, the slower Heinkel and Dornier heavy bomber groups would be taking the fight inland to air bases and the cities, and they needed the fighter support.

A loud pilot, Lt. Kriegel, was standing in the middle of the room, weaving a little from too much champagne, demonstrating with his hands his techniques for the fights ahead, which he was quite sure he had invented.

"The Spitfire patrol is so..." he held out his left hand with three fingers spread, "three together. Our schwarm comes from the sun, from above..." He held his right hand high and behind. "The Spitfires see us. They roll over in diving formation, to keep the carburetors full...one, two, three..." He rolled his fingers one after the other, dropping his left hand, representing the British planes. "Now, the trick. Two 'Willys'..." His right hand made two fingers for the German Messerschmitts, "stay in straight dive so Limeys turn back...now, second rotte 'Willys' come low and up..." swinging his right two fingers up from below, "three Spitfires with their bellies wide open...boom, boom, boom... Three Limeys down, one pass... Ja?!"

He held out his hands looking for applause at his clever maneuver. Miki walked past carrying a couple of scotches.

"Ack, ack, ack..." Miki said with a knowing smile, pointing with a tinkling scotch glass to the Lieutenant's lower hands. "You forget the second Spitfire formation. As you pull up for the bellies...you are wide open. The Brownings take the brilliant head off your shoulders at the neck, Ja?"

The other pilots laughed and the young officer looked chastened. "Ja, Herr Major Staffelkapitän..."

Miki carried the scotches to Kellmann and Von Schleich. Kellmann was now a captain and Von Schleich a general major. He was not Miki's direct superior, but had influenced his moves through the command, and he liked to keep an eye on his protégé.

"The morale is good," Von Schleich took a sip of the scotch, a single malt that Miki had been saving from reserve.

"Soon it will be German, not Scottish," Kellmann joked.

Miki was in less of a jovial mood. He looked around the room at the young men he had been guiding, and knew that many of them might soon be dead.

"So far we have come against fresh pilots in a new plane. This plan to attack England will be the test. The British training gets better and now they have experience with our tactics," he nodded to Lt. Kriegel, "their pilots will get better."

"I don't think we will attack," Von Schleich offered confidently. "Hitler believes the British will settle for peace rather than face the bombs. He has been teasing them with this coastal raiding."

"I've given up trying to fathom what Hitler believes," Miki said. He had looked into the national leader's eyes on two occasions now. He had been moved to five operational areas in two-and-a-half years, five borders and killing men of seven languages. "I point my plane where I'm told."

"That is the smart thing, Miki. You will probably outlast us all."

Lacy came in carrying a tray of hors d'oeuvres. She had dismissed her temporary helper girl who was now pregnant with one of the officers' children. She was more comfortable with fewer eyes around the manor, in any case. As she had set the tray down, Lt. Frische, a bit drunk, grabbed her, and pulled her onto the couch.

"Hey, Miki, when we're done with England, maybe we go on to America, so we can all get ourselves beautiful American wives."

Lacy extricated herself from the pilot's drunken grasp, trying to ignore the remark, but even Miki was uncomfortable with it. "You'd better hope the Americans want to stay at home with their own wives."

"It's alright. He's a little drunk," Lacy said casually.

Frische started to sing the anthem, "Deutschland, Deutschland, Uber Alles..." The other fliers joined in, singing in chorus.

Miki smiled at Lacy. "Like the old college days, eh?"

"Unfortunately." Lacy was distracted, and wanted to leave them to their revels. "Does everyone have everything they need?"

"Some a little more than they need, I think." Miki was mostly amused by it, but his mind was on the move ahead. He had judgments to make now, who would fly, and who might die.

Lacy went down the hall with the singing voices coming from the great room, filling the rooms on the first floor. She hesitated at the cellar door and checked to see that no one was watching. She opened the door and went in, locking it behind. The flying officers were not the only guests in the house.

Von Schleich held up a hand to stop the loud singing, which had turned from the heroic Nazi anthems to bawdy drinking songs of the beer halls.

"Making a toast, Herr General?" asked Kellmann.

"Listen!" commanded Von Schleich. Miki could hear it, too, now, a low distant hum. They were puzzled by it for a few moments, but then knew what it was. It was the steady drone, in vibrating harmony, of aircraft engines drawing closer. Bomber engines. Then, in the distance, they began to hear the rumbling thumps of the first bombs falling, across the river.

They rushed to the windows and peered out. They could see the exhaust bursts of nearly two hundred British Blenheim bombers in formation over the valley. The bright flashes of bombs exploding began to appear all over the valley beyond the trees, with a rapidly increasing thump, thump, thump!

Searchlights flickered on as beams began to crisscross the black cloudless sky. The flak gun on the corner down the road with the young soldiers had cranked into position and began firing into the sky.

The bombs exploded across the Ruhr Valley. Houses, shops and factories exploded in glycerin and cordite bursts of flame.

As the pilots watched, the bombs seemed to be marching across the valley toward the house. One of the young pilots hurried toward the front hall, stumbling, drunk.

"Let's get to the field!" he shouted.

Miki knew they could do nothing. "It is forty minutes to our planes. It will be all over by then."

Lacy came into the room. She met Miki's eyes, trying not to let fear overcome her.

"Everyone to the wine cellars," Miki ordered.

"The wine cellar?" Lacy hesitated. She didn't know what to do.

"It will be tight, but we'll fit, until it passes."

Lacy stood with a rising dread as they all started to head for the hall, knowing what they would find there. She had to do something.

"Now, there's a brave bunch of Germans!" she said sharply loud. They had been singing anthems of bravery and glory after all. "The Fatherland's best, soldiers, fliers, conquerors of Europe and God knows what else, hiding in the basement!?" They stopped, looking at her. Some were incensed and insulted.

Finally, Kellmann grinned. "She's right. What are we all, Jews?!" He grabbed up a bottle of wine from the table. "I have all I need to drink. Let an English bomber try to hit me in the eye. If he can, we surrender!" The other pilots grabbed bottles, glasses and cigars, and headed for the door outside, laughing.

Miki grabbed Lacy by the arm. "What is the matter? This is not you."

"Maybe I don't know who I am anymore, Miki." She stared at him, with a distant emotion. "You're gone most of the time. Maybe you don't know who I am, either."

Miki studied her defiant face. He was bewildered. He knew how to make a machine do exactly what he wanted. He didn't understand this. She had been increasingly more secretive. He had even wondered if she was having an affair, but had dismissed it.

"At least you should wait in the cellar," he said, truly worried for her. "I don't know what I would do without you."

"Yes, you would, Miki." She knew he cared for her, but had long come to suspect that deeper emotions were a stranger to him. "You would point your plane where you were told."

The party gathered on the grounds, the pilots drinking, and with their cigars between their fingers, pointing out the planes in the sky as the bombs continued to fall across the valley beyond, judging the altitude and armament of the Blenheims, and how they would attack them if they were in their planes.

Miki stood with Von Schleich. They could see the dark shadows of the Krupp works and the machine shed buildings of Miki's father's plants, a vast dark space in blackout, surrounded by workers houses and village streets now lit by bursting bombs.

"Look, they miss the factories and blow up the houses," Von Schleich pointed with his cigar.

Just then, the roar of the twin Rolls-Royce engines of a Blenheim drew near above and then the loud whistle of falling ordinance. A bomb exploded in a bright burst harmlessly in the woods, then another, on the other side.

The Luftwaffe pilots cringed for a moment, with the thundering bursts shaking the ground under their boots, but then laughed nervously as the rumbling aircraft motors flew beyond them.

Kellmann held up his drink and shouted at the sky, "Here! Here is my eye! Come on!" But it was only one bomber that had flown afield of its target and rumbled onward to rejoin its wing.

Lacy took Miki's arm, breathing again, her pique subsided, hiding her fear.

"I wish you were in the cellar." He said, calmly, but with a confusion of troubled thoughts that had been on his mind since Belgium. "Maybe I should not have brought you here."

Lacy smiled. "If I am to be blown up, here with my husband, that is what is supposed to be."

"I love you, you know. Do I tell you that?"

"Not enough," she said, but was glad to hear it. "But I know you do."

She slipped her arm around him and held close as the bomb thumps seemed to fade, leaving burning fires in their wake.

~~~

CHAPTER TWELVE

Westhampnett

Aaron, Donovan and Wilson said goodbyes to Charlotte, Darlene and Anderson on a train platform at Penn Station before heading back to Canada, through Montreal to Halifax. Donovan kissed Charlotte goodbye, having to lean past her bulging belly.

"One thing you always had, dearest, was timing," Charlotte said with her usual wry style and turned to Aaron with a hopeful caution. "Don't let him shoot himself."

"Don't worry," Aaron reassured her.

"And leave some girls for the English boys. You don't want us Yanks to get a bad reputation over there."

"I've decided to become a monk." Aaron crossed his chest. They thought he was joking, but he wasn't. He'd buried his screw up with Lacy with a string of girls for almost four years now, but none of them had reached him. It had been odd, but half the time when he had to call them by name it was Lacy that came to him. The training regimen and constant flying over the last six weeks had been a salve over an open wound, and he would leave the girls behind for a welcome celibacy.

His father was there to see him off. "I'm sorry, pop. All that money for school. I know this isn't what you wanted."

Karel Miller had tears in his eyes. They had buried Aaron's mother six weeks before. She had grown

166

increasingly ill over a month's time and then was gone. It was a rapid cancer. Karel was alone now, and saying goodbye to a son he knew he might also never see again.

"It is more. You make me proud. I know your mother is proud."

An uncomfortable goodbye that might have lingered was interrupted by a baggage handler Wilson had offered a tip to carry his two trunks aboard.

"What are you taking, Wilson?" Donovan asked. They had paid their own passages on the ocean liner, but as Canadian Commonwealth RAF pilots, had mostly jettisoned the trappings of a former life.

"Never know what the weather's going to be like," Wilson grinned. "Might be a party or two."

Aaron had winked at Charlotte, "See, nothing to worry about. Tea and cakes. London in the summer season."

The train ride was two days and the Duchess of York, a passenger liner, painted gray to hide from the U-boats, sailed from Halifax, Nova Scotia on the 10th of July.

After arriving with the troops at Liverpool and a train to Euston Station in London, the college boys had seen a London Theater show and tipped a couple of pints in a West End pub before the whistling shriek of a 1,000 pound bomb turned the building next door to a burning pile of rubble and flame.

They left from Baker Street station the next day for RAF Uxbridge. They had been highly scored in their Canadian class and Command was anxious to have them on the line. Familiarization training was hurried. Three days in a Hurricane before assignment to 65 Squadron of

Group 11, RAF Tangmere, Surrey. They had three sorties in the Hawker "Hurries" before the Spitfire Mark IIs arrived and their unit of 65 Squadron was dispersed to Westhampnett near Chichester when the Fighter Command II Group headquarters Tangmere was divided into satellite fields.

The squadron had been in the thick of it since the first Hun raid on Dover in the second week of July. Daily sweeps of the coast and practice maneuvers had turned to short pitched battles, over in minutes. The German Stuka's were easy targets if caught before making their bombing dives. They were not nimble and had little defense armament. The German command had provided little fighter support for the coast raids. The 110 Messerschmitt twin engine fighter-bombers were only slightly better, but were being used as light bombers to attack the air fields and defense positions.

It wasn't until the last week of July that the first wave of 109s began escorting Heinkel 111s across the channel heading for the Thames Estuary and southern airfields that the air fight began in earnest.

The pilots who lounged in chairs outside the dispersal shack looked like experienced old men, though many of them not yet twenty-two years old. Aaron and Donovan were old grand dads at twenty-four years old. The oldest of them were Squadron Leader Reginald "Dimples" Boothe at twenty-seven and Flight Lieutenant Tom "Biggles" Biggle at twenty-six. They had laid their leather flight jackets over the back of the chairs and lounged in their white cotton flight suits over the blue RAF uniforms and turtle neck sweaters.

Biggle was a fireplug of a young man, beefy and gruff, from Auckland, New Zealand, who had only been flying since June and took no end of ribbing for his name, similar to a famous fictional flier from the last war, while Leader Boothe had left his second year at Oxford in 1937 to join the flying service. They had made a few Yank jokes when the Americans arrived, but they had worn thin. Except for Billy "Flak" Ackers, a lanky kid from Slough, who couldn't seem to get enough of needling them.

"I'm telling you, a country what don't play Cricket ain't civilized! Not those ruddy blokes runnin' about with leather buckets on their heads."

Boothe was as usual relaxing with the London Times. It didn't come every day, and he didn't have time to read it all the way through most days, anyway. It was such a ritual with him that if a fresh paper didn't come, he would re-read yesterdays', or the day before. He would laugh out-loud and make a joke about some play in the West End, or a reported politician's speech. The jokes were usually bad, but said with a certain verve that made them comforting.

"When was the last time you had a Cricket bat in your hand, Ackers, old darling?" he said.

"Ain't sayin' I got a fine education as you ruddy lot. All I'm sayin' is..."

"What rot!" Boothe shouted. The others looked at him, as he rarely got excited about anything. He showed them the paper. "The Air Ministry says we're shooting down Jerry three to one!"

Biggle stood up and bent over. "Do they mention the piece of my arse that bugger "Javelin" shot off last week?!"

Aaron and the Americans glanced to each other, staying quiet.

Boothe pointed to the paper with a grin under his thin mustache, "Says here, arses are four to one! Believe that, my darlings, and I'll eat the Blessed Virgin."

"You've tangled with the Javelin?" Wilson asked, trying to stay casual.

"How do you know it's him?" Donovan asked.

"My darling," Boothe said with a serious turn, "if you should ever find yourself close enough to tell, we'll sing a jolly bottoms-up and fare-thee-well to your dear old soul."

"At least the bloody Hun was kind enough not to blast me, bobbin' in the water, not like some of those bastards." Biggle had been picked up from the channel by a trawler after being shot down and spent three days in a field hospital before being returned to the line.

"When was this?" Aaron asked, focused. He wasn't sure he believed it.

"Got back in kit the day before you lot showed up."

Boothe clicked his tongue behind his teeth. It was an odd habit whenever one of his pilots reported an unconfirmed kill or sighting. He'd lost almost a full front upper jaw in a crash landing in his early training. He tried to hide the scars with the moustache.

"Biggles claims it was him. Reports show the 26 Hunter group full complement at Pas-de-Calais. Javelin's got to be there, now. Got the damned thing painted on his nose. If you see it, means his guns are firing up your bum. If he doesn't hit you from the sun, he gets in close and they say he doesn't waste a bloody shot."

The Operations phone line jangled in the dispersal shack. It was a jarring racket and they knew what it meant. It had been ringing almost every day at about ten-thirty since last Thursday. They stopped in mid-chat to listen. The Ops Sergeant leaned out the small window.

"A flight, B flight, scramble!" He rang the ready bell alarm.

Boothe neatly, but quickly, folded his paper. "A sinner's work is never done. Off we go, my dears."

The others jumped up and ran to their planes, pulling on their leather flight jackets over their coveralls as their crews answered the call of the ready bell, starting the engines, until a row of twelve props were spinning.

Aaron and Donovan were in Flight Group A with Boothe, Ackers and two fresh pilots, Rogers and Campbell. Wilson was in Flight Group B with Biggle and Flying Officers Chivers and Simmons.

The pilots settled into their cockpits. They grabbed their flight caps with oxygen hose and communications microphones from where they hung on the windshield. The procedure was routine now, almost second nature.

Boothe twirled his finger and the Spitfires rolled out to the grass runway. The first section of three Spits roared down the runway at the same time and rose away, the wheels tucking into the wings. The other sections rolled out and followed, Biggle was the flight leader of B Group.

The Spitfires in formation climbed at full throttle toward operation altitude, rising through the puffy clouds over the English Channel off the white chalk cliffs of Dover. They could see the other flight groups from Tangmere and Merton rising ahead, toward the rendezvous point. They flew in V formations, two "Vics" forming a group, with the second flight group about a mile behind and above the first.

The Operations Radio officer spoke over their headsets, calling out their guidance from his radar reports.

"Pinewood Leader, twenty-four hostiles at Angels two-two zero..."

The senior leader, Boothe, answered for his group, "Roger, Ops. Pinewood Leader. Angels 2-2-0." He acknowledged the altitude height of twenty-two thousand feet and kept his climb. He glanced in his mirror and back through his bubble glass canopy to see his flock of birds tucked behind him.

"Alright, darlings," he called on the radio, "twenty-four fat ones for the fryer. Keep it tight. Chatter to a dull roar, please. Red Leader to Blue Leader, did you copy?"

Biggle glanced to the flight group of six ahead and banked a few degrees to course. "Only twenty-four, Dimples? There's your three to one. Piece of cake." He checked his flight group. He had begun to expect Wilson to always be a little out of form. In truth, he didn't think the Yank would last very long.

"Close up, Blue Four. Don't lag. You're the cherry pick, so keep your eyes peeled for the escort."

Wilson nervously looked around the skies for the black specs across the channel. He throttled-up to pull in tighter to the formation.

Aaron was flying in number two position behind Boothe. His eyes searched the blue above the whip cream puffs of clouds. He was the first to spot them, the dots of planes, two dozen Heinkel 111 bombers flying in chevron formations of three, over the water, already heading toward the English coast. Aaron had the best eyes and was usually the first to spot them.

"Tally ho, Red Leader. 10 o'clock horizon."

Boothe looked off to his left front quarter and saw the dots growing quickly. They were still about a thousand feet above.

"Eagle eyes, Red Two. Alright, my darlings, here we go. Shoot for the pilot or the engines. You could put forty pounds of lead into the airframe and they'd still bloody fly to Aberdeen..."

He tugged the straps of his flight oxygen mask and banked toward the bombers, still climbing. The flight of Spits behind Boothe's number 5 arced over, one following the next, keeping formation to slightly above the Heinkels' flight altitude so they could attack at dive speed.

The nose gunner in the bubble glass nose dome of the twin engine bomber saw the specks coming at them from above and ahead.

"Spitfeuer!" He called out on his intercom. He swung his gun around, shaking as he released his trigger catch and waited for them to enter his sight range. He was glad he'd peed into his cup before they left the French coast. On his last attack flight, he had survived but spent the whole trip back to base with a soaked flight suit.

He tried to lead the first Spitfire formation as he'd been instructed, but they would be gone in a flash once they got close enough. He began firing anyway.

The Spitfires roared down toward the Heinkels as their pilots began to break formation. Tracer bullets streamed out from the nose and flank machine guns, every sixth shell marking the track of the bullets toward the attacking fighters. The tracers would allow the gunners to adjust their fire, but they also let the attacking pilots adjust to the firing pattern. Boothe was pleased some pissing-his-pants frightened Hun bastard had started shooting too soon, so he could arc away from the firing stream to a fatter target.

Aaron eased down in a drifting bank, as the machine gun bullets from the defensive guns spit out toward him. He dialed his gunsight to the Heinkel 111's wingspan to accurately judge the distance. His gunsight came around until the cockpit bubble of the Heinkel filled the space between the parallel lines of his sight.

He flipped the safety guard from the firing trigger on his stick and his finger squeezed the red firing trigger. The plane jerked and bucked under him with the recoil as the eight Browning machine guns in the wings fired, shooting eighteen pounds of lead a minute in a synchronized burst.

The bullets smashed through the glass bubble of the Heinkel, turning the nose gunner's chest into a bloody pulp as he jerked with the lead. The bullet stream ripped up into the pilot sitting above him at the controls, tore off his kneecap in a bloody explosion, and sparked around the cockpit like dancing fireflies. One of the bullets bounced off the airframe and tore into the side of his head, ripping off his eye socket.

The Heinkel rolled over into a dive like a dying quail to the sea.

"Good shooting, Red Two!" Boothe called through the radio.

The other Spits dove through the formation of bombers with all their machine guns firing. The engine of another Heinkel began to smoke and cough, losing altitude, leaving a trail of smoke.

Donovan, in number three slot, fired at a bomber with his bullets striking metal before the Spits, at 240 miles-per-hour, shot right through the smoke and twirling propellers of the bombers at 180 miles-per hour for a closing speed of 400, just for an instant close enough to see the faces of the flank gunners firing at them.

The first flight of Spitfires shot through the bomber formation, emerging underneath as the second formation came on behind them. Aaron glanced to see Donovan just off his tail.

"Breaking right, Irish. Coming around."

"Right on you, Brick."

Aaron banked hard right and pulled his stick back for a circling climb for another attack. The two Spits pulled up to bank around, back toward the bombers.

Wilson held his breath as his flight group raced down toward the bombers, into the stream of defensive fire.

"Keep tight, Blue Four!" Biggle urged him to stay close.

Wilson shoved the throttle open as the Spitfires ahead of him began firing and the defensive MG 81 fire traced out toward them. A bullet hit his wind screen, chunking a black mark out of it. He flinched as it just grazed the glass. The Spitfire just in front of his left wing, Will Simmons, was hit with tracers. In a split second it exploded, engulfed in an orange ball of flame from the severed fuel line from the tanks, but the plane stayed on its trajectory. Simmons' screams came shrieking over the headphones. Then the ball of burning metal fell away and was gone.

With bombers and streaming tracers rushing at him, Wilson pressed his trigger, firing his guns with nothing particular in his sights. He closed his eyes as they cut through the bomber formation. He waited for the collision, or the searing burn of a 7.92 bullet hot from the barrel. After a half a moment, he opened his eyes. All he saw was the water of the English Channel below.

A Heinkel smoked to his left in a falling dive to the sea.

"Good shooting, Wilson!" Biggle shouted in his headphone. Wilson was only full of terror for a moment as his flight banked away. He pulled back on his stick to follow.

"Oh, Jesus!" Wilson said to himself. He must have actually hit something, and he wasn't dead. The thoughts washed over him in quick succession, until Biggles' voice brought him back to the task.

"Keep formation, round again."

The sky was filled with crisscrossing smoke trails as the Spitfires danced around the scattering bombers.

Aaron's Spitfire, with Donovan on his wing, swooped down on a Heinkel, firing.

Blue flashes of bullet hits sparked across its surface from the guns of both planes. Donovan's firing hit the wing root. The wing sheared off the bomber and it tumbled over, flaming, rolling on its side toward the sea.

"Whoo-hoo! One for the Irish!" Aaron shouted encouragement.

"Where are the fighters?" Donovan asked, worried and amazed they had been so undisturbed.

Aaron had been wondering, too. He looked up through his canopy, but the sky above was clear.

"Who the hell knows," he said and pushed his stick over, coming around on another bomber, bringing it into his reflector sight. He fired.

In the fuselage of the Heinkel, the bullets punched through the aluminum side, with holes of daylight charging forward through the plane, peppering the flank gunner, ripping into his flight overalls. The blue sparks of shells hit the doors to the bomb bay where the load of 500 pounders were still in their racks.

The Heinkel exploded in a sudden blast of sheering metal and flame from the belly. It veered off course and slammed into another bomber, taking them both down.

The Heinkel flight began to turn off course, heading back across the channel, only half of them still flying. They had no hope of reaching their target without fighter support, which never came.

"Got 'em on the run, now, boy-oes!" Biggle shouted.

"I'm out of ruddy ammo!" Ackers voice was giddy over the radio.

"Trigger happy, Ackers. Trigger happy," Boothe scolded good-naturedly as he surveyed the sky. There was still no sign of German fighters. He was getting low on his ammunition counter as well. "Guess the Jaggers are on holiday. Lucky break. Anybody with ammo, clean up a few stragglers and let's go home."

The Spitfires settled in over the hedgerows at the end of the field and touched down on the grass. Aaron taxied to his position on the flight line and shut down his engine. He climbed out of his cockpit as Donovan taxied in next to him. As Aaron dropped to the grass, Boothe sauntered over.

"Forget everything I ever said about you Yanks," he grinned. "Damn fine hunting."

"Thanks, darling," Aaron kidded.

They looked up as the second flight of Spits came in to land.

"I say, old dear, your chum's about to land without his wheels," Boothe remarked without amusement. Wilson was the last in the formation approaching the field. His landing gear was up.

Wilson was in a daze. He had been completely shaken since turning back. He had followed his wing man in blind oblivion. He had been picturing in his mind a collection of images of Simmons burning in his cockpit and the bullets from his gun exploding through the German crews. He hadn't seen it but imagined it as if he was there with them.

Aaron ran out to the runway, waving his arms.

"Shit, Wilson! Wake up!" he shouted.

Wilson looked ahead to the landing field and could see Aaron standing there, waving his arms over his head. He thought Aaron must be congratulating him. He waved back, as his plane sank lower toward the grass.

Boothe climbed back on his wing to try to get to the radio headset he'd hung on the canopy frame.

Aaron extended his arms down to his sides.

"Gear!" came Boothe's shout through the radio.

Wilson looked down to the gear crank.

"Jesus!" he suddenly realized as the grass came up closer than it ever had before, like he was sinking into it. He pushed the throttle and pulled on the stick.

The Spitfire settled just inches off the grass, with its propeller almost mowing the lawn, before the engine roared and it started to pull up. The Spitfire zoomed past Aaron and rose back into the sky.

Aaron waited with Donovan, Boothe and Biggle as Wilson taxied his plane around and feathered the engine.

As he sheepishly climbed down from the cockpit, they all sang in a chorus.

"Let's hear one for the old Martel... He flies to Heaven and lands like Hell..." It was a common song for mistakes.

Boothe grinned under his moustache and clicked his teeth. "You buy the drinks, I'm afraid, old darling."

The pilots lounged around on oil cans and tires as Boothe reported the tally to the operations sergeant.

"Nine Heinkels confirmed. Two probables. Six damaged, unknown. Two more for me. One laggard old bucket for old Biggles." He needled Biggle. "Not your day, Biggles old dear, must have been sitting sideways on your bum!" He looked to the Americans with some admiration. "One and a half for the Irishman. Four and a bloody half for Miller!"

Sergeant Ellard looked up from his report form, not sure he heard right.

"You can give my half to Donovan," Aaron said nudging him.

"Four?!" The sergeant whistled through the space in his front teeth. "You got a bleedin' ace on your hands, you have!"

Boothe grinned at Aaron. "Luck. Luck, pure as soap." He nodded to Wilson, who was sitting quiet. "And one for the Martel. Nerves of steel." He clapped Wilson on the shoulder. Wilson flinched, hiding his "nerves of steel" behind a sheepish smile.

"Losses?" the sergeant asked, his pen poised over the boxes.

"One aircraft and pilot. Simmons," Boothe said, subdued.

The sergeant checked his boxes for aircraft and pilot loss and wrote the name on his sheet.

"Get us a replacement quick as you can, won't you?" Boothe said seriously.

"Grow 'em in my garden, Squadron Leader," the sergeant answered without the slightest humor.

The pilots sat in a corner of the pub with full pints they didn't have to pay for. The locals would always offer whenever they came in, but would rarely try to talk to them as they had before the fighting started. They would just hold up their pints from across the bar. Occasionally some girls might try to strike up some cheek, but while the comradery seemed like young men burning off steam as they laughed and joked, there was almost always someone missing from the group who had been there the day before, and often a new face they might see only once.

Wilson sat at the bar, staring into a glass of Scotch. He didn't like the warm beer very much and insisted on buying it himself. He had bought a round for the house. His hand holding the glass shook and he was glad it didn't have any ice, or it would have sounded like a fire alarm. The other pilots were chumming with some girls on the other side of the pub, but he sat by himself. He threw the drink back as Aaron slid onto the stool next to him. Aaron slapped him on the back.

"Congratulations, buddy. You're a fighter pilot!"

"Yeah." Wilson nodded, but without joy or satisfaction. "Jesus, Aaron, what the hell am I doing here?"

"What do you mean?" Aaron asked, knowing his friend was shaken from the day.

"I'm not you. Maybe I thought I could be." He wiggled his glass for the barman. Then he looked into it, swirling a last bit of liquid in the bottom. "All those years watching you and Miki go at it. I wanted to be up there. Or I thought I did. But I'm just a fan. I should be on the ground, cheering, instead of..." He looked to Aaron with a darkness in his eyes. "I'm going to die here."

Aaron met his questioning, worried gaze. He'd thought about it a lot himself, but he'd confronted it long ago.

"Have to die somewhere, old buddy. Trick is to accept it. Once you do, any day you don't die is another day you live. Really live. It's a bonus. Let tomorrow take care of itself."

Boothe came over, waving off the barman as he reached for the plain label Scotch bottle from his rack. "Alright children, one more drinkie is the capper. Up at first light!"

The pilots jeered and moaned from their corner across the pub. Boothe was a stickler. The "Marme", they called him.

Wilson didn't sleep much that night. He laid in his bunk with images of the day's flight flashing behind his eyelids, Simmons' Spitfire exploding next to him in a ball of fuel flame and his screams over the comms. He twitched uncontrollably all night as if trying to correct the control stick.

Aaron lay awake for much of the night, too, as he often did. But it wasn't war or death that he thought about. He remembered days past, days of he and Miki. When a local in the pub would buy him a pint he would remember his beer drinking challenge with Miki.

"Winner gets the girl," Miki had toasted.

He thought of that moment in the dark parking lot of Luigi's when he realized he'd destroyed everything that mattered, Lacy hurrying away in the dark as he called after her while he pulled up his pants from screwing Charlotte.

"Crash and burn." Miki was right. And the bastard took advantage, cutting inside when he flew off course and closed for the kill. The Javelin. Had Miki stolen her, or had Aaron let her go? Had Charlotte just been an easy excuse, that he didn't deserve Lacy, or that deep down believed he would ultimately disappoint her? It was a constant question for which he had no good answer.

~~~

CHAPTER THIRTEEN

Beef Wellington

A fog hovered over the old cracked asphalt airfield at St. Omer. The 109s of II Group of the 26th Jagdgeswäder were parked along the edge of the field, partially under the trees and covered by camouflage nets. They had moved from their initial grass field base at Audembert for better supply. It was morning and operations wouldn't begin for three hours. A meeting had been called.

Miki was at the Operations Building, standing before GeneralLeutnant Von Schleich. His old mentor had been promoted again, reporting now to Berlin for readiness in the west. The hunter group command had been taken over by Colonel Johannes Fink. Werner Mölders was commanding the 51st Hunter Wing and Adolf Galland was in charge of I and III Groups at Marquise. All three of them had their baptism in Spain. Galland had been a ground bombing officer, but had switched to fighter groups after Poland.

The most recent bombing raid had been a fiasco. The three fighter commanders all complained that flight control needed to be better coordinated, but the command structure which required the controllers to report to Berlin before assigning field commands had slowed the system.

"We lost fourteen aircraft without fighter support! Twenty-three crew lost! Seven pilots wounded! Not a bomb dropped!" Von Schleich was unusually cross. He'd been up half the night with Kesselring chewing his ass from Berlin, so much invective for almost three hours, and he could only hold the receiver away for a time, but could not hang up.

"With respect, Herr General," Miki spoke up. He had agreed among the others that he would take the point with Von Schleich's field inspection tour as he was best acquainted with the General.

"Communications are faulty. We did not receive our orders until twenty minutes after the planes left their bases. Then, we were directed to a rendezvous where there were no planes."

"I want no excuses, Hauptmann. If the planes are up, you will find them."

"We are not allowed to change vectors on our own, Herr General. That is the directive of Central Command."

Von Schleich stepped closer to Miki, standing at attention. Four command level flight control officers were watching the exchange. The old fighter ace had a sly twinkle in his eye. He knew the problems. He had been complaining himself for weeks about the inefficiency.

"Are you suggesting, Hauptmann, that Central Command are fools?"

"Herr General. I would never question the intelligence of Central Command." Miki said.

"You are an excellent liar, Hauptmann."

"I never lie to a senior officer, Herr General, unless I am sleeping with his wife."

"Of course not, Hauptmann." Von Schleich tried to suppress his smile at the game they played. He would report back to Kesselring that he had passed his concerns to the front line pilots and that his message was understood. He would not suggest that the pilots' directive be changed, as it had come from Hitler, but he might slip the idea into a later report on efficiency.

The other command officers returned to their bases to be on station by ten o'clock. At eleven-twenty the horn sounded, in three short blasts. The aircrews began pulling the camouflage nets from the planes and started the engines, as the pilots dressed in their flying suits and scrambled from the old farmhouse across the field they had taken as a barracks.

Miki climbed into his cockpit. The fog had still not lifted, and the reported ceiling above was 15,000 feet until mid-channel. The flight pattern had become routine now. Take-off at half mid-day or thirteen hundred at the latest. Assemble with the bombers at the rendezvous point over France at 15,000 to 18,000 and climb to 21,000 to 24,000 feet. They had about 90 minutes mission time, with a half-hour to cross the channel. The red panel fuel warning light would come on at 1/4 fuel, giving them a half-an-hour to reach the French coast or splash into the sea.

The weather this morning was at operational minimum, and Miki thought the bomber crews would have a bad time of it, even if operations command did manage to coordinate the right rendezvous point.

Miki's crew chief, Flight Sergeant Schluss, fastened his straps. "Good hunting, Miki."

"If we can see what to shoot, Oberfeldwebel."

Schluss had been with Miki for the past two months. They had first met at Schliessheim and Miki had requested him as his chief for the France station. He had arrived with the new BF 109E-4 planes. The newest version of the Messerschmitt fighter had added a higher compression engine, the Daimler-Benz 601N, which provided 1175 horsepower and another 30 miles per hour in speed at level flight. It was a significant improvement over the E-3s, but required higher octane fuel and more particular maintenance, cleaning the fuel injection lines after each flight mission.

Miki had convinced command he needed an experienced crew chief and Schluss was glad to be with the Javelin again. He was sure Miki was going to be Germany's top ace soon, and he would rise with him. Miki now had thirty-five victories. Werner Mölders was ahead of him with thirty-eight and Galland was keeping pace at twenty-two, but most of his were ground attack and not aircraft. Mölders wasn't flying today as his machine had suffered damage to its undercarriage on the poorly maintained runway at Audembert and Miki could possibly pass him in victories.

A fog bank hugged the French coast line like a cotton wall. The 109s of II Group punched out of the fog, pulling wisps of cloying moisture with them. They rose toward the blue, gaining altitude, twelve planes in three formations of joined pairs, spreading five hundred meters apart. The radio crackled with the coordinate for the day.

"II Group intersect 14th bomb wing, sector 2-6-3."

Kellmann was flying on Miki's wing.

"Think we find them today?" he only half-joked.

Miki was fresh from his dressing down of the morning. "We'd better, or else we fly to London and turn ourselves in."

Miki looked off his left wing and saw several specks also rising into the sky in the distance, in the same direction.

"III Group."

"So, we have company. We all get lost together with Major Galland." It was Frische from the second rotte formation, "if the Javelin beats Mickey Mouse today, I buy the steaks."

Adolf Galland had been flying with the Walt Disney cartoon character on his nose since Poland.

"I think Beef Wellington," said Miki.

"Maybe we all fly to London for dinner!' Kellmann laughed, "With Churchill!"

The Spitfires of Pinewood Squadron roared in formation off the chalky coast at Folkstone, in a slow graceful bank to altitude, cutting through the corners of puffy clouds. One of the formation groups was only a pair as they had yet to replace the lost plane and its pilot. The alarm had been early and Boothe hadn't read his Times. It was yesterday's and a new corporal had tossed it away that morning, tidying up the dispersal shack.

"Pinewood Leader, count sixteen hostiles your vector, Angels Two-One-Zero," came the vector call from the Ops radio.

"Only sixteen?" Ackers radioed. "Is Jerry runnin' out?! Maybe he ran out of fighters, too."

"Wouldn't count on that, Ackers, old dear," Boothe cautioned. He knew they had been very lucky on the last few flights.

Donovan scratched his fingers into on his flight cap. His head had been itching for days. "What do you guys make these hat liners out of?" he asked.

Several laughs came over the radio comm, "Best Scottish wool, boy-o. It's imported, including the lice." It was Biggles on the radio as Donovan found another place to scratch. "Just don't be caught scratching with a Hun winkin' at you!"

Ahead of them, Boothe could make out the wing of Heinkels rumbling toward the coast. They had been supplemented with Dornier 17s. That was good, Boothe thought. The Dorniers had a slower cruise speed at altitude so the Heinkels had to fly slower, so they didn't leave them behind. They had come out of Gravelines, headed for South End. Jerry varied his target route from day to day. That was probably why the earlier flight had missed their fighter support. He looked higher in the sky above the lumbering bombers, but could not see the hunters he was sure must be with them. He didn't see any. He hoped that maybe there was a problem with Jerry's flight control.

"Tally ho, darlings," he radioed. "Job at hand. Here we go."

The Spitfires split into two flights and dove from 24,000 feet on the bomber formation. The machine gun fire filled the sky from both directions. The Spits diced through the bombers as the German gunners fired at the dodging and diving British fighters. Some of the German gunners hit their companion planes as they desperately swung their swivel mounted guns. The first Heinkel arced down toward the sea in a trail of smoke.

Miki and his Jäger Gruppe were cruising at 26,000 feet. Air control had given them the right coordinates, but the bombers had not held at their rendezvous point for the fighters to join them. It was probably because of the Dorniers. Miki had to calculate the vector heading in his head to catch them. He didn't bother control, because they would just say he was complaining again.

Miki was mulling the problem when he saw the smoke trails of the Spits attacking the bomber wing below to the northwest. He pulled his goggles down over his eyes and checked his gun firing switch. He selected both the cannons and the guns for the first attack. At high speed dive, he would only have an instant for the first kill. He would switch to save ammunition for a dog fight when he could out-fly the enemy.

The eight 109s of the schwarm pushed over to dive in attack formation, pairs in sections of four with a lead and wingmen each, like a well-rehearsed ballet.

Flight Officer Chivers banked his Spitfire on a Heinkel, bringing his gunsight to bear.

"One fat Heinie in my sights, Blue Leader, attacking now." It was his last radio transmission. As he steadied for his attack, moving the reflector sight divider lines over the bomber ahead, suddenly, blue flashes sparked on his right wing. He looked over for a moment, puzzled, wondering about the odd color. It was the magnesium lead alloy of the German bullets reacting to the aluminum of the wing. He thought it was oddly beautiful before he realized.

"Oh, God..." he said to himself just as the red hot flash of the explosive cannon shells burst across the wing, smashing holes through the aluminum so that he could see the channel below. Then, the faster moving machine gun projectiles smashed the glass of his canopy behind his head, the bullets smashing into the metal below the canopy, cutting bloody holes in him, spattering his blood on the instruments and the canopy in explosions of flesh, before shattering his instruments, then dancing across the other wing.

Bloody and dead, Chivers fell over on his stick and the Spitfire pitched over into a dive toward the sea. It had taken two and half seconds.

Miki's 109 roared past the killed Spit, straight through the formation and banked around for the next kill.

Boothe called urgently on his radio to his group.

"Buster! Buster!" he shouted. He instantly rolled off his attack path before he would be hit. A trail of machine gun trace just missed his wingtip. He had reacted just fast enough. He squinted to see the next formation of Messerschmitts attacking out of the sun.

The Spitfires of II Group broke off the bombers to fight for their own lives as the 109s slashed through them, firing short bursts then arcing away for another attack.

"Look out, Red Two! Got one on you!" Biggles called out to warn Aaron.

Bullets from a 109 sparked on Aaron's wing and canopy. He instantly rolled and banked as the 109 dove past him and banked away. Aaron pulled hard on the stick, the G-force mashing him into the seat as he brought his plane around in a tight bank to intersect on the 109, banking the opposite way.

Aaron leveled his wing in the climb and lined up, sighting the intersecting the 109. He fired his eight Brownings. His arcing bullets in a trail across the sky flashed on the 109's fuselage in the distance. Smoke began to pour out of the 109's exhaust through the oil cooler. The Messerschmitt fell off, rolling into a spinning dive for the sea. On the way down, a small figure tumbled from the plane. The pilot had bailed out. Aaron circled around to watch him fall until his parachute opened before the machine splashed in.

Aaron thought about taking the Nazi bastard out of the fight. He could dive and shoot him while he drifted in the parachute, a hanging duck. The Germans sometimes did it to the British pilots. But then he thought, they were close off the English coast and a British trawler would pick him up, if he didn't drown. He could sit out the war in prison camp and tell his grand kids about how he got his butt kicked by a Yank. And aside from chivalry, if he dove down to the sea, the battle would be over by the time he could climb back to altitude. He pulled his stick and banked back to the fight.

Donovan brought his Spit around on a 109, lining his sight, but as he pressed the trigger pin the 109 flicked away and the bullet stream shot past. He rolled and dove, still after the fighter. He fired again, but the 109 flicked off the other way. He missed again.

"Hold still, dammit!" Donovan shouted as if the German pilot should cooperate in his own death. He lined up again, finger reaching for the firing button, but the 109 pulled up and snap-rolled on its side, then turned in a sudden sideways hard G bank and was gone. It was the split-S maneuver the German pilots had practiced over and over in France against the Hurricanes. Donovan tried to follow, but as he pulled inverted Gs his engine started to cough and flutter. The Merlin engine's gravity fed carburetor couldn't fight the force of an inverted turn. His plane started to stall and drop off. All he could do was straighten the wings into a half loop and pull out at the bottom. The German, with his fuel injection Daimler-Benz, had escaped.

As Aaron climbed back up into the fight he could see Wilson's Spitfire in a straight shallow descent as a 109 banked around to line up behind him.

"On your tail, Wilson!" Aaron called out on his comm.

"Wilson checked in the little mirror attached at the top of his canopy. He looked over a shoulder. He couldn't see it. He looked over his other shoulder. Nothing there either.

"Where?!" he asked, a bit confused.

"Right behind you!"

Wilson looked again to his right and could now see the 109 racing up on him, growing large, the swirl of its prop spinner almost hypnotic.

"Get out of there! Don't fly straight for Godsakes!" Aaron warned.

The 109's cowling machine guns flashed fire through the blur of the spinning propeller. Bullets streaked past Wilson's canopy, just over his wings, the velocity pushing the air so they looked like fireflies in the daylight.

"Pull up!" Aaron shouted again. Wilson would be dead in a second if he stayed where he was.

Wilson closed his eyes and yanked back on the stick.

The Spitfire instantly arced into a power climb as the 109 hurtled past, its prop just missing the tail of the Spit by inches.

Wilson held the stick back with a terror grip, with his eyes still closed, until the roaring of the engine pitched higher over the fading prop fighting the thin air of the flight ceiling. When he opened his eyes, he could see nothing but blue sky outside his canopy. It was dizzying, with no reference to where he was except the sensation of his back pressing hard on his parachute pack in the seat back. The plane was standing on its tail, climbing strait up. He thought for an instant curiously looking at the blue, that it wasn't England any more, but it might as well be New Jersey. Then the engine sputtered, starved of fuel as the carburetors quit. The propeller fluttered and nearly stopped, just half-spinning in a wind forced carousel. It was suddenly very quiet. Wilson could hear his own breathing.

"That's not good," Wilson said to himself.

As the Spit fell over onto its back, Wilson could see the clouds and ocean above his head. He looked around in a momentary daze as the upside down ocean and clouds began to slowly turn as the plane entered an inverted flat spin, turning faster like a platter and dropping from the sky. Wilson pulled on the stick, but it had no force at all. He racked it back and forth trying to control the plane, but it seemed completely disconnected as the world turned faster and faster below, growing closer. Then, the first thought of his training came to his mind. He pulled the stick straight back, straining to pull it into his chest, holding it there until it hurt, hoping and waiting as the topsy-turvy world spun around. Finally, the plane continued over from its back until the nose pointed straight down toward the sea.

Aaron watched Wilson's Spitfire diving straight down toward the channel water like a rock, its wings slowly twirling out of control. He wondered if Wilson had passed out.

As the sea rushed toward him, Wilson pushed the stick against the spin until the turning slowed to almost straight, then yanked back to pull out of the dive. Aaron watched as Wilson's Spitfire slowly started to pull out of the dive with a thousand feet before the water. He would save himself, but as he did, a 109 arced around into an angled dive. The German pilot had been watching, too. He was going in for the kill of a confused and distracted pilot, closing as the Spitfire pulled out of the dive.

"Right, Wilson! Bank right!" Aaron shouted.

Barely breathing again, Wilson heard Aaron in his headphone and this time didn't wait for a reason. He threw his stick over.

Wilson's Spitfire banked over into an arcing right turn. The attacking 109 banked hard to follow, closing in for the kill, but Aaron had been watching him all along. He dove down from above them, vectoring in on a 45 degree tack. The 109's belly was flat and open for Aaron as it turned on Wilson. The exposed light blue underside of the fuselage filled Aaron's gun sight. He fired.

The bullets ripped into the 109, dancing on its skin, passing through the fuselage into the bottom of the pilot's seat and into the wing fuel tanks. The 109 fell off in an inverted spin toward the sea with the pilot dead and exploded in flame as it went down.

Wilson looked through the top of his canopy to see the exploding 109 and Aaron's Spitfire diving around.

"Thanks, Brick," he said over his comm, relieved.

"Wilson..." Aaron's voice wasn't warning this time but seemed to be just getting his attention. He looked forward through the windscreen glass. Ahead of him was a 109 pulling into a climb from an attack. It was fat and flat in his sight.

"Jesus..." he said in surprise and squeezed his finger on the trigger pin. The bullets streamed from the guns on either side of his canopy and ripped into the wings and canopy of the rising 109.

Blood spattered the cockpit glass of the 109 as its left wing tore off, fluttering past Wilson's peripheral, before the destroyed machine tumbled away out of view.

Wilson could only blink in disbelief. Had he hit it, or was it Aaron?

"Good shooting, Blue Four!" Boothe congratulated over the comm.

"Uh...thanks, Squadron Leader," was all Wilson could say, still not fully comprehending he had downed a Hun.

As Boothe pulled out of a turn, he could see the speck of a 109 coming straight for him.

"Come on, Jerry, old darling," Booth said with relish as he leveled his plane toward the on-coming enemy. The two planes closed at 500 miles an hour on level altitude. He lined the 109 in his reflector sight, waiting just a moment. He fired and his bullet stream shot out toward the 109. The 109 fired with its cowl guns. Its bullet tracers whizzed past Boothe's canopy bubble.

The two planes raced toward each other, head on, both firing as they closed, but neither being hit. Boothe held his finger on the trigger as the 109 raced toward him, larger and larger, determined to get him first or make him chicken turn, right into the bullets.

Bullets chunked black marks out of Boothe's canopy, sparking and exploding on his wings, but he kept charging, firing. If he turned, he would fly right into the cannon shells.

"Oh, bloody hell..." was the last they heard over the comms as the two planes slammed into each other head on, exploding and tumbling off in opposite arcs toward the sea.

"Squadron Leader?! Squadron Leader?! Red One?!" Biggles called out on his radio, but there was no answer and the burning wreckage of Boothe's Spit tumbled from the sky. Aaron and the others all watched the leader's plane splash in the sea.

Lt. Kellmann brought his 109 around in a diving turn on a banking Spitfire. It seemed distracted by the other falling plane of a comrade. Kellmann lined up his sights. The fuel light on his panel had been red for the past two minutes. He would have one more chance at a kill before turning back to base. He didn't even know whether the bombers had gotten through, but here was a British pilot fat in his sights.

"Beef Wellington," he said to himself with a smile as he pulled on his trigger. He was out of cannon shells so only the cowling guns fired.

Bullets suddenly sparked on Aaron's wing and rattled in the fuselage behind him, spitting chunks of metal around the cockpit. He could feel them hitting the metal back plate behind the seat. He would have been dead if it wasn't there.

"Shit!" was all he could say, thinking he'd been stupid.

The left wing outside his canopy sheared and was gone. The plane rolled over onto its back, falling into a tumbling spin toward the sea.

Everything was suddenly quiet, except the whistling of the wind. Aaron looked out the top of his canopy at the sea above his head slowly turning, while puffy wisps of clouds flew past as he headed down. The stick was loose in his hand.

After an instant of strange wonder, Aaron reached up for the canopy release and slid back the plastic bubble. The rushing wind surrounded him as he slammed a fist against the restraint release on his chest. He slipped out of the cockpit.

His body tumbled out from the broken Spitfire as it spun now wildly out of control. Aaron could feel himself tumbling over and over as the world flipped in a blur, until the cords of his parachute streamed out and yanked him, almost breaking out of the harness. The straps through his legs snapped against his balls. He almost blacked out from the excruciating lightning bolt of pain shooting through his body.

The white mushroom canopy filled above him, until he was dangling in the sky, with the churning waters of the channel down below his boots.

As Aaron hung in the air on the straps of the parachute chords, fighting the pain and wondering if he'd ever screw again, he could hear the growl of an airplane engine growing louder. He wriggled to spin in the cords to see a 109 coming at him through the wisps of a cloud, growing larger.

Kellmann lined up his sight on the body of the pilot dangling helplessly from the chute, drifting toward the sea. As the body grew larger, Kellmann reached his finger to the firing trigger. Waiting. Closer. Closer.

"Ack, ack, ack," he said, but didn't pull the trigger. He was out of ammunition anyway, only four bullets left on the counter and the red fuel warning light glowing at him. "We do this again sometime," he said with a grin as if the other pilot could hear him.

The Messerschmitt roared past Aaron, not firing. It waggled its wings as the prop wash buffeted Aaron in the chute straps, before it arced back up into the clouds and disappeared.

The churning waves rushed up toward Aaron's boots. He splashed into the ice cold water, sinking under a wave for a moment. He had caught his breath before he splashed in and held it until he thought his lungs might burst. Then, without a lot of effort he bobbed to the surface on his flotation harness.

He looked around the sea, alone. He looked to the sky. The planes were all gone, nothing but trails of smoke and condensation in the drifting clouds, now turning back into a thick overcast. He floated and was pretty certain he wouldn't sink, but the water was so chilling, it bit into his flesh. The one thing he was glad about was the cold of the water seemed to numb the shooting pain in his crotch, and one of the first real prayers of his life came to him. "Thank God for small favors."

Biggle gave his report to the Ops Sergeant at Westhampnett dispersal. Donovan, Wilson and Ackers sat in the chairs outside the shack. They were silent, in their own thoughts while their machine crews refueled their planes and repaired wing holes with fabric tape. Jerry could make another attack before the day was over.

"Miller, one Heinkel confirmed, one damaged, two nines bagged, confirmed." Biggle recounted the damage to the enemy first. The losses would come after. "Wilson, 109, confirmed."

Donovan patted Wilson on the back. He smiled half-heartedly.

"Biggle, one Dornier 17, confirmed. A Fat Pheasant," he only half-joked. "Boothe, one Heinkel confirmed, two damaged."

"Losses?" The sergeant moved to his second report sheet.

"The skipper and craft lost. Chivers and craft lost. Miller, craft lost, pilot missing. Ackers thinks he saw a chute."

The sergeant wrote it down solemnly, marking all the right boxes. The crew chief leaned in the door.

"Refueled and armed."

His timing was good as the dispersal phone rang at that moment. The sergeant picked it up. He wrote down the altitude and vector on his report sheet.

"A flight, B flight scramble," he said to Biggle, just across his desk.

"Tell dispersal we can only put up A flight."

The sergeant nodded at Biggle and reported into the phone. "Can only manage A flight from 65 II group W, sir?" He waited for the response. "Right."

He hung up the handset. "Manage what you can, Squadron Leader."

"Right, then, off we go."

The others slowly stood from their chairs, the exhaustion and fear showing as the dispersal bell rang.

Biggle roused them as best he could. He was in command of the squadron now. "Lively, now, the Hun ain't quit, yet. Let's finish him off. Alright? For the skipper."

"Piece of cake," Ackers said, managing a chipper smile, though he didn't feel it.

They trotted to their refueled planes and roared off into the sky for yet another sortie.

It was two days later when a supply lorry rumbled up to the gate. Aaron was riding in the back with a couple of fresh pilots, Tom Brinley and Dennis Hicks. Biggle sauntered out to the meet them as they hopped off with their fresh kits and an innocent look in their eyes.

Biggle waved for the replacements. "You lot can store your kit in billet four. We might even be able to find some planes for you, if you're lucky." The new pilots lifted their gear and headed for the tent billets.

Biggle grinned at Aaron. "Went for a lovely swim and sight cruise, eh, Miller?"

As they shook hands, Donovan trotted over from the mess hall with a big grin.

"So, the Brick didn't sink! All in one piece?"

He wouldn't tell them about the strap. It still hurt. He had floated in the water for only four hours before a trawler came across him. He had been in a recovery hospital in Maidstone for thirty-six hours of mandatory observation.

"How's Wilson?" he asked, looking for his other friend. He'd worried about him

Donovan and Biggle exchanged looks. Biggle shook his head.

"Damn the luck..."

"What?" Aaron asked, worried even more they'd gotten him.

Donovan grinned a mile wide. "You won't believe it, Aaron. The little cocksman bagged another one! A reconnaissance plane. Almost ran into the thing coming back after sundown."

Biggle laughed, "If that boy ain't a natural born talent, I don't know what is."

Wilson stepped out of the mess, munching on a chicken leg. He waved it.

"Got some new kites comin' in. Fresh from the assembly line." Biggle took Aaron by the arm and walked with him a little. "I'm SQL now, you know, with the bloody Old Darling gone. I want you to take B flight."

A pair of Spitfire Mk IIa's angled on the forty-five for landing on the field. They turned to look.

"Which I speak, would be them. Take a look over 'em. And if none of the bolts is missing, take your pick. We'll give the new Martels the buckets."

He held out the Flying Officer bar patch for Aaron's uniform. Aaron took the promotion with silent nod.

Charlotte and Darlene sat on a blanket on the lake bank watching the rowers. Charlotte was about ready to deliver, shifting uncomfortably to find a good position. The New Brunswick newspaper had just published the story of the local heroes who had crossed the ocean to join the fight. The bold headline had declared "American Boys Aces in the Battle For Britain". The article had a few inaccuracies and some outright deceptions at Air Ministry request.

Charlotte and Darlene both had letters which were a little more accurate. Wilson still wrote regular letters almost every week. They could take almost a month to arrive. Donovan was a little less regular writing to Charlotte.

"Robert says he's doing fine and not to worry." Darlene read Wilson's letter first. "He's shot down three German planes! Doesn't say much more about it... Usual stuff about Aaron... Send socks! What does Jerry's say?"

Charlotte had read through it twice. She encapsulated. "Doing fine. Hates the food. His head itches. When's the baby due? Saw London on a leave...what's left of it, he says." She took another look at the scrabbled handwriting. "Aaron's been made the leader of his flight group and he's shot down eight planes! Aaron, that is. Jerry has three or four... I don't know what "confirmed" means. Send socks."

"Are they making them fly in their bare feet?!" Darlene's letter from Wilson mentioned socks, too.

"Maybe it's getting cold over there." Charlotte looked up at the September sky, trying to picture planes flying across it, and imagining Donovan among them.

The belly of a banking 109 flashed past Donovan's windscreen, too fast to get a shot. He pressed the firing button, but the machine guns fired into thin air. Donovan chased the 109 above the low drifting cloud ceiling, over the channel. He tried to line it in his sights as he fired his guns in short bursts. The 109 dodged to the left, then the right, trying to escape, the wings of the plane flitting in and out of the gunsight.

Donovan's gun stream missed off one side, then the other. Finally, the 109 settled between the wingspan lines of the sight for a moment as it held a turn. The Spit could turn tighter than the 109, but the German plane which could accelerate faster would soon be gone again. Donovan led the sight just ahead of the nose spinner spiral and squeezed the firing button. The bullets sparked across the cowling and the wing root, before the 109 was gone from his gunsight.

The 109 banked away from the Spit, trying for a diving S. Donovan flicked his stick for a half-roll to fill his carburetor with fuel before pulling a hard diving turn, but it was long enough for the German to escape. Just as Donovan was cursing his luck, as the

Messerschmitt tried to get into cloud cover, the 109's engine began to smoke. He'd gotten a lead into a cylinder. The enemy kept flying, but was losing altitude, drifting downward toward the deck, passing through a cloud.

Donovan was sure it was going to splash, but he needed to observe it to report a confirmed kill. He'd had three unconfirmed in the last two weeks and really wanted this one. He watched the cloud, straining. Then, the 109 passed out below it, still descending, but turning back toward France. Donovan banked over it, keeping it in sight. He would follow it down, because it would take too long to get back to flight Angels.

"Irish, stay with the group," Aaron's voice came over the radio comm.

"I want to eyeball the splash. You're getting way ahead of me," Donovan answered, keeping after the wounded 109.

"Let it go," Aaron ordered. Donovan kept toward the French coastline. He'd give it another minute. He needed this one and he was so sure. Finally, the enemy plane skimmed the water, its shape reflecting on the glistening waves, then, splashed in.

"Alright!" Donovan shouted, "There's one Kraut eating bastard confirmed!"

He pulled his stick back to his chest and shoved the throttle to climb back up through the clouds. He'd lost a thousand feet. He looked around the sky, but couldn't see the other Spits.

"Where'd you go? Blue Leader?" There was no answer on the radio. He thought Aaron and the boys were playing with him. Pretty soon they'd congratulate him and he'd have to buy the pints. He thought he would write home to Charlotte and brag about his score and wondered if it would get there before the baby came. She had sent him a handful of baby name suggestions in her last letter. He didn't like any of them, but he would pick one to make her happy.

"Okay, play hide and seek!" he said, "jealous bastard!" His head itched and he scratched his flight cap trying to get at it through the layers of leather and wool.

"Son-of-a-bitch!" He couldn't get his fingers deep enough to reach it and pulled off the cap, cursing the Scots and whoever invented sheep.

As he scratched, his plane flew lazily through the clouds. The radio was silent. Maybe the battle was over and the Jerries had all headed back.

The German command had thrown waves of bombers at London and the docklands for six days. The Germans had the worst of it, at least in the air, but just better than a draw. The Squadron had lost seven pilots. Rogers and Campbell a month ago, a kid from South Tyneside, Boothe. Brinley and Hicks, who had arrived with Aaron, were gone. They had been replaced by two more fresh faces straight out of training. One of those was gone, too. Biggle, Aaron, Donovan and Wilson were all that was left of the "originals." But it felt like the tide was turning.

The Javelin had been busy. Miki, it seemed, was now a pure killing machine. They had not seen him, but his distinctive marquee had been reported by 54 Squadron and 213 Squadron. Pilots in Hurricanes had apparently been his favorite targets. Eight Hurries had fallen victim to the wing cannons of the German ace. He had only been confirmed for three Spits, but he seemed to be flying missions further north than their area.

Donovan hopped over little rising puffs of clouds cutting his wing through the mists, curling the vapor in his wake. As he punched through a puff, flying through a cloud valley, another plane appeared in his canopy from behind, flying right beside him, pulling up almost wingtip to wingtip.

"Okay, peek-a-boo. You got me," Donovan said through the radio, thinking it was Aaron or one of the boys who had been keeping silent on his radio, messing with him. He looked over his shoulder to see the spiraling cork-screw nose spinner of a 109. A Javelin in a fist like a lightning bolt was painted on its side just below the cockpit and over the yellow cowling.

Miki looked over at the careless, joyriding fool in the Spitfire. He was close enough to shout at him, to tell him he was a dead man who should be paying attention. He saw the distinctive red hair and freckled face. It was very familiar. The Princeton fight song came into is mind. He usually sang it just before a kill, but it suddenly popped into his head with nearly forgotten images. He'd given his GeeBee racing plane to Donovan. Could this be him, now flying for the Brits? Then, he was sure it was.

Donovan caught himself staring at the cowling of the Messerschmitt, flying level next to him, and the pilot inside the cockpit in his gray flight cap and oxygen mask. The pilot waved his hand.

"Christ!" Donovan shouted to himself, thinking how careless he'd been. He yanked the stick over hard, diving away. The Messerschmitt rolled and dove after.

Donovan shoved the throttle wide open, dodging and weaving to get away. The 109 kept right with the Spitfire's every move, dodging through and around the clouds. He waited for the searing burn of the cannon shells. How could he have been so stupid?!

Miki easily threw his stick, anticipating Donovan's every move. He pulled in closer, closer, lining the Spitfire in his gunsight.

"Fight for Old Nas-sau. Fight for our ivy halls," Miki sang to himself inside his mask. His finger moved to the firing trigger, in rote practice, just pure instinctive muscle memory now. He pictured in his mind where the shells would strike and burst through the fuselage and cut off the tail wing. His finger rested on the gun trigger, almost caressing the stick in his hand.

Donovan flung his plane around, desperately trying to get away. He looked over one shoulder, then the other. The Javelin's prop was always right behind, matching him maneuver for maneuver.

"Shit! Shit!"

The Spit was in Miki's sight for the perfect shot, but he lifted his finger off the trigger. He smiled inside his mask, but kept on his pursuit, just enjoying harrying old "Irish", teaching him a little flying lesson.

"Ack, ack, ack," Miki said to himself, then pulled back on his stick.

Donovan pulled out of a hard turn and looked over his shoulder, no 109. He looked over the other, nothing. He cringed, waiting for the bullets. Nothing. Puzzled, he looked out his canopy, all around the sky. Miki's 109 was nowhere to be seen. Finally, he breathed again, thanking God. He promised himself he'd go to Confession.

"Shit," he said aloud, realizing something must have happened to his radio, and turned back for home.

Donovan's Spitfire banked over a cloud into clear air, the white chalk cliffs ahead of him. He'd have a hell of a story to tell. He couldn't believe he'd actually seen Miki, and was still alive! He found himself smiling at the thought of them all coming this far, to find themselves on opposite sides in the sky. He lined up his course toward East Bourne and Beachy Head

Suddenly, a 109 dove out of the high overcast and its guns fired. The bullets and cannon shells ripped into Donovan's plane, exploding on the wings, sparking on the cowling, and shattering the canopy.

Donovan's right thigh exploded in a gush of blood. A bullet cut across the side of his head, throwing him against the canopy with the force. Another bullet tore through his left arm, just below the shoulder.

Lt. Frische pulled his nose up and banked away as the Spit's engine smoked and the enemy plane began an out-of-control decent toward the sea.

"Ja! Beef Wellington!" Frische said to himself, satisfied with the kill. He was sure the plane would crash into the water or the beach, but his fuel warning light was red and he couldn't linger to watch it, or get shot himself. He couldn't wait to tell his buddies over drinks how he had caught the careless British pilot napping.

As the sun sank lower in what was promising to be a beautiful sunset, the Spitfires of 65 Squadron settled on the field. Two. Four. Five.

Aaron feathered his engine and hopped out. He looked at the other planes taxiing in and looked out toward the horizon below the sinking sun. Biggle came over from his plane.

"Was the Irish with you?" Aaron asked.

"His comm went silent, but I saw him off to the south for a bit."

They headed over to Operations where the sergeant stepped out of the doorway.

"Anything from Red Two?" Biggle asked. The sergeant shook his head.

Donovan pressed his hand on the blood flowing wound in his thigh, trying to hold the stick steady with his left arm, but it was going numb. The corner bone of his eye socket was gone, and the blood was wet and slick on his face. He could only see out of his left eye, as the right was dangling.

The engine sputtered and groaned. Oil spattered on his windscreen. The plane was shot so full of holes it was hard to imagine its holding together, but he crossed the coast, passing low over the long shadowed green pastures of West Sussex.

Aaron, Wilson and Biggle stood out on the grass of the field, watching the sky. Biggle checked his watch.

"We'd better report it in," he said and started toward the operations shack.

"No. Wait," Aaron said. His sharp eyes could make out the small shape against the orange-flare on the bottom of the gray clouds. He pointed out to the horizon. The others could see the tiny outline of a Spitfire, low over the trees.

Donovan tried to hold the sputtering, rattling, dying machine in the air, skimming the trees and hedges, determined to make it to the field. If he could just hang on, he'd make it. Home to base. Home to Charlotte. Maybe she'd had the baby already, and the news was in a letter crossing the Atlantic. He'd read it soon, in the corner of the pub, while the other guys were drinking, lonely bastards. Maybe she had already picked a name and would tell him in the letter.

He peered out his one eye, blinking away the blood, and trying to restrain the bucking control stick.

He remembered the landing procedure. He released the pressure on his thigh to crank the landing gear. The handle was slippery in his hands. His boots slipped on the wet cockpit floor as he pushed the rudder pedal, hard to the left, trying to hold the yaw, but it was fighting him. A tail surface must be gone.

As the sputtering Spitfire settled toward the hedge at the threshold of the runway, the undercarriage legs opened from the belly, locking into position.

Aaron and the other pilots watched the plane, lining up over the runway, amazed it was still in the air. Wilson cheered, shaking his fist in the air.

"Alright, Red! Hang in there! Almost home!"

Donovan struggled to hold the stick back as the plane settled toward the grass, lower and lower, clearing the hedgerow. Under the shattered instrument panel, fuel spurted from a punctured fuel line onto the puddled floor. A spark arced from the dangling wires of the instruments. The fuel ignited. The cockpit filled with flames. Donovan shrieked in searing pain as he was engulfed. He still had to hold the stick steady, or he'd crash. It was the only thing he could keep in his mind as the fire burned him.

The pilots watched the aircraft settle on the grass, landing as if nothing was wrong, until it rolled past them, flames licking out of the shattered cockpit dome.

Desperately, they ran toward it as it spun to a stop on the grass. Aaron was the first to reach it, jumping up onto the burning wing.

"Donovan!" he shouted as he reached into the flames through the shattered canopy, cringing from the pain, hitting his fist on the searing hot harness release and pulling Donovan out through the canopy.

They fell to the grass. Donovan's flight jacket was burning. Aaron's jacket arms were burning with the fuel. The others rolled them in the grass, throwing their flight jackets over them, rolling them until the flames were out.

Aaron held his friend in his arms, but Donovan was almost unrecognizable. His exposed flesh was a mass of blackened peeling skin. He hadn't been wearing his flight cap and his bright red hair was just a mass of singed black.

Aaron cried as he held his friend. He hadn't cried in five years. "Irish," he whispered, "why wouldn't you listen?"

To his surprise, Donovan opened his one eye, white and blue against the black. He opened his mouth, taking a gulp of air, a rasping rattle.

"Miki..." he gasped. "Aaron. I saw him! Miki. He waved..." his lips almost curled into a smile, then eased into the lax stillness.

"Irish!? Donovan?!" Aaron called out at him, but he didn't answer or move. The blood from his thigh artery had stopped flowing.

Aaron held him, cradling him in his arms. He looked up to the twilight sky in anguish and rage. It was war and they were enemies, but how could Miki shoot a friend. It was a betrayal. They had known they might encounter each other. Sightings of the Javelin had been in action reports from Eastbourne to Kingsdown, but somehow, Aaron had thought it was like sighting a ghost.

"Miki," he said with a breath, a curse.

~~~

CHAPTER FOURTEEN

Berlin

Lacy sat on the train surrounded by good Germans going about their lives while the war news reported great successes in France and the imminent collapse of the English defenses. They were not hearing about the bomber crews falling from the sky into the Channel. Miki would call every two weeks. He often wouldn't say anything at all about the campaign, usually reporting that he would be sending her something he had seen in a store and thought she might like, or to just put away in the cellar. A crate or box would arrive a week later. Sometimes he would say simply that he had to write a letter to the family of one of his pilots. He would say, "you met him", one of the brash and eager boys who had been drinking in their parlor. Lt. Kriegel had tried his clever maneuver, and Miki had been right. He had paid the price.

He had asked her in one of his calls two days ago if she had any more letters from Wilson. She had told him that of course they had stopped after May and asked him why. He had said he thought he had seen Donovan from school in a plane. They had had reports that Americans were flying for the British from the south coast and that an American pilot, just known to them as "the Brick", was racking up ace scores, and he was sure it was Aaron. Donovan must have come with him. Lacy didn't get much past the idea of Aaron flying in a death machine with

Miki's duty to shoot him down rolling in her mind, before she had just repeated that it was all news to her. She just told him to be careful as she usually did.

The journey from Essen to Berlin had taken six hours, and the old Imperial Palaces of Potsdam were just now passing by the windows. Lacy thought she might try to stop on the way back as she had heard much about the San Soucci Gardens which had been open to the public since the last of the Hohenzollern emperors were blown to the dust of history by the defeat of the last war.

Lacy had written to Herr Speer to take him up on his offer to show her his vision of the city. She was interested in architecture, of course, and design, but that was not all she intended. She needed to see, and if possible, obtain a copy of the new Reichsfluchtsteuer stamp required from the Finance Ministry for exit approvals since the war declaration.

To her surprise, Speer's answer and invitation were effusive. He said he was "delighted" to hear from her and remembered their earlier encounter with "distinctive pleasure". He had invited her to a dinner at his house in the Schlacttensee District. It was a little out of town by a lake common for swimming and only a few miles from the Olympic Stadium. A car would collect her from the main railway station, a solid and heavy iron hatch-work building from the late 19th Century erected by Emperor Wilhelm II. Speer had curiously asked her to take note of the building and the district of government buildings around it, and the now domeless, still fire-damaged Reichstag Parliament building across the plaza, which he referred to as architecture from the Gründerzeit. Lacy was unfamiliar with the term, but later learned it was the economic industrial boom of the second half of the

19th Century from where Miki's father gained his wealth and when the kingdoms of old Germany united in the empire. She could have changed at the Zoo Station, which was closer, and she was not entirely clear why he had asked to her make observations. She had been concerned that Speer perhaps might have had fanciful ideas of her coming to him for some romantic adventure, but as it turned out he had something else in mind altogether.

The car drove her through the city and the residential districts, passing the stadium which now seemed nearly abandoned. She had expected to arrive at some ornate grand villa, but as they drove up to an address, his house was, she thought, a decidedly modest one for a man of his stature in the government. His official title on his letterhead was Inspector General of Buildings and Construction for the Capital, but he was responsible for the far more. The house, while set in a pleasantly landscaped yard, and finely framed with hand-worked eaves and trim, consisted of one dining room and attached living room and just three bedrooms. It was incongruous with the man who built with such soaring columns of grand imposing scale.

"We wanted to avoid all that," he said when she asked about it, "the official pomp and all the stiff circumstance. To tell you the truth, I had to borrow the mortgage from my father. I do not take an architect's fee for my official buildings." She found it surprising when every official she had encountered seemed to be grasping all they might gain from a rise in stature.

The walls of the house were decorated with another incongruity from his public designs, soft and moody landscape paintings of woodland scenes and river streams with ancient falling down castle ruins and misty meadows.

A cook served a formal three course meal of recipes Lacy recognized as being from the Baden region, south along the Rhine. His wife, Margarete, was gracious and it seemed to Lacy, reserved and a bit shy, in contrast to Speer. The dinner was punctuated with conversation, mostly from the famous architect who seemed as interested in revealing himself as he was in interviewing her. He certainly had enough official information about her at his disposal.

"You came to Germany by the Hindenburg, I understand?"

"Yes. I was horrified to see it destroyed. It was an amazing experience. Max Schmeling was on board with us. To think, now, of all that gas, terrible."

He nodded. The tragedy of the Lakehurst landing had been a very serious blow in Germany, not just the horror of it, but a blow to the national pride as well.

"When I was ten years old," he said with almost a wistful sadness, "one of the zeppelins used in the bombing air raids on London was stationed near our house in Mannheim. My parents liked to entertain and the captain and his officers would come for dinners. My brothers and I were invited for a ride. We had to pass through the corridors inside the hull between the bags to reach the control gondola. I was so impressed by the technology and to rise with such effortlessness. The captain made a turn over our house, and the officers waved a sheet from the gondola for my mother watching from the ground. It was thrilling, but for several weeks afterward, I would wake in night terrors that the airship would go up in flames and crash into our house." With a small laugh, he poured wine in her glass. It was a story he apparently had told many times.

"From the vineyards of near my family," he said, holding up the bottle with some pride, then, nodded to a photograph in a frame on the wall of the Nazi eagle adorning the stadium of Nuremberg. "It is ironic my largest early commission for the Reich was the Zeppelinfeld of Nuremberg."

"I haven't been there," Lacy said with honesty, but without comment of what she really thought, "but I know it well from Miss Riefenstahl's film." The film "Triumph of the Will" of the great Nazi rally at Nuremburg had been shown over and over before cinema features.

"It was built to hold three hundred and forty thousand persons. I proposed that as many events as possible be held at night, to give greater effect to the lighting spotlights. And perhaps to hide a bit the party members, many overweight Bavarians with bulging bellies from lots of sausages." He smiled as if to point out his joke. She wondered how much he knew of her experience with Leni Riefenstahl's filming at the Olympics.

"I was impressed by the Olympic Stadium," she said, thinking to offer the compliment.

"That wasn't all original with me," he demurred, but whether in modesty or by way of excuse, she couldn't be sure. "Hitler didn't like my predecessor's design for it. Werner March was a Bauhaus modernist. Hitler tends more to the classical, so I added the stone facings and columns."

"You also designed the German Pavilion for the International Exposition in Paris," Lacy thought to prime him a little.

"Yes. 1937. Did you visit?"

She recalled the great standing column of smooth stone reaching to the sky with the giant Reich eagle perched on its crown in the shadow of the Eiffel Tower beside the Seine River. It stood directly across from, and just a few feet higher than, the Soviet Pavilion with its statue of the glorified worker on its top.

"Miki and I went to the Exposition, just before he went to Spain. He's been back to Paris since then, I haven't." Miki had sent her gifts from the city from his visits, but Paris had another meaning now. "How did you become interested in architecture?"

"My family had a summer house in Heidelberg, on the Schloss Wolfsbrunnenweg. I would detour on my way to school across the park of the Heidelberg castle to admire the ruins and look down on the old city with its crooked streets. Perhaps that's where my interest in architecture began and my passion for collecting landscape paintings, especially the works of the Heidelberg Romantics." He gestured to the paintings on the walls. They had art in common, though not exactly taste.

"On my way to school, when I was seventeen, I met Margarete." He reached across the table to take her hand. She smiled softly. "Her father was a successful craftsman. He was renovating an old building and I admired the craft of the wood-working. Such skill with the hands. We fell in love, but my class-conscious mother frowned on the relationship. She felt that her family was socially inferior."

"I understand that very much," Lacy said, remembering her mother's tone whenever she said a word about Aaron, and her own relationship with Miki's mother, for whom she seemed to be a distant alien.

"You come from Princeton. Do you know the rowing club there?"

"I am very familiar with it." She smiled at the question, the image of sitting on the grassy bank with Charlotte and the other girls, watching Aaron and the boys on the lake, rising with a warm memory.

"My way to school led me past the clubhouse of a rowing association,' he said. "For two years, I was coxswain of the racing fours and eights."

"I have many friends who are oarsmen," Lacy said, with a common connection. "Some, I'm very fond of. I still exchange letters, but that's become difficult." She had not received a letter from Wilson or her mother in over a year.

"Yes. I'm sorry." It was a simple response, but Lacy thought it was odd. It seemed as if he was sincere, but was he actually apologizing for the war? Had he seen her letters? How many in the Nazi Reich administration had been watching her and even reading of her schoolgirl friends' wedding announcements?

"Miki didn't row," she said, turning from the questions in her mind. "He preferred the individual sports."

"Yes," he nodded, "such a symbol with his javelin. I, myself, had a frail constitution as a boy, but when I was sixteen I advanced to the oars in the shells. I was seized by ambition and spurred to a performance beyond what I thought I was capable. With a team, the individual's flaws can be out-weighed. In common action there is a requirement of self-discipline."

It occurred to Lacy that he was revealing some private part of himself for her benefit. But was he expecting her to take a lesson from it? Some form of instruction? And it was strikingly almost the precise opposite of Miki's view. She wondered about his politics. He had seemed to her entirely unlike the other high members in the party she had met.

"May I ask, Herr Speer, how you came to join the party?"

He thought about the question, seeming to turn it in his mind. Lacy wasn't sure he would answer and wondered if she should have asked at all, but then she thought about the woman journalist from the Hindenburg and how she had presented the formative days. She had heard Frau Lindl's story of rapturous revelation so many times, she thought she'd like to hear it from one so close. Finally, he rose from his seat to pour the last of the wine bottle into their glasses.

"The first time I saw Hitler was 1931," he finally said, simply. "I was teaching then, at the Berlin Institute of Technology. It was advertised he would speak. The meeting was at a rather dirty beer hall. It seemed as if all the students in Berlin wanted to see and hear this man. He was wearing a blue suit, I recall. Not at all like the posters with the military uniform and the caricatures of the opposition. I was very impressed with the reaction of the students. When he spoke, it seemed he was speaking candidly of his anxieties about the future."

"I was from an upper-middle-class family but we did not escape the food shortages of the war. We had wealth, but no acquaintances in the countryside. My mother became very inventive with turnip recipes. We called it the winter of turnips. At night, all the way from

218

Mannheim, we could sometimes hear the distant rumble from the Krupp guns of the siege at Verdun."

"After the war I had a very strong nationalistic sentiment. The French who occupied the Ruhr in 1923 were conceited and cruel. Perhaps it was revenge for the guns, this I understood, but with the demand for war reparations, the inflation was unbearable. Milk was 250,000 marks for a bottle. A school meal could cost almost a billion marks! Hitler talked of this. I don't recall his words as much as the mood he created. It was as if it didn't really matter what he was saying, but the enthusiasm he projected with his feelings, almost seemed to physically carry his meaning. It swept away any reservations I had from some of his unpleasant positions. Here, it formed in my mind, was hope. Instead of endless unemployment and deprivation, caused by the outsiders in our midst, we could move to a recovery of our economy and our destiny."

"And that was enough?" Lacy asked. It seemed so clinical.

"Some friends and I went to a demonstration at the Sportpalast where Goebbels spoke. The Doctor was much different, with his phrase-making and formulations, but the crowd was whipped to a wild frenzy. When the hall emptied, the police squad trucks of the government were waiting and the mounted police rode into the crowd on their horses with raised batons. My friends were beaten. It affected me deeply and the next day I applied for membership in the party."

"You know, of course," he added with a half-bemused afterthought, "Hitler came to power with only a thirty-seven percent popularity in the last national election." Lacy couldn't tell whether he admired it, or not. It seemed more a curiosity to him, that it was likely the last vote would Germany ever have.

After the intimate and cordial dinner, Lacy said goodbye to the Speers and a car drove her to the Adlon Hotel, which was directly across the Pariser Square from where she was to meet Speer the next day, for what he had promised was to be an exclusive treat. She could see his design for the Reich Chancellery out of her suite window. The grand hotel of Berlin was sumptuous, although Lacy wondered what Miki had meant about the beds when he stayed there. Maybe he was used to his flat and stiff military mattresses that made the puffy goose down of the luxury hotel seem lumpy.

The lobby in the morning was filled with light through the glass dome. Her breakfast was a reminder of home, prepared by the staff to her American tastes, eggs and toast. The American Embassy was a doorstep away so the hotel was well used to the customs of its staff and ambassadors who met officials at the hotel dining room. The American Ambassador had left in 1938, in protest after Kristallnacht, but the consular mission remained. Amid the tinkling and clatter of coffee demitasses and silverware were military officers of general rank with their swastika armbands, sitting across from diplomats and businessmen in custom-made suits from far-off countries, in cheerful conversation. It seemed as if Germany had indeed mastered the world.

At ten o'clock, Lacy walked across the Pariser Square, which took its name from the last time the Prussians had captured Paris, after defeating and chasing Napoleon back from Leipzig in 1814. She took a moment to walk by the Brandenburg Gate with its bronze Roman chariot erected to commemorate the victories of the Second Empire, and through which triumphant soldiers would march in parades down the Unter Den Linden.

Speer was waiting for her at the steps to the Academy of Arts across the square from the gate. His appearance at his home was an informal, if not crisp and tailored, suit and tie. He was now dressed in his working brown uniform with the armband and hat with insignia of his civilian rank, above even the generals she had seen at breakfast.

"Frau von Steuven, I hope you had a pleasant evening," he greeted her.

"I did, thank you."

"Shall we go inside?"

He gestured toward a door in the academy façade where a Wehrmacht solder stood guard with a Mauser slung over his shoulder. Lacy wondered what could require an armed guard at the Arts Academy. The solder executed a sharp heil salute as Speer unlocked the door with a key from a small chain in his pocket.

He led her through a darkened hallway with only daylight through some high upper windows of the gallery. There was no art on the walls but in the center of the marbled parquet floor, below the high coffered ceiling, was a table display holding a massive scale model of Berlin. Not the Berlin she had just seen outside the door, but the one envisioned by Adolf Hitler through his chief architect.

"Isn't this the Art Academy?" Lacy asked, puzzled.

"It was. Now, it is my office, in the other wing." Speer stepped to a series of light switches on the wall near the gallery arch. As he turned the switches, a series of spotlights in the ceiling coffers came on, bathing the models in a bright directional glow.

"The lights are to simulate the direction of the sun in late summer," he explained as the last of them flickered into brightness, illuminating the models of Hitler's new Imperial City of Berlin, meant to rival and emulate ancient Rome as the center of the world.

"Hitler chose this particular building because he can reach it from the Chancellery by way of the gardens without being seen by the public. He had private entrance doors installed, down that hallway." He pointed to another gallery hall where another model seemed to fill the space. "Sometimes he invites dinner guests to see it. No one is allowed to view this without the express approval of the Führer."

"You asked him?" Lacy was surprised.

"For the wife of one of his most ardent heroes? He remembers you, you know."

"I only spoke to him for a half a minute."

"You don't give yourself enough credit." He smiled. It was a compliment. She was still only twenty-three. "I am to report to him your opinion."

"Why would he want my opinion?" Lacy looked at the tables of models, stretching through the series of halls.

"Let me show you."

Speer proceeded to take her on a tour of the scale model of the planned city. The buildings were like doll houses, reproduced in meticulous detail, and painted to simulate the materials to be used. Whole sections of the grand new avenue plan of the Under Den Linden were laid out in successive tables that went on for a hundred feet through the former exhibition rooms of the Academy of Arts.

'I promised Hitler that this project would be completed by 1950."

"1950? All of this?"

"He loves his architecture. He studied in great detail the city plans of Vienna and Paris. In Vienna, the imperial city of the Habsburgs, he admired the formal buildings of the Ringstrasse and in Paris, the grand shopping avenue of the Champs-Élysées."

"Everything is so big," she marveled, looking through the miniature scale windows into vast interiors.

"He thought of this project in medieval proportions. The cathedral of Ulm has thirty thousand square feet of floor area, but when the building was begun, only fifteen thousand people lived in Ulm. They could never fill the space. So the building was constructed with the future in mind. In comparison, a meeting hall for a hundred-fifty thousand people could be thought of as small for a city of millions like Berlin."

As he led her toward one of the models, she realized why he had asked her to make observations of the railway station. At one end of the grand boulevard was a great central railway station with steel ribbing showing through the copper cladding and glass to offset the great blocks of stone of the rest of the avenue.

"In ancient times all roads led to Rome. Here is to be the rail center. The main station is to have four levels of tracks linked by escalators and elevators and will surpass New York's Grand Central Station."

At the farthest end of the wide boulevard model was a huge triumphal arch.

"The old gate of Brandenburg is of a former time, and to Hitler's mind, not worthy of a great nation."

Lacy was stunned by the scale of it.

"It is to be four hundred feet high, five hundred and fifty feet wide, three hundred and ninety-two feet deep. The Arc de Triomph of Paris would fit within its arch and all one million eight hundred thousand of the German war dead will be chiseled in the granite. Personally, I am most happy with the railway station as it is the most practical in function."

Lacy thought of the scale of the project and the ego of it. "And why does he want my opinion?"

Speer took her along the main avenue, pointing out spaces between the large formal buildings with green park plazas and little figures of people.

"An avenue consisting solely of ministries would be a dead and lonely space. We have allowed for a luxurious movie house for premieres, another cinema for the masses, accommodating two thousand persons, a new opera house, and a concert hall, a twenty-one story grand hotel, luxury restaurants, and even an indoor swimming pool, built in Roman style to be as large as the baths of Imperial Rome."

"There would be quiet interior courtyards with colonnades and small luxury shops set away from the noise of the street to invite pedestrian strollers. Electric signs will be employed throughout, like your Times Square. The whole of the avenue has been conceived by Hitler as a sales display for German goods, which might exert a special attraction for foreigners."

"Can you afford to build all this? In ten years? With a war?"

"The total cost estimate of the rebuilding is between four and six billion Reichsmark. Spread over eleven years, this means about five hundred million annually to be allocated." He paused at her reaction. "I made my budget calculation on what percentage of the total tax revenues of the Prussian state King Frederick Wilhelm spent on his building program in Berlin. We will finance that from the state budget. The rest is from an annual fund allocation. The Finance Minister has been placing 60 million annually into the fund."

"Everyone said King Ludwig II of Bavaria was mad because of the cost of his palaces. Today, most tourists go to Upper Bavaria just to see them. The entrance fees have long since paid the amount of the costs. It is Hitler's plan that the whole world will come to Berlin to see the buildings. Americans in particular always seem impressed by the cost of things. It is his belief that if we tell the Americans how much the Great Hall cost and maybe exaggerate a bit, and say a billion and a half instead of a billion, they will be wild to see the most expensive building in the world."

Lacy understood now. And she was flabbergasted. Hitler planned to pay for the capital of the new German Empire by tourists coming to admire his vision and American wives shopping on his grand boulevard.

"Can you finish all of this by 1950?"

"I have promised my wife a trip around the world when it is finished. It is a small consolation for not seeing me so much at home. We planned to present a World's Fair at the half-century to invite the whole of the world to come and see. But I'm afraid my Margarete will have to wait a bit longer. The adventures in Poland and France and now England have somewhat postponed our deadline for the time."

Lacy knew what it was to not see a husband, and she doubted the promise of a travel trip would be sufficient to placate his wife. She thought of her father. How he would react to this great plan. How he would organize it. Finance it. Debt costs and amortizations. She thought of her purpose in coming to Berlin.

"This is all very impressive. May I see the engineering plans? My father would love this?"

Speer led her through the galleries and through a door, guarded by another soldier on duty on the other side, and locked it behind. They climbed a grand marble staircase where the sound of typewriters clacking echoed off the stone in a cacophony of clerical activity.

She engaged him in the details, trying to seem as interested as possible.

"How do you plan to get the materials?"

"Himmler has offered to employ his labor camp prisoners to increase production. He has proposed a brickworks be set up in Sachsenhausen under SS direction for supplying granite blocks. I have doubts this will be sufficient, though it will save on costs." Shocked by the idea, Lacy suddenly envisioned herself making bricks, in prison pajamas, if her plan failed. She said nothing.

He led her to his suite of offices on the second floor of the Generalbauinspektor. Blueprint plans were spread out on long tables. Financial budgets were in book volumes on shelves and accounting sheets spread out on the desks of clerk accountants.

Lacy could see the dark ink stamp of the Finance Ministry on the budget documents. She wondered if she could memorize it enough to be able to recreate it. It was not so different from the previous stamp, but could she take the chance of missing a detail? She looked over the plans Speer showed her with a pretense of fascination. One of the smaller prints had been approved with the

226

stamp marked on its corner and signed by Finance Minister Johann Ludwig Graf von Krosigk. She needed a distraction.

"Herr Speer," she turned to him, leaning against the drafting table, "may I ask you something?"

"Of course."

"I was on the street in Essen the night of November breaking glass."

"Yes?"

"I was wondering if you had experience with it here in Berlin?"

He turned away for a moment as if the question made him just a bit uncomfortable. Lacy thought it might. She had spent a dinner with the man and thought she had started to know him. And while he was turned away to think about it, looking out a window to the street below to formulate an answer, Lacy reached her hands behind her back to fold the drafting budget approved top sheet and slip it into the top of her skirt. She held her breath, glancing around the office. But none of the busy clerks or accountants had seemed to notice.

"The Jewish pogrom took place during the Chancellery project," he said, still seeming to be focused on something inconsequential. "I did not see much of it, I was very busy, but I did drive past the ruins of the Central Synagogue and thought it was sad."

She couldn't quite tell exactly what he thought was sad.

"When I first met Hitler, he only mentioned Jews tangentially. I rarely thought of them and I had many Jewish friends. The Communists were the threat. There are few Communists left."

Then, curiously, he laughed. "Himmler is running around the country with crews excavating prehistoric sites, trying to prove an ancient mythological foundation for the German people. With every clay pot and stone axe he finds, he only proves our forefathers were gathered around fires when Greece and Rome were at the height of culture." He gestured around at the blueprints and elevation illustrations. "We build our culture."

Lacy looked at the cold imperial designs of towering, smooth-faced stone edifices, massive in scale and heavy with the weight of grandiosity, with Nazi iconography at every turn, and thought about the airy and romantic paintings of old Heidelberg landscapes which adorned his walls at home. It occurred to her maybe she knew what he thought was sad, even if he didn't fully acknowledge it. Perhaps he felt a gradual loss of himself to his work and his society.

Then, she noticed an odd blueline drawing that didn't seem to go with anything else. It was of an ironwork arch for a gate with words spelled out, "Work makes you free" - 'Arbeit macht frei'. She didn't know what it meant, or what structure the gate was intended, but thought it was the perfect antithetic of what she saw in the man before her, and in Miki.

Speer stepped out of the doors of the Building Inspector's office with Lacy.

"I will leave you here," he said. "What might I tell to Herr Hitler?"

"About what?" Lacy was confused.

"Your opinion?" He gestured from the steps of the Academy out to Pariser Square and the Unter Den Linden, intended to be transformed to the great plan of the Third Empire. "Do you think American wives of your class would like to come to Berlin for shopping and to stroll on our avenues in the new Germany?"

Lacy tried to picture the new buildings in place of the ones she saw in front of her. Down the street was an open space of rubble where once a building stood, destroyed by a British thousand pound bomb in a raid two months before, like a broken tooth in a grimacing smile. She thought of the crumbled workers apartment buildings in Essen around the factories and bomb rubble store fronts in Mulheim. It suddenly came to her mind that replacing the old buildings with new ones would be easier if they were all bombed into flat empty lots.

"I'm sure they would be impressed, Herr Speer," was all she said. "We like shopping."

She shook his hand, feeling the stiffness of the folded purloined finance plan document in the back of her skirt. She stepped away to go down the steps, feeling the eyes of the soldier on duty with his Mauser.

"Frau von Steuven..." Speer called out to stop her. She hesitated, wondering if the paper was protruding from her skirt or forming an impression in the back of her blouse. She turned back. He came down a step toward her.

"Yes?" she asked.

"Before you go back, you should stop at the San Soucci Palace Garden and visit the Zoo."

Lacy smiled, relieved. "I intended to. Do you have plans for them as well?"

Oddly, all the tension in Speer's face seemed to slide away, as if a release. "No. Not currently."

"I have a few hours to enjoy the city before going back to my little corner," she said. "I would like to remember it."

Lacy did explore the city. She especially liked the Chinese Gate of the Zoo with its stone elephants and the giraffe enclosure with its Moroccan Palace theme. She walked along Prinz-Albrecht-Strasse, just a few streets from the Adlon, past the iron-spiked gates of the Reich Security Office of the Gestapo, taking up two full blocks of the city.

She had waited for them to show up at her hotel room after the document had been discovered missing. There was a knock on the door and when she opened it, outside in the hallway was a black unformed SS officer. She waited for him to arrest her, but instead he simply handed her a card, then saluted her with a sharp and crisp heil, before turning to march down the hall under the crystal lamps. It was a typed and signed thank you note for her enthusiastic reception of the future of the empire on Reichsführer stationary with a hand-doodle of a dog's head in one corner and the signature, Adolf Hitler.

~~~

CHAPTER FIFTEEN

Martlesham

The boys were in the pub, drinking, in a good mood. They had been grounded by a thick soup which hung over the channel from a cold storm front moving across the continent. No one would be flying for the next two days. The room was loud and full of cheerful smiles and free rounds like it hadn't been since June. It was the 16th of September, 1940. In the past day, two massive flights of German bombers and fighters had been turned back from London. It had been a last ditch assault by the Germans and had by all reports been a decisive failure. Fighter Command had reported a hundred and eighty-five German craft brought down with only forty home craft lost. The weather would forestall daylight raids for the next week. Winston Churchill had come on the radio to declare that the Battle for Britain was over. The pilots of II Group had performed well. Wilson had shot down two Dornies, but Aaron wasn't celebrating among them.

Aaron stood alone at the grassy edge of the chalk cliff to the sea. He had missed the biggest aerial battle of the 15th. He had been grounded that day. His hands were still wrapped in bandages and a dressing covered half of his right cheek. When he'd heard the reports of the number of craft, he had ripped his bandages and got his kite up anyway, but by the time he'd reached altitude it was over. He now looked up at the gray empty sky of low hanging clouds. A strong wind was blowing, chopping the waters into white caps. Aaron closed his eyes, in almost a prayer.

"We won, Irish. We won," he silently said to a lost friend.

The war was not over. It had really just begun, but something had passed. The Germans were not sending over waves of bombers now in the daylight, but flying packs of fighters with single bombs. They were fast and hard to catch, but the single bombs did only modest damage and their targeting references seemed to be out of date. The field at Westhampnett had been hit and the runway was in bad shape. The group was moving back over to RAF Tangmere.

Aaron looked across the churning water into the misty haze with a burning hatred he had never felt before. He felt a desire for revenge, which was a new emotion for him. He blamed himself. He was the one who had convinced Donovan to leave his life behind and follow him to war. If it wasn't for him, the Irish would be home with Charlotte and maybe a new son.

"I'll find you, Miki. I'll find you. I swear I will," he said softly to himself, promising to some distant uncaring God who let good men die in flames.

Across the channel, Miki stood on the pier at Pas de Calais which stretched out over the sandy shore. He looked into the thick gray miasma blocking the view to the white cliffs. Kellmann and Frische stood with him. They had all survived the last days' fighting. Frische had barely made it back to base from his last coastal raid with an oil leak from an anti-aircraft shell.

Kellmann raised a bottle of French wine he had pilfered from the cart of a passing monger. He took a drink and passed it to Frische. The newly promoted Oberleutnant tipped the bottle. He had been telling over and over again the story of the careless pilot he'd surprised at the English coast. He had risked running out of fuel to catch one off-guard and was rather proud of himself. Miki had asked him about the markings on the plane, but didn't say very much when he had told him the number. He took the report of a kill, but Frische couldn't report that he'd actually seen the plane destroyed.

"No dinner in London with Churchill," Kellmann said with a forlorn loss.

Miki nodded. The invasion of England would not come anytime soon, if ever. He knew what was next. He looked to his comrades, young men turned wizened and hard.

"Now, it will be our turn to play host. Churchill comes for Sauerbraten and Frois Gras."

He turned and walked away.

Charlotte had lain in the hospital bed holding her son against her in one hand and clutching the letter with her other. She had read it three times until she had let it fall to clutch her newborn son, kissing him as she cried, her fingers feeling the fur of downy red hair. Darlene tried to comfort her. She had been at her side through the worst of the labor, and had struggled with herself whether she should give the letter to her friend or keep it until she was stronger. She had decided she really couldn't wait. Charlotte's mother had said a letter had come, and if it was kept a secret, she would know anyway. It was from Aaron and not her husband.

"I wish there was some way I could apologize for failing you, Charlotte. But I can't. All I can promise is to make up for it." The letter had been written on an official RAF paper. "I wanted you to know he died bravely, a hero, here and back home, and that his last words were that he loved you."

The pilots of 65 Squadron filled the pub with raucous laughter, singing the old pub songs. There were new faces now, young men eager to fight, who had not seen real action. They had come from training in the last two weeks, but the air had been quiet. It seemed that it must be true that the Huns had given up on an invasion.

Aaron, Wilson and Biggle, the "old men", sat on stools together at the bar. The barman filled three glasses with his best Irish whiskey. Aaron's bandages were down to tape around his fingers and a healing burn scar covering his lower cheek.

Biggle raised his glass in a toast. "To Boothe, Donovan and Ackers... Rogers, Campbell, Chivers, Simmons, Brinley, Hicks...all the darlings..."

Aaron and Wilson raised their glasses, looking at the golden liquid sloshing in the cut glass.

"Absent friends."

They tossed back the whisky. Biggle brushed off the Flight Lieutenant bars on Wilson's shoulders, and tickled the Flying Cross medal on Aaron's tunic.

"Aces all around. Can't say I've enjoyed flying with better." He looked at Aaron's bandages. "How're the hands?"

Aaron flexed his fingers. "Hurt like a son-of-a-bitch. But they can still send a Hun to hell."

Biggle took the bottle from the barman and poured more whiskey. He raised his glass with the others.

"Sendin' the Huns to hell!"

They tossed the drinks back.

"One Hun in particular," Aaron said, darkly, and drained the last of his glass, thinking of the letter he had written to Charlotte and promised himself he would never write another like it.

Biggle jabbed a thumb into Aaron's chest, winking at Wilson, "This boy·o's got his sights set, alright. Killer shark. Sixteen kills, but the big one's still out there."

Aaron was silent. Wilson slapped his back. "We'll get him."

Biggle set his glass down. He had had new orders in that morning's pouch. "Have your chance soon enough." He couldn't help from a sneaking smile. "Something's up. Group meeting next week. I'm supposin' we'll get to see a bit of France, before we're old."

He poured another round.

The rain was coming down in buckets as pilots and officers hurried into the Operations building at RAF Martlesham. November had turned cold and wet. The Luftwaffe had almost completely ceased daylight operations since September and concentrated on raining hell on London and other cities at night. The bombers were now coming from deeper bases in Belgium and Holland to the east. 12 Group had put up fighters at night, but with little success at finding the bomber groups before they could unleash their loads. The barrage balloons and anti·aircraft were as much or more effective.

The planning auditorium was packed with flyers, sitting on folding chairs and any available space, group commanders and select squadron leaders. The room was peppered with Britain's top aces.

Doug Bader was there. Bader was 65's new boss. He had recently been reassigned from RAF Duxford of 12 Group to command of 11 Group RAF Tangmere. He had been a proponent of Leigh-Mallory's "Big Wing" tactic of putting up a mass of fighters to meet the Germans, but the boys of 11 Group under Air Chief Parks readily complained that they were often late to the fight, as it took too long to join up. Bader had lost both legs in a crash of his plane, but had returned to flying and was an inspiration to his fellows as a fighter pilot, and the units were still getting used to the tactic coming to the south where they dealt more with the quick hit attacks of the Jägers.

"Sailor" Malan, leader of 74 Squadron was there. A South African, whose first name was Adolph, Malan used his nickname as much as possible. He said he liked to leave some of the bomber crews alive so they could fly back to base and tell their comrades what hell it was to face the Tommies.

Robert Stanford Tuck was there, too. He was now commanding the Hurricanes of 257 Squadron at Coltishall. Tuck was a little fellow of dashing Brit style, even though his parents were Jewish and he was not a product of public school.

One of the American Eagle Squadron pilots was there, too. An American businessman in London named Sweeny had sponsored some American fliers to come over. Enough had arrived now to form a squadron.

This was the first time Aaron had met them all in one room. And they all listened in anticipation as the fresh plan for operations was to be announced.

Aaron, Wilson and Biggle sat together at the back of the fifth row while Group Captain Levingham paced on a gimp leg on a small stage set up with an easel, with diagrams on paper and another with aerial reconnaissance photographs.

"Jerry seems to be concentrating his attack on nighttime shellacking of London and on our shipping lanes. I know you are all still catching hell, but the Air Marshall has come up with a plan to give a little back what we've gotten."

The pilots whistled and cheered.

Levingham folded back a sheet on the easel, revealing a map of Northern France, Belgium and the Rhineland. There were colored dots, mostly along the coast, around Paris, and the Ruhr region.

"Of course, Bomber Command isn't up to strength yet for all we've got in mind, and the sotted weather, but you lot have been sorted out to switch from defensive operations to bomber support. Over the next few months and on into the spring, we'll begin selected offensive attacks on Jerry's coastal positions, continuing on deeper and deeper until we can catch him sleeping at home." Levingham waited for the cheers and the stomping of feet to calm.

"Targeting will, of course, not be your concern, but we've managed to round up some recon photos to give you a look at what we have in mind. Now, we have a lot to cover, so if I can have your undivided attention for the next three or four hours..."

The plan for bombing operations was laid out for the pilots. It was an overview and assignments wouldn't come for weeks, but at last they felt the war had turned. They couldn't do much effectively against night bombs, but they could now work to stop them on the airfields and hit them in the supply lines.

After the briefing, the pilots milled around the tables laid out with charts and organizational plans. Reconnaissance photographs were pinned to cork boards and laid out by regions on the table. Wilson pointed to a photograph of Paris.

"Been there," he joked. "I hope it still might be left before we're done."

Aaron glanced at it, but his attention was focused on another board with aerial photographs of the Ruhr Valley. There was a photograph with the city of Essen marked with a wax pen and several factories circled.

Wilson stepped over to see what Aaron was looking at.

"Wait a minute," he said, something catching his attention. He jabbed his finger into one of the circles.

"That's the Von Steuven Works. Miki's dad's operation," he said with a certain recognition.

"Yeah, it's got a big fat X on the roof," Aaron said facetiously. It wasn't identified on the photograph, but he thought Wilson could be right.

Then, suddenly excited, Wilson pulled the pin out of the picture and took it off the board, looking at it closer. He pointed to the corner of the photograph, outside one of the circles.

"Jesus, Aaron," he exclaimed. "That's his house!"

"Who's house?" Aaron asked.

"Miki's."

Aaron looked at him like he'd gone nuts.

"You've really got to stop mixing Scotch in your milk, Wilson."

"No. I'm not kidding. Lacy described it in one of her letters." He traced his finger on the photograph. "You go down this road from the factory, turn at the old church, and it's in a woods above the river. Look. See...?" He pointed at the steeple from the air with an anti-aircraft flak unit marked.

"That's gotta be the old church." He moved his finger to a large manor on an open space of land by the river. "Who else is gonna live in a house like that?"

Aaron peered closer, fascinated. Wilson must be right.

"Son-of-a-bitch..."

Lacy drove in the Mercedes saloon car toward Essen, turning past the Flak battery and the old church, as she had been doing for almost a year and five months now. The soldiers manning the gun had changed from seasoned Luftwaffe troops to Home Guard older men and some boys from the Hitler Youth. Two extra guns had been added to the battery, but while the search lights had come on many times in the past four months, the guns had only fired six times, all but two of them false alarms. Berlin had been bombed, but no bombs had fallen on the Ruhr since 1939, and Lacy suspected that the flights over were photography missions. But they all knew the bombs would come when winter was over and the dark skies cleared. England had not been invaded and had not surrendered.

Lacy had made the trip to Essen on nine occasions since Miki had left for France. Three families from Duisburg, two from Essen, a young couple from Oberhausen, and three families who had come to the network from Dortmund after an arrest was made there.

Lacy had been worried about receiving "guests", as she liked to call them, from that far. She had been debating with herself whether she should stop. She had worked out a system with Frau Lindl that she only needed her for three days a week, now that Miki was away, and she could close down part of the house.

The recent snow clung to the sidewalk of Tentelgasse as Lacy walked from her car, parked in the usual place. The city seemed quiet.

As Lacy stepped in the door of the tailor shop, she was surprised. The shelves were empty, with hardly a thread left. It looked as if the shop had been ransacked and all the goods carted away. She started to go out again quickly, but a man stepped from the back.

"Ah, Baroness..." It was a familiar voice. Lacy stopped. A jolt of dread shot through her spine, but she didn't let it show. She turned as casually as she could. It was Stenhoffer, the Gestapo agent who had come to her house. He stood just outside the curtain to the back room. The sewing room also was bare. Had the tailor been arrested, or had he just packed and left after the arrest of the comrade in Dortmund?

"Where is Herr Lublin?" Lacy asked as haughtily as she could manage. "I was expecting a length of damask on order."

"Herr Lublin has been arrested."

"What on earth for?" Lacy asked, allowing her American accent to heavily flavor her German. She thought it best to seem as lost and unaware as possible. "He was a very sweet old man. What could he possibly have done worthy of arrest?"

Stenhoffer was silent, just watching her, observing. She couldn't just say nothing, or she might show her fear

"Well, he did get a seam crooked sometimes. I've had to come back many times for corrections. But I didn't think to complain to the state. Did someone else?"

"The charge is espionage," Stenhoffer finally said flatly. "Would you care to come with me, Frau von Steuven."

It was not a question. He gestured to the door. Lacy could now see the other agent outside, waiting across the street. The thought of running left her as quickly as it had come.

Lacy sat in the small office alone. There were no furnishings other than her chair, a desk and a photograph of Hitler posing with a dog on the wall behind the desk. She looked at it, wondering if it was the dog he had sketched on his thank you note to her. She doubted she would be shopping on his boulevard.

She had been brought to the Reich Sicherheitsamt national police office at Kaiser Wilhelm Platz. Nothing had been said in the short journey of five blocks, but Lacy had thought about how close they had been to the security office and its bloody alley where enemies of the state and the unlucky were summarily shot and hauled away by a truck.

The door opened and Stenhoffer came in. He stood behind Lacy a long moment. She wondered if he would just shoot her in the back of the head there, without bothering to go outside where it was cold and snowing. She finally turned and looked at him. He stepped to her right and sat, rather casually she thought, on the edge of the desk. He flipped through a pad of notes in his hands.

"Herr Lublin has revealed to us a full list of those conspirators to whom he has transmitted forged documents. We have all the names." He ran his finger down the pad, apparently reading a list and stopping at a name. He looked over the pad at Lacy with a chilling certainty.

"Frau von Steuven. Would you like to now cooperate with our investigation?"

"I don't know what you mean," she said as simply as she could, trying to hold the dread at bay. She had lied to her mother often enough about petty things, and had been operating as an agent conspirator now for a year.

"To whom have you transmitted documents?"

Lacy sat, silent.

"You should be aware that espionage is a capital crime," Stenhoffer just held the pad and stared at her, trying to seem kind, "those who cooperate fully, receive due consideration for that fact. If you help us, that will go well for you."

Lacy focused on the pad in his hand. "I don't have any idea what you're talking about," she said.

Stenhoffer smiled, "Ah. Perhaps you believe that because you are married to a hero of the Reich and have friends in Berlin, you are immune. Let me assure you that is not the case."

Lacy wondered how much the local Gestapo knew of her Berlin excursions. She had been twice, since her afternoon with Speer. There were other documents and stamps she had needed for transits through occupied France and Holland. Lublin had been the conduit back to the network, but she had become the chief operator of the ring in the west, with her position and access to state departments.

"No," Lacy said, with the slightest shrug. "I just don't know anything about it."

Stenhoffer sat silent a moment, staring at her. Then, he got up with a coldness which sent a shiver through her. He went out of the room and closed the door. After a moment, a gunshot boomed in the next room. Lacy cringed, shaken. She sat alone, for what seemed like an eternity, time ticking in slow motion, until the door opened again and Stenhoffer stepped back in, wiping the powder residue from a hot Luger. His under agent also followed him into the room and stood by the door, with his arms folded.

Stenhoffer sat in the chair behind the desk, pushing the note pad to one side and placing the Luger with deliberate ceremony in the center of the desk. He fixed his eyes on Lacy, folding his hands and allowing her to think about her situation.

"Herr Lublin has paid the price. Now, Baroness, may we put aside this nonsense and discuss your involvement?"

Lacy looked at the gun on the desk, like a dinner table centerpiece, meant for effect. She thought that she could plead for mercy, or she could try to run and push past the agent at the door. Or she could trust her instinct.

"If that is the price of cooperation with the Gestapo, mein Herr," she said as indignantly as possible, "I think I'd rather not. Except to the extent of informing you once again that I am...or was, a customer of Herr Lublin's fabric and tailoring. He made several suits for my husband and I know nothing of any documents. If you have proof otherwise, kindly show it to me." She rose from the chair, standing as tall and straight as she could. "If not, then I will have my husband inform Berlin that I have been held against my will and treated to a most disgusting display of brutality."

Stenhoffer fidgeted a moment. He picked up the Luger. Lacy waited for him to point it at her, but instead, he slid it into a drawer. He, too, seemed to make a calculation of his options. Finally, he turned to the agent in the doorway.

"Take Frau von Steuven to her car and give her an escort to her home." Then, he simply went out.

Lacy breathed a moment. She gathered her purse and gloves and followed the other agent out. As they passed the room next door, the door was open and the room was empty.

Lacy allowed herself a secret relief. It was all show. She had guessed right. If the arrest of the man in Dortmund had resulted in him giving them a name, he would only have known Lublin. There would not have been a list. If Lublin had been arrested and talked, Stenhoffer would not be calling her "Baroness", which could have been passed among some of the escaping families, but from his tone, he seemed to think more insulting than a courtesy. She and Lublin had agreed that if either of them were caught, they would have signal names. If he had been arrested and talked, Stenhoffer would have known that Lublin referred to her personally as 'Madame Kester', and the "Lark Bird" as his codename for her in the network.

As she drove back to the estate, Lacy thought about what to do. Lublin must have escaped. She knew he had been prepared for that. The Gestapo may not even have any proof, just the name of the shop overheard. But he might be caught. Then what? She couldn't just pack and leave. Could she? Could she make the excuse to go home to visit her parents? She would have to apply for an Aus Visa and leave through Spain or Norway. But that would raise suspicion and what penalty would Miki have to pay? Miki was home again. Maybe she could talk to him about moving to France. She could say she wanted to be near him. Then, she thought of the irony. She had not gone to see Lublin about documents. There were no more exit documents for Jews now and there would be no more "guests". Her days as an agent were over. She had actually gone to pick up some cloth.

"Is something wrong?" Miki asked. Lacy was looking through the curtains to the little Volkswagen parked under the trees outside the gate. She suspected it would not go away again for some time.

"No. I was just wondering about the weather. The snow looks like it might let up." She turned back to Miki in his major's uniform, relaxed and holding a whisky.

"Yes, by tonight. And I must fly back to St. Omer in the morning. It is only one hour, but the weather..." He smiled. "Let's go to bed and build a fire."

He had only been home for a few hours and would be gone again. She had accepted that he might never come back. It was almost pure luck he had not already been killed. Many of his men had been. His friend, Colonel Mölders, one of the "Spaniards" as they liked to call themselves, and Germany's top fighter ace, had been killed. Not from British or French bullets, but crashing into a factory chimney flying home for a ceremony. It all seemed so senseless.

"Don't you ever think about what it is you're doing, Miki? What your country is doing?"

"I think about it. But what is there for me to do?" He was surprised by the question.

"Complain. Speak out."

Miki growled in a burst of sudden feeling. He thought about it almost every time he pulled the trigger, or more precisely, when he was deciding between machine guns or cannons.

"To whom, Lacy?! Who should I speak to?! To whom should I complain?!"

He paced, gesturing around with whisky sloshing in his glass. "This is my home. My country. I defend my country! Whether I agree or not. I see it in your eyes when I come home to be with my wife, this question... 'My husband's job is to kill...does he care?'"

He stepped close to her and reached to her face, looking at her with his own questioning. "In these eyes where I should hope to see love, I see this question. And I wonder, what is the price of the answer?"

Lacy was afraid of the answer as well. She wondered if she should tell Miki about her interview with Stenhoffer. Did he know already? Could they have contacted him or questioned him? He seemed to be completely unaware of her secret life. Or were they just that good at lying to each other.

It was a bitter cold day at the Jagdeswäder II Group field as the crews worked on the Messerschmitts under camouflage nets. Two of the new Folke-Wulf 190 fighters had arrived with promises of more. They had a higher rate of climb than the 109s and a tighter turning radius. Miki had flown one back from Paderborn from his trip home and was impressed, but the armament had not yet arrived. He was still more comfortable in his "Willy". He would assign the new planes to the better of the younger pilots.

Only three fighter groups were left in France with the job of defending the German occupying forces from the Spanish border to Belgium and Antwerp. Since opening the front to the east, most of the fighter units and nearly all the bomber groups had been sent to the Russian theater or Sicily. The British had been sending probing raids across the "stream", and night bombing raids to Düsseldorf, Hamburg and Cologne.

There wasn't as much snow now. It had been cleared into small piles, but some frost still clung to the grass. Schluss blew on his fingers as he hammered a wrench on a stuck valve fitting. Some small pine branches had been hung on the camouflage netting as Christmas trees. It was Advent and the holiday was just three weeks away. A mechanic was wrapping a present to send back home.

Suddenly, there was a building roar from the sky. A Spitfire streaked low over the field, firing its Brownings. The bullets strafed along the flight line, striking the planes and tearing through the netting. A bullet ripped through the mechanic, flopping him like a bloody doll and bursting the wrapped box into fluttering pieces. A fuel can exploded as the Spit arced back up toward the overcast sky.

The alarm horn began to blast as the crewmen ran for cover. The pilots dashed out of their warming bungalow. Miki came out, waving to the crews.

"Start them up! Get them in the air!" he shouted.

Schluss threw down the cowling of Miki's 109 and quickly cranked the starter flywheel. He reached in the cockpit to switch the magneto and start the engine. As the propeller kicked over another Spitfire roared in low, firing and strafing along the planes. Two bullets ripped into Schluss' back, bursting him open. A bullet sparked off Miki's 109 and hit the next one, blowing off a wheel strut. Schluss flopped over, hanging half in the cockpit.

Wilson eased back on his stick, climbing again above the field. He looked back behind him to the chaos of the flight line in his wake.

"Piece of cake. Should we take another run?" he called on his radio.

Aaron was in the lead Spit, banking away from the field. Flak guns began firing from their positions to the north of the field. "Leave it for the bomber boys. We caught 'em with their pants down. Let's see if we can find some targets of opportunity."

As the German pilots tried to get into the planes still undamaged, from the sky came a deeper roar as two twin engine Bristol Beaufort bombers banked in to line up on the field, at a higher altitude, flying through the ack-ack fire.

The first Bristol passed over, releasing its bombs. They tumbled and exploded along the field, raising plumes of earth, concrete and flame. One bomb hit the warming bungalow. Another bomb hit a fuel truck, igniting a ball of fire of precious high octane fuel, which spread burning liquid to men and trucks parked nearby.

Miki jumped up onto the wing of his 109, grabbing his crew chief by the collar.

"Schluss?!" he shouted, but Schluss was dead. His instinct taking over, Miki let him slide off the wing to the ground and climbed into the cockpit. He revved the twelve cylinders, apparently undamaged. He twirled his finger in the air to his pilots, then gunned his engine, rolling out toward the runway.

The second Bristol roared in overhead. It released its bombs and they tumbled from the bomb bay.

Miki accelerated his 109 down the runway. The bombs exploded up the runway behind him, as if chasing him. As the bomber passed over, a 500 pounder tumbled in front of Miki as he raced toward it with his tail just raising off the ground. It exploded in front of him, tearing the field into flying earth. Miki pulled on the stick just before his wheels hit the crater and he plunged through the explosion debris, rising off the ground.

The Folke-Wulf following him was not as lucky, as another bomb hit it dead on, blowing it to pieces.

The two Spitfires roared low over a rail yard where a train of boxcars was parked on a siding. They fired. Bullets chunked through the wood and pinged off the metal of the train. Something in one of the cars exploded, sending shattering shards of wood in a burst radius.

"Whoo-hoo!" Wilson shouted in his radio. "That wasn't cheese in that railcar, that's for damn sure."

"Confirm one transpo," Aaron answered

The Spits zoomed off, back up into the sky, one banking off left, the other, right, before disappearing into low clouds.

Wilson looked around in the thin clouds. He couldn't see Aaron.

"Hey, where'd you go?" he asked.

"Where did you go?" Aaron answered. He looked at his fuel gauge. "Meet me at coordinate Charlie 12. Fuel's low. Time to go home."

"Right." Wilson answered. He pulled out the map from his seat pocket, trying to fold it to the right page, and flew through the thin fog of clouds at 500 feet.

A young German soldier, Hans, was at the wheel of a Volkswagen Kubelwagen, driving back from Lille to Watten. In the back seat were some wrapped boxes, Christmas presents for his superior. He slowed when he saw a French girl walking along the side of the road. She was carrying firewood in one arm and a bucket of hens' eggs in the other. As he pulled over by her, slowing to a stop, he could see her pregnant belly bulging from inside her brown coat. She first stepped back from the car, nervous. He reached over to open the door, and beckoned her to get in. She was nineteen and pretty. She didn't speak any German and he knew little French. She shook her head, no.

"Allons" he said, gesturing and smiling as kindly as he knew how.

She was wary, but he had a kind face, and he looked only to be her age. She could see the boxes with wrapping in the back, and thought maybe it would be okay. She had more than a mile to walk and the wood was heavy.

She climbed into the passenger seat. The young soldier helped her toss the wood onto the floor in the back, but she clutched the egg bucket tightly over her slightly bulging belly. The boy laughed and reached over to close the door, brushing past her. She smelled of Lilac water and barnyard loam. He thought he might like to kiss her, but he had a girlfriend waiting for him back home in Lingenfeld. She was pregnant and must have a French boyfriend, he thought, or maybe he'd been killed fighting. He closed the door and shifted the gear stick.

250

Wilson dropped below the clouds, looking at his map, trying to figure out where he was, banking between a pair of low hills, toward a town with a waterway. He glanced to his map, then, looked over his wing toward the village, trying to match it to the map. There was a military base near Watten along the Calais Canal which carried barge traffic to the harbor at Dunkirk. The Kraut pilots had done a lot of damage to the Brits along here and Wilson thought a little payback was in order.

As he followed the canal he could see a German military vehicle driving down the road. It was one of those boxy little jeep-like things, toodling down the road without a care. There were no transports, but it must be carrying some important dispatches about troop movements. It had the black cross of the Luftwaffe on the gray painted hood, underneath the spare tire.

"Piece of cake," Wilson said to himself.

As he drove along the narrow road, the German soldier glanced over toward the French girl. She hadn't said anything and he thought about asking her name. She smiled at him. It was a pleasant, if cautious smile. Maybe she thought he was good looking. He would never know.

Behind them, the Spitfire angled along the road, dropping low, racing up. They never even heard it behind them over the rattling of the Volkswagen's rear engine. The flash of eight wing Browning machine gun muzzles flashed simultaneously, and silent. The bullets ripped and tore through the car, tearing through the girl's pregnant belly and the young soldier's head, splattering eggs and blood on the shattering window.

The mangled Volkswagen rolled off the road and crashed into a low stone wall, flipping on its side as the

Spitfire whooshed back up into the sky, pulling up over the town.

As Wilson banked around the church steeple in the middle of town, he looked again at his map, sure now that it was Watten. He pulled up to gain some altitude before defensive flak could spot him.

Wilson's Spitfire broke out of the low cloud formation into the clear, joining up with Aaron's Spitfire.

"Where you been?" Aaron asked over his radio. "Thought I'd lost you."

Wilson looked over to Aaron in his cockpit, back in pair formation. He chuckled, "There's a couple of Jerries that won't be going home for Christmas!"

Aaron glanced over. He was a little ticked off.

"Well, while you were out joyriding, one of the Krauts got off the field and took out one of the Bristols!"

"Shit. Sorry." Wilson apologized over his comm. Then he asked, "Hey, does a jeep count toward my score? That's Transpo, right?"

"Wehrmacht or Luftwaffe?"

"It was air support. Had the black cross."

"Yeah, it counts. Did you confirm it?" Aaron asked.

Wilson chuckled again. "It was a kill for damn sure."

Back along the road beside the Calais Canal, the Volkswagen laid on its side with the wheels still turning and the dead soldier's bloody arm lying across the dead pregnant French girl, like an embrace. She had a large hole through her belly. Her name was Evette.

~~~

CHAPTER SIXTEEN

Ghent

The snow was falling heavy now, casting the Essen train station in a pall of winter white. A train with box cars sat on a siding, with steam slowly hissing out of the engine as it heated the boiler, wrapping a white cloud around the black and red painted metal.

Young army soldiers herded a line of people with yellow Stars of David pinned to their coats, loading them into the box cars. It was all very neat and orderly. The soldiers took their luggage and set it aside by the tracks as they urged and even helped the older ones onto the cars. Other soldiers picked up the luggage, traveling cases and boxes of personal belongings, and carried them to another box car on another siding.

Lacy stood on the passenger platform across the tracks, waiting for the train for Düsseldorf. She held a small paper in her hand with an address in the Golzheim district and a doctor's RX symbol on it. She didn't want to drive to the appointment as she would not be in good condition to drive back.

She watched the activity across the train yard. No one else seemed to be paying much attention. First class businessmen to Düsseldorf, third class workers going to Wuppertal, and families traveling in second class were all waiting for the passenger train, but none seemed to care what was going on.

Lacy stopped a railroad official passing with a cart of first class luggage.

"Excuse me," she asked, "where are they taking them?"

The official looked over to the Jews being loaded on the train with its engine pointed to the east.

He shrugged, "Away." Then, he continued down the platform, checking his schedule.

The locomotive of the arriving passenger train from Dortmund approached down the tracks toward the station, slowing to the platform, backpressure from the steam releasing on the concrete ties and gravel of the track bed. The flickering shutter of the windows obscured the activity on the other side of the yard. The doors opened and passengers disembarked. Waiting passengers stepped on board.

Lacy looked down the platform as the passengers got on. There was a man in a long brown coat over his black suit and a Homburg hat, holding a paper, but not reading, and not getting on the train. She hadn't seen him before. He was a new one. She stepped onto the train in the first class car. The Gestapo agent stepped on the train, two cars back in Second Class.

Steam hissed from the engine pistons and the train pulled out. Lacy settled into a seat and watched the boxcar train as it drifted away. She noticed the soldiers at the boxcar with the luggage, sliding the door closed. There was no engine. The luggage, travel bags and personal goods weren't going anywhere.

Lacy thought about the agent who was now following her. She wondered if he would go to visit his mother and his family on Christmas. She didn't care if he was following her. What she was doing was illegal, but it certainly wasn't espionage. She mostly worried that the Gestapo might report to Miki, but she doubted it. She would tell him, if she had to.

The weather had shown signs of clearing over the channel and the fighter groups had expected a call to come. It was still cold but they suspected that Bomber Command was itching to take a lick and wouldn't miss the chance.

Aaron and Wilson gathered with the senior pilots and squadron leaders of II Group and III Group in the meeting hall at Martlesham. On a large board on the stage was a map of the channel shore to the Rhine with a bright red circle in the middle, over the center of Belgium. Group Captain Levingham jabbed his pointer in the center of the circle to a red dot.

"Here is our target, the rail junction at Ghent. As the weather clears, we expect Jerry to try another go at us. We've had reports he's moving elements east, but that may be a feint just to catch us up, so we're going to put him out a bit. He gets his fuel and material resupply by train across the Rhine from the Ruhr, mainly through this junction. This will be in daylight. There are heavy defenses of flak anti-aircraft, both 37 millimeter mobile units and the big 88s in static batteries. And let's not forget our old friends of the 1st and 2nd Fighter Groups of Jerry's 26th and the 3rd Group of the 51st."

Aaron and Wilson looked at one another and mouthed at the same time, "Miki".

Levingham pulled over a small map on wheels with details of the rail yard, with buildings, track junctions and the defense positions.

"Needless to say, this is going to be a rough go. But I know you're up to it. Damn eager, I'm sure. And just a reminder, if you take a hit and have to go down, keep inland, you won't make it to the coast. Harder to get out, but less chance of the Hun catching you in your chutes. Right, then, the Operations Sergeant has your coordination assignments and rendezvous points. Tally-ho."

"Tally-ho!" they all shouted.

The sergeant handed out envelope packets to the squadron leaders. Aaron and Wilson accepted theirs with tense grins of anticipation. They were to lead a spear of 14 Wellingtons from Honington.

It was just after dawn as the clearing sky over the channel filled with bomber groups from six RAF Bomber Command bases in flights of Bristol Blenheims, Wellingtons, and the new Mosquitos from Horsham. The Spitfires and Hurricanes climbed in formations to rendezvous off the East Anglia coast.

Aaron's Blue Squadron and Wilson's Red Squadron flew to join the flight of bombers at the rendezvous point off Clacton-on-Sea. Painted just below Aaron's canopy were twenty-three black victory crosses in rows of seven. Wilson's Spit had eleven. Biggle was missing from the formation.

Aaron checked his vector map. The Wellingtons they were shadowing were better as long range night bombers, too fat and slow for daylight, but the planners calculated that this objective was not a sprawling German city, and they would only be over the target in flak range for four minutes. The faster newer bombers would have to fly slower so the Wellies could keep up. Aaron thought it was a mistake, but Bomber Command wanted the poundage the Wellington could deliver.

"Blue Leader, on course to co-ord 326 Victor, climb to Angels 240." Aaron called on his comm.

"Roger, Squadron Leader. 2-4-0." Wilson answered from his flight of four off Aaron's wing to the south east.

"Today's the day, buddy. I feel it," Aaron said cheerfully. "Today's the day. Too bad Old Biggles isn't here for it."

Squadron Leader Biggle had been shot down somewhere near Dieppe. The last words they heard from him over the comm were, "I'm in for it". No one had seen a chute and they didn't know if he was dead or a prisoner. They wouldn't know until the war was over, if any of them made it that long.

"Yeah," Wilson answered, seeming a little nervous as he searched the sky, "absent friends." Wing Leader Doug Bader was gone, too, his craft lost over Calais. They had heard that he'd parachuted without his legs, so some of the boys dropped him one on a harrying sortie.

The horn blew at II Group, St. Omer. Miki and his pilots ran to their planes as their crews in their black coveralls had the props spinning. It was early for a raid. The spotters in their channel barges had reported a large flight to the north headed toward the Belgian coast. Their heading indicated a target of Ghent or Antwerp. It could also be the Rhine or Ruhr, but that was unlikely in daylight. With their reported speed and range, at full throttle, the hunters could catch them at Ghent or turn them away from Antwerp. The II Group's 109E's had been replaced with the F Friedrich. The wing cannons were gone, replaced with the improved single motor cannon through the spinner. The fire power was less, but the reduction in weight and drag allowed faster speed and climb.

The 109s took off from the field in pairs, one group after the next, forming in staffels of eight. As Miki climbed at the lead of his group, turning east toward Ypres, where German guns had turned the city to rubble in the last war where troops had slogged in muddy trenches and clouds of poisonous gas for four years. No such clay feet for Miki's pilots of the Luftwaffe. On the tail rudder of Miki's Javelin were rows of yellow victory chevrons. There were sixty-two. It had been a busy year.

There were no bombers now to rendezvous with, just the hunter fighters. They could dial their fuel injectors to rich and climb to 18,000 feet in six minutes, lean out and push full throttle at 600 kilometers per hour, easily outrunning the lumbering British bombers.

The ancient city of Ghent in central Belgium was the capital of the wool and silk trade in the days of medieval kings and queens, and still seemed frozen in the Middle Ages, with Gothic church steeples and canals of brick and plaster filigree houses. The railways came well after the city had lost its old glory and bypassed the old city center, but now the junctions through the rail yards just to the west were uniquely situated for goods traffic between Northern France, Holland and Western Germany .

The rail yard was a beehive of military activity. Snakes of rail cars on tracks crisscrossing the yards were moved about by switch engines, formed of an array of box cars, tank cars and flat cars loaded with trucks, artillery, tanks and barge boats.

Mobile .37 mm anti-aircraft guns were are set up on sandbagged flat cars on side rails from one end of the yard to the other. A tower supporting the .88 mm artillery raised two of the big guns above the tree line. Barrage balloons dangled in the sky on cable tethers. At 9:45 in the morning the air-raid sirens began to whine. Soldiers rushed to positions. The air defense crews cleared and loaded their guns, searching the sky of low cloud overcast with a few breaks of blue. There was no sound of planes, yet, just the wailing siren.

The bomber formations rumbled through the sky, above the cloud deck. Small patches of green lowland fields and hills were visible through breaks below. The twelve Blenheims from Abingdon were the lead group, with the anti-aircraft guns their primary targets, to clear the way for the Wellingtons of the main assault.

The 109s of II Group were waiting for them. They banked over and dove from high blue. Defensive machine guns fired out of the Blenheim turrets at the swooping planes.

The wing of Spitfires and Hurricanes banked over and dove on the first group of German fighters. The fighters banked and dodged through the blue sky as the bombers keep flying toward their target. The anti-aircraft guns began to fire and puffs of exploding shells burst over a section of broken clouds. The bombers flew right into the midst of the black puffs.

As the rail yard came into view through the clouds, a Blenheim bombardier pressed his eyes to his bomb sight. The shining lines of cross-hatch rails trailed through his view finder until he spotted the flashes of the guns on the rail cars. He pressed his bomb release.

Explosions began to rip along the outer tracks, marching toward the yards until one of the mobile gun units burst into a cloud of metal and bodies. More explosions pocked all around the yards, blasting boxcars, tossing them off the tracks, ripping up track in showers of earth and steel. A tank car exploded in a thundering flash of flames. A bomb whistled and the switch office on stilts over the main line track exploded, tossing the switchmen crashing through the windows to the tracks below. The remaining gun batteries fired into the sky in a stream of fire, but a marching pattern of bombs blasted through the yards as the Wellingtons unleashed their loads.

The Blenheims of the lead wing had taken the worst of the Luftwaffe fighters and were falling from the sky, but they had done their damage on the defensive guns and had drawn the German fighters down from their hunting altitude. As the Wellingtons were reaching the target and releasing their bombs, the Spitfires of 65 Squadron bounced on the 109s, now vulnerable. Aaron lined up on a 109 from above and fired his Browning into the cockpit. The 109 flipped over on its back and augered into the ground below.

A 109 banked around, lining up on the tail of Aaron's diving Spitfire. Bullet hits sparked on Aaron's wing and one round chunked into the fuselage by Aaron's seat, spitting pieces of hot metal through the cockpit and cutting his shoulder.

With the sudden searing pain, Aaron instinctively pulled his stick back and over in a hard climbing turn. The 109 streaked past his upside wing and as he looked over he could see the Javelin emblem blazoned on the cowling before the fighter banked the opposite way.

"Miki," Aaron said out loud to himself. He threw the stick over to follow.

Aaron's Spit rolled over-the-top, coming around after Miki's 109. He banked inside Miki's wider turn. As the tail of the 109 with its sixty-two yellow victory hatches rose up into Aaron's gunsight, Aaron pressed his trigger.

Miki could see the Spit with many black crosses under its canopy coming at him, guns flashing. He recognized the markings of 65 Group.

"Aaron," he said to himself with a long expected meeting of an old friend. He flicked his stick over, just as a bullet sparked off the rib of his canopy and another chunked through the fuselage by his feet.

Miki's Javelin snap-rolled and arced back into a climb. Aaron's Spit stayed with him, pulling up and around. He fired again, but the bullets streamed off into the sky as the fighter maneuvered under Miki's skilled hand.

The two planes seemed to dance in the air, flicking one way then the other, in sliding turns, rolling, looping. They cut through the other fighting planes like they we're standing still. The bombers had dropped their loads and were turning for home or falling from the heavy .88 air bursts. The fighter groups now focused on each other.

Aaron banked around on Miki's tail, climbing for altitude, lining up his gunsight for an instant.

"For Irish!" he shouted and pressed his firing button. But the 109 was gone from his crosshairs, suddenly flicking into a bank and diving out of its climb.

As the Javelin suddenly fell out of its climb, Aaron's Spit flew past. An instant later, the Javelin was rising on Aaron's tail. Aaron saw the 109 behind him, with its spiral spinner and yellow nose. He could just make out Miki's face between the cockpit supports. He was wearing goggles and black leather flight cap, but Aaron knew him like a brother.

"Shit," he said as the 109's cowling guns and nose cannon flashed fire. Aaron flicked his stick hard. The glowing cannon shells streaked past his canopy as his plane rolled into a turning dive. The world turned upside down and backward as he fell toward the gray cloud deck shrouding the Earth. He pulled back on the throttle to a dead stall, allowing the plane to arc over into a dive into the clouds while Miki's 109, at full throttle, rose into the blue.

Miki watched as the Spitfire dropped into the clouds, disappearing, swallowed. He banked at full speed, almost ripping the controls from his hand to follow before his adversary could escape. He dove into the clouds and the daylight disappeared in a deep sea of gray.

Aaron's Spitfire roared out through the bottom of the low clouds, pulling up just before smacking into a rising hillock. He was now in clear air between the low clouds and the ground, with only a few hundred feet between. There was no sun now and he wasn't sure which direction he was flying. His compass was still dancing around from his maneuvers. He flicked the wings to get a look over his shoulder. For a moment, he thought he was clear, until Miki's 109 punched out below the clouds behind him.

Now, it was just he and Miki, like the old days. Diving low and skimming over the farm fields, over the trees and power lines, he thought about the racing days with he and Miki wing to wing, in a challenge for who was best. It was lucky they survived. He thought about pulling back up into the clouds to try to lose him, or fight it out at altitude, but as the ground rushed by below with the clouds just above his canopy, he felt a charge of energy he had lost. The war was gone. It was just he and Miki now. He looked at his compass, it had settled. He was heading east.

Miki followed Aaron's plane in a low altitude chase. He matched him move for move, wondering why Aaron didn't pull back up into the cloud deck. Then, the thought came to him, "What fun would that be?"

The wings of the two planes almost dug soil as they banked and turned over the fields, past farm buildings, almost flying through barns, but pulling up just in time to miss them. Aaron pulled up just before smashing into a grove of trees. Miki fired. The bullets and cannons cut through the tree branches, just as the Spit cleared them. Aaron wondered if Miki was really trying that hard.

The Spitfire rose up over the trees in front of Miki's canopy, then, dove back down, disappearing. He was gone from the sky. Had the bullets hit? Had he crashed?

Miki only had second to react before throwing his stick over, banking. It was a river. Aaron's Spitfire was roaring down the slope of the channel canyon of the river flowing through the Belgian hills.

Aaron dropped to skim down along the water. He wasn't sure which river it was, but thought it might be the Meuse, it was wide enough. He flew along the channel, turning with the gentle curves of the river, his prop wash churning the surface,

Miki's 109 hung high, following from above. He watched Aaron dangerously following the river. He realized he could dive from height. A smile lit his eyes.

"Fool," he said to himself, though he wasn't sure if he was thinking about Aaron, or himself. He took his finger off the firing trigger and pushed his stick over, diving down to the water.

The two fighter planes roared down the river canyon in a flying "chicken" race, arcing around the turns of the river like flying around pylons.

The old bridges of the Meuse had been bombed in the blitzkrieg of 1940, replaced by floating pontoons, but the foundation stone arches still stood, jutting from the water. They flew underneath two high stone arch bridges as the washes of the planes startled soldiers manning the crossings and rocked stunned fishermen in their small boats as they roared past, six feet over the surface of the stream.

Low on the water, Aaron was coming up on a low bridge, eighteen or twenty feet, he guessed. Should he try it, he wondered.

"Crash and burn," he said to himself. An image of Lacy at the little bridge on the Princeton road came to him. Maybe it would be the last thing he thought. He held the stick forward.

The Spitfire zoomed under the bridge, the prop tips chopped into the water, as the boom off the stone sides pounded his canopy.

Miki watched Aaron go under the bridge and pull up on the other side. He hesitated a moment, starting to pull back, to fly over, but then...

"Crash and burn." If Aaron could do it, so could he. He pushed the 109 lower, rushing closer, easing his

264

throttle. He leveled his wings on the water and shot under the bridge.

Miki started to pull up as his plane cleared the bridge arch. He looked around with a laugh of the old exhilaration he had long ago exchanged for the coldness of killing. He searched the sky for Aaron. The clouds were breaking and the blue patches cracking, but Aaron's Spitfire was nowhere in sight.

As Miki's Messerschmitt slowly pulled up from the bridge, Aaron rolled out of a loop and banked around on his tail. His maneuver had worked, getting Miki to go for the bridge. Now, he was vulnerable. Aaron lined up behind the tail of the Javelin.

The Spitfire dropped down from the sky behind Miki's cockpit. He didn't see it. The eight Browning machine guns flashed.

Bullets chunked into the 109. One smashed a pane of the canopy, spitting glass. A bullet hit the frame of the seat. Miki could feel it searing. If it had been an inch to the left, he would have been dead.

"Shit! Bastard!" Miki shouted. The words came in English as if Aaron might be able to hear him. He pulled up into a roll over the riverbank. Aaron pulled up over the bank of the river after him.

On the road along the riverbank, a German Wehrmacht squad troop transport with two Hanomag half-tracks with orders to report to Antwerp had stopped for a ration break. The young troops had never seen an air battle and were amazed at what they had been watching. The 109 roared up and over them, barrelrolling, so that they could see the pilot in the canopy and the Javelin emblem. They shouted and pointed. It was the hero ace, performing before their eyes.

Then, as the British Spitfire roared up from the river, the half-track gunner swung his MG 42 around and fired.

The bullets chunked through the floor of the cockpit, smashing into the instruments. A bullet ripped through Aaron's boot, tearing off two toes. The engine began to sputter and fuel spurted out of a cut fuel line.

The soldiers watched the Spitfire pull up just over some trees, the engine roaring for an instant as if it might climb, but smoke beginning to puff out of the right exhausts, and the engine cutting out, sputtering.

The Stabsfeldwebel column commander ordered his half-tracks to start their motors and turn in the road. He waved his troops to drop their ration tins and get on the trucks.

Aaron held his plane just off the tree tops, looking at the spilling fuel, waiting for it to ignite. He didn't have time to feel the shooting pain in his foot. He would die of fire or crash if he didn't find a clear spot to put down. The engine continued to sputter and cough. He reached to turn the undercarriage crank, but it wouldn't budge. A bullet must have sheared the mechanism.

Finally, ahead was a clearing in the trees, a bare spot where some helpful Belgian farmer had planted and harvested a crop of cabbages. The engine quit. The cockpit went silent except for the rushing wind in the shattered canopy glass.

The Spitfire slowly sank down toward the earth, with its wheels up. The wings just clipped the tops of some trees before it settled to the ground. The prop ripped through the plowed sod, the belly sliding. A wing caught a tree and ripped off. The rest of the plane spun around, finally sliding to a stop.

It had all happened in an instant. Aaron had blacked out for a few seconds and come to again, shaking the cobwebs from his head. The world had spun out of control, but he was alive and aching all over, especially his shoulders from the belt straps and his throbbing foot. His legs were wet. He thought maybe the cold liquid would sooth his foot, but he realized it was fuel dripping from the line onto the floor, all over his legs.

He slapped the harness release and fumbled for the canopy latch. It wouldn't budge. Something under the instrument panel was sparking. He gripped desperately at the latch. Finally, it moved to release and the canopy popped open.

Aaron lurched out of the cockpit and flopped on the ground where the wing once had been. He tried to get up to run, but the pain shot through his foot and leg. He rolled away, crawling to get distance, picturing the spark in his mind and the fireball consuming him. He kept crawling, and crawling, then turned and looked back to the plane, waiting for the fire, but all was still. Still, at least, until he heard the growling motor of the half-track coming through the woods. The German soldiers were looking for him.

Aaron looked at his foot where there was a hole off to the side of the toes. It was soaked in blood and gasoline. It hurt like a son-of-a-bitch, but at least the gas would stop any infection. And he was glad he was wearing three pairs of socks. The layers of socks which had kept his feet from burning on the hot engine firewall in the Spitfire cockpit now seemed to be soaking up and slowing the blood. He pulled the scarf from around his neck and wrapped it around the hole, jerking it tight until the pain shot through him like a needle, then settled to a throbbing ache as he tied it off.

The shouting voices in German were coming toward him quickly. He reached to the top of his boot and pulled out the .32 revolver stuck there. The gun had been intended to shoot himself if he was burning in fuel flames, but now would serve a more hopeful purpose. He picked himself up from the field, stumbling on the tender foot, farther from the plane. He aimed the revolver at the fuel soaked machine and fired. The Spit exploded in gas-fueled flames and he quickly hobbled off toward the trees at the edge of the field.

Miki was flying at altitude over the woods, looking for where Aaron's plane went. He could see the fiery explosion and rising black smoke in the distance. He started to bank toward it, but his own engine juttered and coughed white smoke, spurting out of the right exhaust with each rotation. With a last look toward the burning fire in the trees, Miki turned his plane to find the nearest airfield, before his fate would be the same.

Aaron limped through the woods as fast as he could, away from the half-tracks and soldiers' voices. A gunshot cracked and a bullet cut a twig by his head. He ducked behind the trunk of a Spruce tree. He listened, mostly to his own labored breathing and the German voices, which seemed to come from all around. He didn't hear the half-track motors. Maybe they had given up. The thought only lasted a moment before he heard the crack of a branch behind him. Suddenly, a gray uniform clad arm and hand grabbed him by the shoulder of his flying jacket.

He spun around, looking into the face of a young German soldier, a seventeen-year-old with pimples on his face. The soldier looked as startled and frightened as his prisoner as he clutched him. He turned his head to call out to the others, but a gunshot boomed, echoing in the trees.

Hans Lempet had joined the Hitler Youth on his fourteenth birthday in October of 1936. He was from Esslingen, a smallish town near Stuttgart. His mother had baked him a cake with his name in the frosting with fifteen candles, fourteen for his years and one for good luck, circling a large black Swastika made of licorice frosting. He had hoped with all his heart to be a soldier one day and finally, just three days after his birthday in 1939, he was assigned to the 705th Heavy Infantry Company of the 7th Panzer Division. He had been in training during the heroic invasion of France under Rommel, but was proud to be in a unit of men who had seen battle, returning from rearmament. When he had seen the British plane going down he had been thrilled with an excitement that he might be the one to capture an enemy pilot who would provide information on the plans of the British air bombers to attack his homeland. He wouldn't.

The young German's face showed a moment of startled and surprised pain. Aaron held his revolver against his stomach, now staining with blood as he stared into the eyes of the young man. The grip on his shoulder released as the boy's life slipped away and he slumped down Aaron's body to the forest leaves at his feet.

Aaron had only a moment to react to the feeling before the shouting voices drew nearer. Another bullet whizzed past his ear before he heard the shot of the rifle. He pushed away from the tree and lurched, hobbling across an opening in the woods. The pursuing soldiers charged through the trees after him. Just as one leveled his MP38 machine pistol and fired a stuttering bark of rounds, Aaron dove over an embankment.

He rolled down the steep hill, tumbling over and over, crashing and stumbling through the brambles, finally coming to a stop in a leafy gully. He looked up to the top of the hill through the tree branches where the soldiers peered down, trying to see him. They had lost sight of him and they spread out along the ravine top to search in a sweep phalanx. There was no way Aaron was going that way. Aaron picked himself up and hobbled through the long shadows of the trees.

Aaron came out of the woods at the edge of a long, narrow clearing where a railway track cut through the forest. A heavy freight train was chugging up the long grade from the river where it had to cross at a temporary bridge low on the water and make the uphill climb. He hid behind the trunk of a tall standing pine as the train engine steamed up the grade and clattered past at a slow and agonizing pace. He waited until the engine was well down the track, then, hobbled from the tree.

He reached for the handle of one boxcar but missed it. He grabbed for the rung of another, snatching it in his hand. It yanked his legs off the gravel, almost ripping his arm out of the socket, but he clung to it, swinging between the cars as the soldiers came out of the woods.

The soldiers looked under the wheels of the train to the woods on the other side. They looked all around. They knew the airman was wounded, he couldn't have gotten far. The freight cars rumbled on down the track, picking up speed as the train reached the top of the grade and headed away to the east. After it had passed, the commander ordered his men to continue their phalanx sweep across the tracks.

Aaron clung to the box car while the train rattled on at a fast clip. The signs on the road crossings and buildings changed from French and Dutch to German. Aaron thought about jumping off, but the train was moving too fast and he didn't know how he would land on his throbbing foot. The train crossed a road guarded by border troops with guns and sandbags, but they were all watching the road and not the train heading back into Germany with the downed flier clinging to it. He was in enemy territory and would find no friends to help him. He decided he would wait for the train to stop at a junction yard and then find a train headed west to the coast. After the guarded crossing had passed from view, he pulled himself up the ladder to the top of the car and laid down as tight to the roof as he could. He was exhausted and drifted in a half sleep.

The train passed through towns of brick buildings. It never slowed and seemed to be on an express route to its destination. It was getting dark by the time the train rolled across the steelwork of a long bridge spanning the wide flat waters of the Rhine, the sun setting through a haze on the river. It finally slowed as it entered a busy switching yard, with tracks dividing, and dividing again, sidings filled with strings of rail cars standing as dark hulks.

The train came to a stop. The cars jerked, as somewhere ahead the engine was changed and the portion units uncoupled. Aaron awoke, with a start. He had passed out. Where was he? He rolled over and pulled himself to the side of the car roof. A station sign read "Düsseldorf".

"Jesus," he thought. He had intended to get off miles ago. He tried to think. He could try to find another train back to the coast, but could he find one in all the hulks waiting on the sidings? Maybe he could try to find a barge heading down the river to Holland. He slid off the roof and hobbled down the ladder to drop off. He knew his chances of getting caught were very likely, with no very good options, but as he climbed down he was able to read the destination placard slid into the frame on the side of the next car. Then, he understood why it had been an express freight. The cars jerked again as a fresh engine was joined ahead. He pulled himself back up the ladder, knowing it would not make any more stops. It was going directly to the factories of the Ruhr.

~~~

CHAPTER SEVENTEEN

Kester

It was getting late as Lacy drove back from town, turning the big Mercedes past the old church. The soldiers at the gun emplacement waved, but she no longer stopped to chat with them. The lights of the Gestapo car following her turned after. Her shadow was now a regular fixture of her life and they made no pretense of hiding.

As Lacy pulled up in the courtyard drive, the house was dark. She had been most of the day in Essen looking for something suitable to mollify her mother-in-law. They had gotten into another argument over America's lend-lease program supporting the British. If American ships carrying war supplies were torpedoed by German U-boats, that would not be an act of war but of self-defense. Lacy had tried to never get into a discussion of politics with anyone, but Mathilde von Steuven could always drag her into one, usually starting with the complaint that Lacy wasn't sufficiently honoring Miki's heroism for the Fatherland. Lacy had difficulty with her mother-in-law's recital of her husband's kill count with every casual conversation of how proud she must be. As she got out of the car and gathered some packages from the back seat, the Gestapo car slowed, shifting gears, then drove on.

Lacy stepped in the front door, closing and locking it. Without turning on the light, she stepped to one of the windows to peek out the curtain. The Gestapo car had turned around and cruised slowly past the gate in the opposite direction for a last look, then drove back toward headquarters to report. She turned back into the entrance, picking up her packages. But she stopped, sensing something. Behind her, in the corner of the entrance way was a form in the dark, just the eyes glistening.

"Lacy..."

Lacy froze at the voice. It was so familiar, yet it could just be a memory of a distant past. Was it just in her mind? Had she been so unhappy in her solitude in a foreign land of such ugliness now, that she had begun to hallucinate? Or was it another fantasy? She had them from time to time, alone at night in the dark.

Aaron limped from the shadow into the half-light from the door window curtains. He spoke again, "Lacy. It's me."

She finally turned to look. Aaron was standing there, under the crystal chandelier and the Raphaelite paintings in a grease-stained blue worker's coverall he had pilfered from a railway yard cart over his RAF flight uniform, battered, bruised, with blood globed on his boot. He was older, but somehow, unchanged.

"I broke in a window," he said quietly. "I hope you don't mind my dropping by like this. I would have called first, but I didn't have the right change."

Lacy dropped her packages to the floor and lurched to hug him, hanging on tightly. He held her body against his, feeling her warmth, smelling her hair. She didn't say anything, but just clung to him, crying, feeling as if years had vanished.

The curtains were drawn closed in the great room, the last light had faded outside and only one lamp burned. Lacy helped Aaron lay back on the divan, to half sitting, leaning back on the cushions. He had told her about his journey on the train box car. He had slept on it for what must have been hours and amazed he wasn't discovered. The destination placard on the car had designated "Essen" and the car had the markings of the Krupp FabrikWerk, so he knew where it would take him. He had seen the old church steeple as the train crossed the Ruhr River Bridge and recognized it from the reconnaissance photographs. He had dropped off the train after the bridge, finding the worker's cart at the Mulheim switching yard and followed the river bank to the estate woods.

"You need a doctor," Lacy said. It was odd to be speaking English again, she had wondered if she could still frame the words.

"Do you know one?" he smiled.

Lacy thought wistfully about Dr. Neuenstein, the only one who wouldn't instantly turn in an enemy pilot, but he was long gone. She had last seen him walking through the trees. She liked to hope he had made it to Rotterdam and onward from there, but had not heard from him, and he could not dare write to her without exposing her.

"No."

Lacy carefully untied the flying scarf cloth from around his boot to look at the hole. He winced, but the pain had numbed to a throb.

"You're lucky I let the house servants go last year. I don't think they would have been as glad to see you." She was glad indeed that she had turned Frau Lindl out. She had come close to discovering Lacy's "guests" twice and suspected that she was informing the Gestapo on her every move. Whenever she planned to be away and had told Lindl, the agents were always there. The trip to Düsseldorf was the last straw. Lacy had worked up a scene about wine missing from the cellar and blamed Herr Lindl. It was unfair, but an accusation of theft was the most explainable reason why she would dismiss them. She felt badly about it, but Herr Lindl was appointed to a maintenance manager position in Duisburg for his party loyalty.

"Are you glad to see me?" He looked at her face to try to read it, but she focused on tending his leg. Finally she glanced up at him, but then back to her task.

"Of course I am. I didn't know if you were dead or alive."

"Still kicking. Ow!" he winced again, sucking air as she pulled the boot off with a last tug. She looked at the bleeding wound through his socks. Lacy held her stomach in check as it turned a little at the sight of his foot, wrapped in a three layers of socks. She tried to remember her first aid courses at St Mary's Hall school and the summer she volunteered at the hospital in Princeton.

"It doesn't look too bad," she lied. "I don't see any bone."

"Or toes, either."

She looked at him. He could always find the joke. "The bleeding as stopped, mostly. That's good."

"Lucky for the socks, I guess."

"Why all the socks?" she asked.

"Engine heat. The boot leather gets scalding under the panel."

She understood. The quirks of a flying machine. Miki always complained about his back and a racking gear that reached into the seat area of his plane.

She pulled off the socks which stank of gasoline. She cleaned the wound carefully with soap and water, and some disinfectant and wrapped it tight in clean cotton bandages.

"You'd have made a good field nurse," he said to encourage her. She seemed distant to him. Sad, somehow.

"I wish I could do something like that," she answered. She remembered the pills she had left over from the procedure in Düsseldorf the doctor had given her, some Dolantin for pain, and Penicillin. She ran upstairs to get them.

He looked around the room of the grand house, fine furnishings, museum art and rich decorations. What a life she must lead, he thought. He couldn't know that to her it was more like a prison.

"So, how's Miki?" he asked when she came back into the room. He had been looking at the case of trophies out in the foyer.

"God, Aaron! You got shot out of the sky and crawled across two countries to have a chat about me and Miki?!"

"Just catching up. It's been a long time."

She looked at him with amazement and reached out to stroke his cheek.

"You haven't changed." She noticed the burn scar on his other cheek, around his neck and the back of his hands.

"A little," he said.

She looked away, trying not to let him see her eyes dampening. She couldn't imagine what the last year had been like for him, or didn't want to. She had imagined it enough with Miki when he was gone and she didn't hear from him for weeks.

"Let's get your jacket off and see about that shoulder." She raised him up to get at his jacket, trying to make small talk. "Robby Wilson wrote. He said that he and Donovan volunteered with you. That was a shock."

"Donovan's dead." Aaron said simply.

She pulled at his jacket but stopped, reacting a moment, then went about laying it aside and looking at the wound.

"I know."

"Then, it was Miki."

Lacy looked at him, seeing the hate burning him, in his eyes.

"You'd kill him, wouldn't you, if you could?"

He didn't answer her.

"God, Aaron, what has this done to us?" She fought back her emotions. "It wasn't Miki, Aaron. He told me he saw Donovan. He could see him in the plane. He said he broke off, but one of his men reported downing a plane with the same markings."

Aaron was quiet. He felt like the weight of his rage was lifting from his soul, but not the guilt. Alright then, it wasn't Miki who killed his friend, but who was it?

"Irish joined up because of me. He always felt he needed to get one-up." Aaron felt the need to confess his churning doubts. "First it was rowing, then, jobs. Dad's money. Me and Miki. He didn't know he had more than I ever could. Charlotte loved him. She had his son, y'know. What have I ever done, except try to be the guy in front.

278

The truth is, up in front, you're all alone. I killed him, Lacy. I did."

Lacy stroked his chest, and held his burn-scarred hand in hers, looking in his eyes. She was glad to know that Charlotte had a baby, glad for someone to know joy.

"Somebody has to be in front, Aaron," she said. "Or no one else would try. I think you gave your friends more pride in themselves than you know. You should read Robbie Wilson's letters."

Aaron laughed, breaking from his brush with self-pity, angry at himself for it.

"Wilson," he said with a grin, "he'll outlast us all. There's one lucky bastard." He thought about Charlotte and Donovan's baby boy. "Well, at least there's someone to carry on the old Irish line."

"My mother wrote that Charlotte was expecting. It was the last letter I ever got from home, before they stopped," Lacy said. She looked away, focusing on his shoulder cut.

"What about you?" he asked.

"What?

"Any little Miki's running around?"

Lacy was uncomfortable. "No."

Aaron studied her face in the half-light of the lamp. She was almost five years older than he had last seen her. She had matured. Some of the softness had left her cheeks, but she was perhaps even finer.

"God, you're beautiful. More than I remembered," he said.

She hesitated a moment, then went back to her nursing work, trying to ignore what she was feeling.

"Would you shut up?! You're such a damn flirt. I'd forgotten, almost."

Aaron just watched her tend to him, feeling her hands touching him, soothing. He smiled and tried to relax. The pain pills she had given him, washed with a swig of brandy, had eased the throbbing in his foot. He was so tired.

The Luftwaffe staff car roared along the road from Mettmann, screeching on the turns of the flat winding road. Miki was alone at the wheel of the car. His plane had a cracked cylinder and it would take four days for a replacement. He had managed to land at a support airfield near Liege. There were reports that units had searched the woods to the east of the Meuse for a downed pilot, but believed he probably died from burns as the plane fuel had ignited on impact. He had called for his driver to get him and thought it would be a good excuse for a quick trip home but had left his driver in Cologne, telling him to enjoy himself for the weekend. Miki had enjoyed the countryside drive to the old estate when he was younger, through the valley where ancient man was named, the Neanderthal, and didn't want to have to put up the driver in his house. He wanted to be alone with his wife. He had longed to see Lacy and have a good fuck.

He turned into the gate of Schloss Kester and skidded to a stop behind the Mercedes. He hopped out of the car. He was exhausted, and anxious for some reason.

Miki threw open the door and charged into the house. It was dark. He looked in the great room and the dining hall. He looked in the back dark hallways which had been closed off for the past three months.

"Lacy...?!" he called out. He strode past his display case of medals in the foyer and took the grand staircase to the upper floor two steps at a time. "Lacy?! I'm home. Where are you?"

He strode down the long hall, through the anteroom to the master bedroom. The door was closed. He reached for the handle, but hesitated. It had been months since he was last home. He had often wondered when he had returned from a mission, still alive, exhausted and trying to wipe the images he had seen through his gun sights the wrath of what his bullets and cannons did to other men, what his wife did, alone in their house while he was at war. Sure, he had seen her with lovers in his imagination, a young handsome soldier from the artillery battery on the corner, maybe, or that officer she had argued with about being too friendly with his men, or one of the boys who would come to the door with deliveries in their crisp Hitler Youth uniforms, too young to fight. Maybe that was why she fired the housekeeper, so she couldn't be a witness to her mistress' drunken sex orgies in the great room, with wine from the cellar and workers from the factory dressed as cherubs and fawns, like those museum paintings in all variety of sexual positions on the family furniture. Or had she fired the old groundskeeper so she could have a hard, young workman around to service her needs, when her husband had abandoned her to kill other men and conquer the world. He grabbed the handle and pushed the door open.

As the door swung open, hitting the wall with a thud, Miki stepped into the dark bedroom. The moonlight from the windows fell across the bed, large and soft with thick down mattresses between the posts. Lacy was there, sleeping, alone in the bed with the stuffed white duvet half covering her soft back in a thin chemise. Miki stepped closer to the bed, into the moonlight from the window, just watching her sleep. Death, exploding flesh and burning men left his mind, as he just watched the one portion of beauty and sweetness left in his life, in innocent repose, breathing in peaceful life.

"Miki?" Lacy stirred.

Miki said nothing for a moment, in his Luftwaffe uniform with his rank markings and campaign medals.

"I drove all night," he said, finally.

Lacy glanced around the room, making sure it was all in order.

"Why?"

Miki sat on the end of the bed. He stroked her foot under the sheets.

"I don't know. I wanted to see you." He was quiet a moment. "Aaron was shot down over Belgium."

Lacy hesitated. She didn't know how to react. She had plenty of practice in lying, to her servants, her friends, to the Gestapo, to him, and maybe to herself.

"Was he killed?" she asked simply.

Miki studied her, trying to read her. He realized that she had changed so much since they had first met. He wasn't sure he knew her anymore. He couldn't read her at all.

"I don't think so. His plane crash landed. They were searching for the pilot."

"Who shot him down?"

Miki got up from the bed. "I did." He paced, rather like a caged animal. "I knew it would come."

"If he wasn't killed, then," she watched him pacing, wishing they were all far away, from war, from their lives as they had become, "it's alright, Miki. It's alright. Why did you come home? You can't think he would come here?"

"No, of course not. He is in the woods in Holland or Belgium, hiding. Or he is captured already. Or he is dead. His plane burned."

Lacy sat silently in the bed. She didn't pretend to cry. She didn't have to. She could see his pain.

"You're tired. I'll make you some coffee. Something to eat?" She rose from the bed, starting out of the bedroom. He grabbed her and held her by her arm. He looked into her eyes, trying to fathom what they said when she looked at him.

"Miki...."

"I came home because... I wanted you to know... I wanted to tell you... that I love you."

Lacy smiled. She touched his face. "I know that, Miki. You don't have to drive all night."

He let her go, pacing again, but something eating at him. He peered out the window at the moon shadowed grounds and trees of the estate with the factory steam and smoke beyond the river.

"It is often in my mind," he confessed, not looking at her, "how I brought you here, knowing you still thought of Aaron."

"Miki, I married you."

"Yes," he said, nodding. "Yes. But...we make love, Lacy. And make love... Yet, we have no children. You get sick and sometimes I think, I hope...but nothing."

Lacy stood frozen, uncomfortable. "You never said you wanted them."

"I never said....about it. But I wonder. I could die before."

He finally turned to look at her, to face her. She was crying, deeply, silently.

"Don't you want them?"

She couldn't answer for a moment. She struggled with the pain of it, her secret. Should she tell him? The Gestapo knew, but her husband didn't. Maybe even Hitler knew for Godsake, but Miki didn't. He was never home except for a few hours at a time while the world around her was turning to a nightmare, where kind innocent people were beaten, burned and pissed on, shipped in rolling boxes to God knows where with their belongings left behind and all of them, Miki in his hero's uniform, his family, and she herself, responsible for madness.

"Lacy," he urged her, wanting to know the darkness between them. "Tell me."

Anger and self-recrimination welled up in her until she burst.

"I will not bring a child into this world, Miki! This place. Where human beings are loaded on boxcars like cattle. Where they kill each other...for what?! Honor? Duty? To what?! A greater evil? I will not bring a child... I...would not!"

She sank to the floor against the bed post, holding her belly where she felt, not pain, but the emptiness. Miki stared at her, trying to understand, but a building ache in his own gut.

"Mine. You would not allow my child. How many? How many, Lacy?"

Lacy didn't answer, looking away from him. She didn't see him leave, but the room was now quiet, only her breathing.

Miki fought off a dark anger as he opened the door of the liquor cabinet in the dining salon to grab the bottle of French Brandy. He had sent home several cases of Remy Martin Louis VIII Cognac from France. He felt a little bad he didn't pay for it. It was confiscated from a Jewish wine shop in Lille. A friend in the Administration for Finance had offered the seizure for his Luftwaffe staffel and he had distributed it among his men. The last of the bottle dribbled out into the glass. He couldn't remember the last time he had drunk it, but there was more in the cellar.

Miki walked down the dark hallway to the door to the cellars. He tried the knob, but it was locked. He was puzzled and angry. He stood back and kicked at the door with his boot. The wood cracked and splintered a little, but it held strong. He kicked again and again with his black leather boot.

Lacy heard the sound of Miki kicking at the cellar door downstairs. She could hear his anger in the crack of the cellar door. She held her breath for a moment as she heard the door shatter.

The wood of the door gave way under Miki's boot. He stepped to the top of the stairs, looking down into the dark. He turned on the light. The single bulb illuminated the shelves and stacked cartons below. He wondered why there were footsteps in the dust on the stairs. Who had been down there in his wine? Lacy had fired the housekeeper, so no wonder the house was dusty, but at least it could be clean for when he came home.

He walked a little unsteadily down the stairs and searched among the cases of wine, liquor and art pieces he had sent back from his various stations. He looked around the cellar, wondering about all the stuff he had accumulated, like the medals on his chest, without caring about them in the least. He found the stack of Remy cases with the red eagle stamp marking them as Reich property and ripped open the cardboard to grab a couple of bottles.

Lacy listened as Miki had apparently gone down into the cellar. She went to the door hurriedly and locked it.

"Aaron," she whispered softly.

Aaron pulled himself out from under the bed, still in his RAF uniform pants and undershirt. He rose to his feet, supporting his weight on the bed post. He looked at Lacy across the dark room with just the moonlight through the tall windows. She met his eyes, silent.

"There's a gardener's shed in the grounds," she said and stepped softly in her bare feet to the window. She turned the latch and opened it. The slight constant whistle through the old sash went quiet as the night air drafted into the room, smelling of cedar and early blooming lilac.

"I'll come to get you, when it's safe."

He grabbed his flight jacket and boots from under the bed and went to the window. He stopped there, looking at her in the moonlight.

"Don't say anything. Please. I'll come when it's safe."

Aaron nodded and climbed out on the window ledge. He dropped his flight jacket to the soft earth of the flowering beds below. He hung by his hands from the water pipe which ran alongside the window and dropped onto his jacket. He tried to land on his good foot, but crashed into the bushes, clattering a loose piece of brick. They waited to see if there was any noise from the first floor, but the lights didn't come on.

Lacy watched Aaron below as he hobbled around the side of the house toward the gardens. It was then she thought to look out to the road, to see if her Gestapo shadow was parked in his spot across the road. They usually left her alone at night, but sometimes would be there at random times. The agent had once nearly startled her to death when she opened the rear pantry door and he was standing in the dark. She didn't know what he was snooping for, and he gave her no answer when she had demanded to know. But the car wasn't there.

Lacy found Miki lounging on the divan, pouring himself Cognac. He had finished off almost a half of the bottle. She stepped up behind the divan, stroking his shoulder with her hand.

"Miki," she said softly. "I don't want to hurt you. I do love you."

He wouldn't look at her, focusing on his display case of trophies in the hall.

"Yes, of course. You love me. I love you. We're together."

"Are you alright?" She didn't know what he was thinking.

"Yes, of course." He threw back another swallow of brandy. "I point my plane where I am told. I have my medals. I am a hero of my country. What else do I need?"

He suddenly got up from the divan and set down the glass. He calmly and deliberately buttoned his tunic. Lacy watched him, bewildered and torn. She didn't know what to say to him. He was right. Yes, of course she loved him, but as what? What did that mean? Her feelings and memories of Aaron and a simpler, sweeter time had come flooding back over her. Miki had never been emotionally expressive, and had drawn even more sullen and distant as his victories and battles mounted. She cared for him, but didn't know who they were together anymore.

Miki, without another word of what he was thinking or what he wanted, or didn't want, strode to the front door, passing his display case. He opened the front door and went out.

Lacy stood at the door watching as Miki climbed into the staff car, sliding behind the wheel. He tried a couple of times to start the motor, the brandy taking effect. Finally, it rumbled to life. He backed around in the courtyard, cracking a fender against one of the plaster figures which lined the balustrade, not noticing, and roared away down the drive. As she watched him drive down the road toward Mulheim, she wondered if she would see him again in the morning, or might never see him again. But that was not new. Every time he came home and left again, she knew he might never return. The uncertainty of it had become so familiar, and nearly unbearable.

~~~

CHAPTER EIGHTTEEN

Agent Horst

Lacy stepped through the twigs and leaves of the grounds now cloaked in the light morning fog which rose from the river and up the slope to wrap the house. It was one of her favorite times. Something about the fog made the rest of the world go away, just peaceful. And it kept the house and her life hidden from the road. She had dressed in a morning coat over her night slip and carried a thick bundle wrapped in curtain cloth.

She pushed in the door of the ancient shed, with its creaking door. It had probably been there since the gardens were designed in the early 18th Century. The old wood had aged and overgrown with clinging vines. Herr Lindl had asked if she wanted it cleaned up or torn down when she first became the mistress of Kester, but she liked it. It had added an old world charm to the grounds.

Morning light came through the cracks between the wood of the shed. At the tap on the door, Aaron got up from where he'd been lying, only half asleep. He pulled away a shovel he'd propped against the door and opened it. Lacy stepped in the door and he closed it behind her. She showed him the bundle.

"I brought..."

Not letting her finish, he took the bundle and tossed it aside. He took her in his arms, held her face and kissed her. She struggled a moment in surprise but didn't try to stop him. She had often conjured it on lonely nights. She allowed herself to melt into it, kissing him back, feelings forgotten or suppressed welling up and released. They sank together onto a pile of tarps, not minding the dried leaves and earth.

They urgently pulled at each other, stripping away uniform and morning coat, the warmth of bodies, wounded and scarred, connected, as one. Lacy pulled him inside her, her disconnected life falling away as the cool blue morning light through the slats cut across their heaving bodies in the dark.

A car drove up the road toward the house. It pulled up across the road from the Kester gate and turned into the path of clear ground at the roadside. Joachim Horst was late to his post. He'd been with the national police for two years. He had been transferred to the Essen assignment from Kassel where he had been comfortable. He resented Stenhoffer for making him follow this woman on her shopping trips. Of course, he was happy not to be fighting in the war. His younger brother, Thomas, had been sent to Eastern Poland, and sitting for hours watching a house was better than that, but he had long given up on catching her at meeting foreign agents. She was an attractive girl, so that wasn't so bad, and he had glimpsed her in the house from time to time on his night assignments. He had often imagined he could just sneak in the back pantry door and take her while she was alone, screwing her all over that decadent furniture as she begged him not to shoot her in the head with his Luger pistol, and made her do things to him his wife never would even consider. Then he would shoot her and toss her in the river, and report that she had escaped. He had often thought about it, until that one night she caught him at the back door, peeping in the windows, and worried for two weeks that she would report him. His wife had always said he lacked ambition, and maybe she was right. He picked up the Zeitung newspaper from the seat and opened it to read of the stunning victories on the Eastern Front, where his brother would probably get a medal, while he would be lucky to retire with a pension.

Lacy pulled the coat around her shoulders, nervous and uncertain, as Aaron stroked her shoulder, lying back, still naked. She looked at him, wanting to sort it out, but not sure what to say.

"Don't," he said. "Don't say anything."

He pulled her back to lying next to him, holding her. She just laid there in his arms, comforted, but only for a moment, before the truth of their situation could not be forgotten. She had thought about it all through the night, and had made her choice.

"I brought one of Miki's uniforms." She nodded to the bundle she had brought. "I can't get forged papers anymore."

"Anymore?"

"It's too complicated." She could have told him about the escape network she had organized, the families she had helped escape, her life with the Gestapo at her heels, the cat and mouse games with the police agents watching her and interrogations at gunpoint in the office at Kaiser Wilhelm Platz, but that all could wait until later. What mattered now was the plan she had to get him out.

"We'll just make do with the uniform," she said. "You'll be an officer heading back to the front."

"What are you talking about, Lacy? I don't speak German. If they catch me in a German uniform, they can shoot me as a spy. It's not a game. "

Lacy hid her nervousness behind a smile and took a breath. She knew it was a desperate plan, maybe even foolhardy. But she felt a sort of desperation of her own, and it was the only way she could think.

"You don't have to speak German. I'm going with you."

"You what?"

"I'll go with you to as far as Antwerp. You can change into civilian clothes there. The Dutch underground can get you to a boat."

"How do you know all this?"

"Never mind. Like I said, it's complicated." She thought of the steps and contact points she had sent other families to follow. She hoped they were still undiscovered.

"They can shoot you, too, you know."

She knew it very well and thought about the alternative. She couldn't hide him for long. He would have to turn himself in. She imagined him in a prison camp, maybe tortured for information. And how could he explain why he travelled so far to the Ruhr. They would know her history with him. They would make the connection. They already suspected her. It wouldn't matter what uniform he was wearing.

"Yes. But I know we can do this."

He was startled by her confidence. She had a certainty he had never known in her.

"What about Miki?"

"He's my husband, Aaron. I'll take you to Antwerp." It was all she thought she could do.

Lacy came out of the shed, pulling her morning coat tight around herself and started to walk back across the grounds toward the house. She stopped as she saw the car on the road through the thinning fog. Her shadow had taken up his position. He was looking right at her. She didn't know how long he'd been there, but it was a good distance to the road through the gray mist. He couldn't really see much detail from there. She turned and went back to the shed.

Aaron was buttoning up the tunic of Miki's Luftwaffe major's uniform. He looked up surprised as the door opened. Lacy looked around the shed and grabbed an ax from the tools. She handed it to him.

"Take this. And follow me. Leave some buttons undone. Pull the collar up. It's cold outside."

Aaron marveled at her. This was a different Lacy than he had known, assured and confident. He left the buttons undone and followed her.

Agent Horst watched the garden shed, now attentive as the lady came out again. He wondered what she could be doing. Maybe he would catch her at something.

Aaron stepped out of the shed after Lacy in Miki's uniform, trying to limp as little as possible on his bad foot. He saw the little car parked across the road by the gate. He wondered what Lacy was doing, surely they were being watched. As they reached the Mercedes in the courtyard, Lacy stopped.

"Wait here," she said, then walked straight down the drive toward the car. She crossed the road and stepped up to the window. She pulled her coat more closely about her with her most indignant gaze at the surprised agent. She gestured for him to roll down his window. He did.

"My husband, Major von Steuven, would like you to leave," she said. "He doesn't appreciate his privacy being invaded in this fashion and intends to speak to your superiors in Berlin."

Agent Horst looked past her to the Luftwaffe major, standing in the distance in the fog, holding an ax. He had seen the Javelin in newsreels and that heroic poster. He didn't look quite so tall in person, but those propaganda and publicity pictures always made people look larger than life. He didn't want to stare too much, and wondered for a moment how far he could throw the ax, thinking about that night his wife had caught him peeping on her.

Horst rolled up his window and started the car. Lacy watched him drive away, breathing again.

Aaron and Lacy stood on platform four of the North Essen station, waiting for the train. Aaron was smartly dressed in Miki's old uniform. It had a few tears and loose threads, but they would only be noticed by another senior officer. The medals, too, might not pass too close of an inspection. A few of them were from Miki's trophy case. The Luftwaffe gave no medals for track and field. A white cotton bandage was wrapped around his throat, as if covering a serious wound. Lacy stood by him in her best travelling coat. They had a small valise between them as if for an overnight trip.

Lacy pretended to fuss with the bandage like a dutiful wife with an injured soldier husband. People on the platform would look over at them, but try not to stare too much. None dared approach them, though a few nodded in honor as they passed on their way to find lower class cars down the platform. Lacy straightened the silver cross dangling in his collar.

"They're staring at us," Aaron whispered, trying not to move his lips too much.

"It's the Spanish Cross. Miki doesn't wear it since he got the Knights Cross. Now, quiet. You've been wounded and can't talk. If anyone speaks to you, just look stern and important. They bow to authority. Any authority. If we meet a general or something, I don't know, salute a lot."

"You're amazing," he whispered, looking away, down the platform.

"And stop talking!" she whispered back as the train came chugging up the track toward them. It slowed to a stop, and they stepped onto a first class coach.

Miki stepped out of the Hofbrau beer house inn where he'd spent the night, mostly drinking, into the center of Essen. His uniform was rumpled, his eyes weary. He hadn't really slept, but had lain half-awake all night, but for a few hours of drinking, in one of the rooms upstairs.

It was a familiar place he liked and had taken his men to while on visits. It was where Frische had met the serving girl, Berta, who used to help at the schloss, until she got pregnant. She had now the little Aryan baby, a girl, being cared for by her parents, as Frische had not the slightest interest in her anymore. He was getting enough French girls pregnant to worry about the one back home who was hoping to go to hotel school. The German hotel business would not be expanding now that Germany had turned on Russia. Miki had thought it was a huge mistake. More and more of the prime Luftwaffe units were being taken off the western defense and moved to the east. He was left with new, inadequately trained replacements to fly against a bombing force that he knew would soon overwhelm them, especially if

America entered the war. All it would take would be one U-Boat torpedo hitting an American passenger ship, like the last war.

He tossed back the remains of a glass of Apricot Schnapps and smashed it in the street. He wasn't sure what he wanted to do, or where he would go. Would it do any good to go home and argue again? Or should he just go back to his base and fly his plane? As he paused to button his uniform tunic up to the Knights Cross at his collar, a man in a black leather coat stepped from a small Volkswagen at the corner. The car looked familiar to him, but not the man, though he was without a doubt an agent of the secret police.

Agent Horst stepped smartly to Miki, checking the name over his uniform pocket just to be certain he wasn't doubling his error, and snapped a smart salute.

"Heil Hitler, Herr Major!"

Miki saluted back, though less enthusiastically.

"I must apologize for this morning, Herr Major. I hope I did not give offense, but it was in the course of my duty."

"This morning?" Miki asked, quite confused.

"At your house. With your wife, Herr Major."

Miki was even more puzzled. Maybe he hadn't recovered from the schnapps, which he really knew better than to mix with brandy.

"What about you and my wife?"

The agent now looked more closely at Miki's features, his unmistakable shock of blond hair, just like the propaganda poster and his height, standing taller than the agent. The realization seemed to come to them both at the same moment.

~~~

CHAPTER NINETEEN

Dover

The house had been searched and an incompletely burned leather flying cap and jacket had been found in the incinerator. Old rail ticket stubs and a telephone exchange number in Antwerp had been found among tailoring receipts in a false bottom drawer in the dressing room. The Opel had been found in North Essen, two blocks from the train station. Witnesses had been interviewed who had seen a Luftwaffe major and a lady boarding the train to Duisburg. Station agents in Duisburg had seen the officer on the platform there, but didn't see which train they boarded, or if they had left the station.

Lacy and Aaron sat in the first class car of the train from Eindhoven to Antwerp. They had changed trains twice and would have to transfer to another local train there. Aaron would change to civilian clothes for the last leg to Rotterdam. He would use the last transit documents Lacy had procured for the family that she could not get out of Germany across to Holland. The two border crossings route was more complicated but harder to trace.

The uniform had done its work. They had passed across the border without anyone asking for their papers, just a salute. Several seats behind them, a pair of officers sat together. They were Wehrmacht and not Luftwaffe, so had not attempted to converse with Aaron. Whenever someone had tried to speak to them, Aaron would just point to the bandage around his throat and Lacy would kindly explain he had been shot through the neck by a 7.92 Browning bullet from an enemy Spitfire he had shot down near the Meuse River. He would thankfully recover, but the doctors had made a critical suture on his larynx and he mustn't speak.

On the occasion when someone would not simply move on, Lacy would describe the air battle as a proud wife. From listening to endless bragging and "hangar flying" of the pilots under Miki's charge at the salons and debauchery parties at the house, Lacy could recite flying tactics and aircraft performance minutia as well as any pilot, and she would describe them in nauseating detail until the listener's eyes would glaze over, and then Lacy would tell them how tired her husband was and could he get some rest, please.

Miki raced along the road in his Mercedes staff car with the big engine straining under the long hood. The wind blew over the windshield, tossing his hair, as he raced along the sleek newly completed auto route highway to the border at Venlo. He didn't know where they were going, but the one clue he had was the exchange number in Antwerp, so that was where he would go. His service Luger was on the seat of the car next to him. He didn't know what he would do with it, but in his distraction he thought he would do anything to bring his wife back.

He had questioned could it be possible that Aaron had made it across two hundred and thirty kilometers of enemy country to find his way to his house? How could he know the way? Had Lacy been secretly communicating with him all along? Certainly, it could be another pilot she was helping escape, but the rankings and unit patches on the jacket that had not completely burned would be correct for Aaron. Miki even wondered, questioned, whether Aaron had led him on the chase into Holland just so that he could get to Lacy. Could that be possible in the middle of a war? Maybe for Aaron. Aaron would be that stubborn, and that foolish, just to win out over him.

He sped on. He would stop at the border crossing to telephone for a report. The Gestapo would be checking every train now between Duisburg and the Dutch coast.

The army officers chatted in the first class car, while on a seat across from them, a businessman read his paper. The car was otherwise empty. Lacy glanced back to the soldiers. One of them seemed to be staring intently at them, as if trying to decide a recognition, although it seemed it was not Aaron's uniform he was looking at, but her. Aaron was facing away from them, so they could not see his face.

Lacy's hands fidgeted nervously. Aaron reached his hand over and placed it on hers. She gripped it, but tried to keep her eyes ahead and not look at the soldier. The soldier stood up, still staring at Lacy and walked up the jostling train car toward them. He stopped at the back of the seat where Aaron was turned away. Lacy's eyes drifted to the Luger at his side, then, focused on his face. He was a junior officer, young but seasoned. Lacy guessed him be about twenty-one. He pulled off his cap and smiled.

"Excuse me," he said politely, "but I could not help recognize you, Frau von Steuven. I do not wish to intrude on you and the Major, but I wanted to be able to tell my wife we had met and make her jealous."

Lacy was puzzled. "I'm sorry. Do you know me?"

The officer explained, fingering the military cap in his hand. "You see, I was a runner in my youth program. I watched the Olympics films many times. I was most inspired by the Major, and his prowess. Der Javelin." He smiled as it rolled from his tongue in the same way as many of the idolizers of Miki's hero status did. He continued, speaking for the benefit of her husband but attempting to not intrude upon him. "And I hope I am not out of turn, but I was young and impressionable, and the films showed his beautiful bride from America cheering him on and looking so admiringly at him. It was inspiring to me. So, I tried even harder at my practices and have won some medals of my own."

Lacy looked at his eager young face in his crisp gray-green uniform with campaign badges and the double lightning bolts of the Waffen-SS on his collar. He had the single diamond pin of a Scharführer, the leader of a squadron. He had risen in the ranks by his loyalty and service to the cause.

"Thank you," Lacy said with kindness. She thought about the last years of her life since that day. "I had to do that many times, over and over, while watching a man eat a sausage, so that you would be inspired to put on that uniform. I guess I played my part."

The SS soldier was a bit puzzled by what she meant. He looked to the famous hero sitting with his back to him, looking away out the window as if not listening to the conversation, his neck heavily bandaged.

"Is his wound severe?" the soldier asked.

Lacy just smiled uneasily. "He'll recover."

Then, the soldier seemed to notice something. A puzzled curiosity came over him. He was looking over Aaron's shoulder at the medals on his uniform tunic. He could just see the tops of the pins from where he stood, but there was something very familiar and very odd to him.

"Excuse me, but why does the Major wear track and field medallions on his uniform?"

Lacy realized he was seeing the medal she had taken from the display case to fill out the tunic. Who would have thought they'd run into another track athlete? She realized it might have been a fatal mistake.

"He's very proud of his achievements. Aren't you?"

The soldier hesitated. He didn't speak. And he didn't move, just staring at the back of Aaron's head, as if waiting, willing him to turn around.

As he stepped a little further past the seat to get a better look, the train suddenly lurched, nearly toppling him off balance. The train was quickly slowing to a stop. The SS soldier steadied himself on the back support of the seat and bent to look out the window.

The businessman put down his paper. "There is no stop here."

The train slowed, with back pressure steam hissing from pistons as it rolled past the angled crossing of a small intersecting country road where a farm truck and a Citroen waited to cross. Aaron slid down the window and peered out ahead. There was a main road crossing ahead where a military truck waited with a squad of soldiers in the back. An officer waited, along with a pair of Gestapo agents, by a car which was blocking the track.

Aaron leaned close to Lacy and whispered, "End of the line."

As the train came to a standstill, Aaron grabbed Lacy's hand and pulled her up from the seat. As they stepped into the aisle, the SS soldier stood in front of them. His eyes registered that Aaron was not the Aryan hero of the nation. Aaron slugged him and grabbed the Lugar from his belt holster as he crumpled against the seats. He may have been a fast runner, but he wasn't much of a boxer.

Aaron pulled Lacy back down the car. The other German officer got up from his seat to confront them, but Aaron shoved the Luger in his face. He sat down again. Aaron took the Luger from his belt and clocked him across the temple with it. As he slumped, Aaron pulled Lacy quickly to the connecting door between the coaches.

The two SS soldiers recovered and began to shout warnings to the Gestapo men boarding the train. The young Scharführer slid open a window and waved to the squad in the back of the truck. They quickly began to muster from it.

Aaron and Lacy hurried through the train, from coach to coach, tripping over legs and luggage. Soldiers hurried after them from car to car. Other soldiers were double quick marching along the side of the train from the front to the back. Aaron came to the door of the third class car. It was crowded. He looked out the window to the road crossing where the farm truck and Citroen were still stopped, waiting for the train to move, their drivers standing out in the road, watching the activity.

"Come on," Aaron said, opening the carriage door, "our ride's here."

He jumped down to the track, landing with a sharp pain from his foot. He didn't have time to worry about it and helped Lacy from the high train floor. They hurried to the road crossing and Aaron pointed the Luger in the face of the frozen Citroen driver.

"You drive," Aaron told Lacy. "My foot's...bad."

Lacy got behind the wheel and Aaron slid in the other side.

The soldiers now saw them as the little car backed up at the crossing and turned around, driving away.

The Squad Command Officer waved at his men and ordered them to get back on the truck. The Gestapo agents had to hurry back through the cars, stumbling over confused passengers.

Lacy pressed the gas as far as it would go, but the little Citroen two cylinder engine couldn't manage more than forty-five. Aaron looked back to see how close they were being followed. They'd had a lucky break. There was no direct road connection between the main road and the farm road they were on with the train stopped on the track. The farm field was bisected by an irrigation ditch, so the detail and Gestapo had to back track to the next connecting road.

The SS Scharführer who had been a runner and a fan told all he knew to the Gestapo agents. The American wife of a national war hero was travelling across borders with an impostor, dressed to appear as her husband, but was not. He described the false medals he was wearing in detail and the bandage on his neck, obviously a ruse.

Lacy drove down the narrow road between bramble hedges, but didn't know where they were going.

"God, Aaron! How far can we possibly get?" she worried aloud. She knew if the Gestapo got to a telephone, every road, at least the main transit points, would soon be blocked. And they could never get across the border with only the documents they had. They would be useless now.

"I don't know," he answered, "just keep driving until we figure it out." He looked at the speedometer. "And go faster."

She almost said something, but thought it was stupid at just that moment to argue about how fast a little Citroen could go. It wasn't a twelve-cylinder Packard. He kept looking out the windows as the trees alongside the road broke and patches of open fields came briefly into view.

"What are you looking for?" Lacy asked as he craned his neck.

"Did you notice those soldiers' uniforms? In the detail on the truck?"

"What about them?"

"They were Luftwaffe security police, right?"

"Yes."

Lacy looked at him puzzled a moment, but then realized what he was searching to find.

Miki had stopped at the border gate at Herungerberg and called in for a report on the search. A couple matching the description of a Luftwaffe Major with the Spanish Cross and a blond young woman companion had been seen boarding a train at Mönchengladbach for Antwerp via Eindhoven. Police had arrived too late to board the train at Eindhoven and a security detail from the Luftwaffe base at Gilze-Rijen was to stop and inspect the train west of Tilburg.

Miki drove like a madman on the road to Eindhoven. He was forty minutes behind the train, as best he could tell from the report. He had navigated to enough rendezvous points at time and speed to have a clear idea of how far he was away from them.

Aaron had spotted the Dornier transport plane banking for a landing from about two miles away. It had taken them a roundabout of turns and dead ends at canals to find their way to the air base, but once on the right road, it became evident by the military transport trucks and material depots that they were near. No one seemed to raise alarm as the little car with a Luftwaffe

Major and a pretty girl driving him passed them. Drivers had saluted as they passed. They had probably thought the officer had been out for a night of "collaboration" with a local girl and had stayed for an extra roll or two before returning to the base.

Lacy was nervous. She had begged Aaron to get out at the edge of the runways to try to get through the fences, but Aaron knew they would be watched and guarded from local resistance saboteurs in an occupied country. This was a desperate gamble, but the German security apparatus, for all its efficiency would be searching for public transportation and closing a net on the roads. It was a bet they had to make, or crash and burn.

The Citroen pulled up to the guard gate stanchion. The Luftwaffe guard stepped from his box to the window as Lacy rolled it down. His Mauser was slung over his shoulder smartly. He looked at Lacy in the driver's side of the little foreign car. The guard smiled at her. He had seen a few girls like her while stationed in Holland, but had never been able to get one for himself. They always seemed to go for the pilots. "Bastards," he thought. He was a tall young man and had to lean down to the window of the little car.

"Can I help you, Miss...?" he started to ask, but then saw the insignia of a major on the arm of the uniform in the passenger seat. He snapped to attention and saluted his sharpest "Heil Hitler", hoping he wouldn't be sent to some Godforsaken base in Poland for hitting on an officer's dolly girl.

"Pardon me, sir," he said. "May I see your identification? The civilian is not allowed, Herr Major."

"Identification?" Lacy asked as casually as she could. At least he had not been warned to look for them. The Gestapo had not fully informed the Luftwaffe. The

Germans had built a war machine on their organization but would fall on the bureaucratic inefficiency of divisions of authority.

"Don't you know who this is?" she whispered aloud as if she might offend her passenger.

The tall guard, a Corporal, leaned over again and looked through the window. He could now see the Spanish Cross.

Lacy leaned closer to him and whispered softly close to his ear. "You have heard of 'Der Javelin?'" A look of reverent recognition came over the young man. He bent down to look at Aaron, obviously recovering from his wounds. He was impressed, but a good soldier.

"Excuse me, sir," he said, "but it is my duty. Your orders?"

Aaron hesitated uncertainly, then, reached to the flap of his tunic pocket. He unbuttoned the pocket and took out a paper, unfolding it with one hand and holding it for the guard to see. It was a Luftwaffe pilot training order. The guard looked at it across the car. Aaron held it close, but did not hand it to him. It was one of Miki's old orders for Paderborn. If the guard looked too closely he would see the old date and the wrong airfield, but it had the red eagle stamp of Luftwaffe High Command and the signature of Feldmarschall Göring. Lacy had copied it from Miki's Knights Cross citation. The guard stared at it, but whether he truly recognized it, they couldn't tell. Aaron refolded it and put it back in his pocket.

Lacy whispered again. "His foot is sore and he can't walk far. I'll just let him off at his office." She smiled sweetly, asking a favor.

The young corporal could have made a decision that would have kept him from a firing squad. He could have ordered a car to the gate to take the new training officer to his quarters. He could have insisted that a civilian could not enter the base, and made the famous war hero get out and walk on his injury. At his court martial it was suggested that he could have taken the weapon from his shoulder and shot the woman. But it was the action he took next for which he would be executed.

The guard rose to attention and saluted, "Heil Hitler." He smiled and winked at the pretty woman in the driver's seat and waved for the gate to be lifted. Lacy smiled her thanks, and the little car drove through the gate onto the bustling airbase with Dornier transports and Heinkel bombers parked on the runway aprons.

Miki slowed his Mercedes staff car at a check point road block set up by Luftwaffe security at the intersection of the highway from Eindhoven to Tilburg. After assuring his identity to the soldiers, they told him the British pilot impersonating him and the woman had been stopped on the train but had escaped by a car. Miki asked the squad leader if a security alert had been made at the airfields. The leader looked at him, bewildered, as if it was insane that an escaping enemy pilot would try to gain access to a military installation.

"Idiots!" Miki cursed to himself under his breath. He knew Aaron, how he thought, what he would do. They thought like Germans. The squad leader looked even more puzzled. Miki ignored him. He calculated that he was still thirty minutes from Rijen. If Aaron succeeded, he would be too late. He got back into his car and slammed the door. He turned around in the road, rumbling over the divider and raced back the way he had come. The fighter defense squadron of Jagdeswäder 21 was stationed at Eindhoven.

Lacy drove through the camouflage netting covered machine shops and hangars to the grassy edge of the concrete runway apron opposite two Junker 88 bombers with mechanic crews bustling in overhaul repair work. Further down the line, beyond where crewman were unloading supplies from the Dornier which they had seen landing, was an ungainly looking plane, smaller than the bombers with an overhead wing and a twin tail boom, a Junkers 120 Reconnaissance plane.

"There," Aaron pointed.

The Citroen rattled along the runway edge to the plane. The flight mechanics looked over at it in curiosity, but had their work to do.

Lacy stopped behind the tail of the plane. Aaron hopped out of the car and hobbled to the wing of the Junkers. He opened the cockpit door hatch and found the crank behind the seat. It was a two-seat tandem plane with a pilot seat in front and passenger seat behind. He flipped on the magneto switches, calculating that they had just a minute or two before the ground operations tower spotted them, if they hadn't already. The alarm horn hadn't sounded yet, so he had hope. He hopped to the engine cowling and shoved the crank in the starter slot. He turned it and the engine sputtered and started with a petulant whirring of the single blade propeller. The engine seemed strong and fit.

Aaron turned to Lacy standing at the car with the door open. He held out his hand for her.

"Come with me."

Lacy shook her head. "I can't Aaron. I married Miki."

"Of everything that could possibly matter in this bloody, turned-over world, is that it, Lacy?" Aaron pleaded. "They'll shoot you. They won't give a damn who your husband is. I've never loved anyone but you. Maybe for the wrong reasons at first...but there's no one I've thought of when I get up in the morning, and when I go to sleep at night, but you. Even with someone else, it's your name that comes in my head. Every time I climb into a cockpit. When I'm flying low, I can see you, driving along a Pennsylvania highway. When I'm flying to a mission point, I think about the creek or the fountain. I should have asked. I should have been the one to ask."

"It's too late, Aaron," she said, unable to find a better answer. She wanted to go with him, to hold him, be with him, but she was frozen by a sense of duty and commitment.

The alarm horn began to sound. The security force would soon be on them. Aaron made a last desperate plea.

"Lacy, listen to me..." He looked up to the sky, in bright haze overcast and breaking low clouds. "Up there or down here, your life can change or end in a moment. And in one stupid moment I screwed up the only thing in my life that ever counted for anything. I know you care about Miki. But only you know what you really feel. If ever there was a moment for either of us... It's your decision."

Lacy still hesitated, crying, looking at his extended hand, his face.

A base guard Kubelwagen was driving down the runway toward them. Aaron saw it, but didn't say anything, waiting for her. He would wait until they would both be caught. It needed to be her choice.

Suddenly, Lacy reached out and took his hand. He pulled her close for a moment, wiping the tears from her cheek and kissed her, even as the guard car was coming on them. They had cut it close, climbing into the plane, Aaron in front, Lacy behind. Aaron closed the door.

The Junkers' propeller roared and pulled out onto the runway just as the security guards reached it, swerving just past the turning wing. The plane spun onto the runway, pointing west and roared to speed. The security guard arrived in the Volkswagen, but too late. The plane was already down the runway.

The security soldiers watched helplessly as it lifted off into the air. They could have shot with their guns, but didn't. They had responded to the intrusion and had seen a senior officer pilot taking a civilian woman on board a trainer. They joked about how much trouble he was going to be in with High Command for taking a girl on a joyride. The Second Lieutenant thought he might throw a little scare into him, but they assumed he was probably drunk and laughed as they got back into their car. They wouldn't connect the arrival of a new training officer with the search for an escaping British pilot masquerading as a Luftwaffe major until a general bulletin was distributed an hour later.

Aaron guided the little plane off the ground, rising into the air. Lacy looked out at the ground below, grass and trees falling away, and the open space of the sky surrounding them, like sinking upward into the firmament. A pressure pushed her down into the seat. She had not felt it before. She had seen the sky from the windows of the Hindenburg, but that was almost like standing in a building. This was different. She realized, as if it were suddenly a revelation, after years of loving and living with fliers she had never been in a plane. She reached forward to Aaron's shoulder.

"You never took me flying with you," she said in almost a wistful wonder.

"Let's hope it isn't the last," Aaron answered back over his shoulder. He was comforted by her touch, but worried. The fuel gauge registered just under a half tank.

Miki's Mercedes raced onto the airfield at Eindhoven and skidded to a stop at a pair of 109s parked for refurbishment. The squadron had been scrambled to intercept a radar track of a flight of Blenheims vectored toward Amsterdam. It would turn out to be a false alarm, just a flock of geese. The radar was new and unreliable.

Miki stepped out of the car to a mechanic working on one of the 109s.

"Warm the engine," he commanded.

The mechanic saluted. "But, Herr Major, it cannot fly. There is a fuel leak. The other is worse."

"How long?!" Miki demanded.

"I'm working as fast as I can, Herr Major."

Miki paced, cursing, looking into the sky to the west.

He checked his watch and strode over to the maintenance shack. He picked up the phone receiver and dialed the direct exchange for Gilze-Rijen. When he identified himself, he was told of the incursion and description of the intruders. When asked what should be done, Miki thought about all he could say.

"Inform your superiors. Send a report to regional command," was all he said.

"Ja woll, Herr Major," was the response. Miki clicked his finger on the cradle and dialed the exchange for Radio Observation Coastal Section.

An operator sergeant answered the call. He listened carefully to Major Michael Baron von Steuven, Staffel Commander, Air Defense Wing, Group 26.

"Ja, Herr Major. Should I alert Fighter Defenses?" He listened. "Ja, Herr Major."

He saluted in rote reflex to no one in particular, then hung up the phone and sat back down at his station to finish a roll and coffee he was having for his midday snack.

Miki paced near the Messerschmitt as the mechanics worked. He was a man beside himself. He looked at his watch again, calculating in his head the climb and cruise speed of a 109 versus a Junkers 120. He had taken young pilots up in the craft as a trainer with the two tandem seats, to demonstrate bank angles and stall recoveries before they killed themselves in a high powered 109 or Folke-Wulf. Training schools were now sending fresh recruits with almost no air time to the front line, dressing them in uniforms and calling them pilots. All the real pilots were being put into bombers. This was an older 109E and not an F, with 120 less horsepower. It would be twenty minutes to Gilsen and Aaron could reach the Channel bay at Vlissingen before Miki could overtake him. But would he head for Margate on the Kent coast south of the Thames channel, or Harwich in East Anglia? After leaving radar range, it would only be a coin toss. He could not wait any longer.

"Put a patch on it!" he shouted to the mechanic, fussing with a connector ring.

"But Herr Major…" he tried to object, but saw the look of intense determination in the Javelin's eyes. He could tell he would not be deterred. He ripped a rag into strips and wrapped it around the connector, and wrapped that in tape. It would still drip, but the cloth would hold it for a time, long enough for a mission.

The mechanics prepared the cockpit straps and removed the chalks, without the skill of a real ground crew. Miki stepped on the wing root with his boot and launched himself up the wing to slide into the tight cockpit. He primed the injectors and turned the ignition switch to off. Two of the mechanics cranked the starter flywheel with the handle, another attached the battery cable. Miki switched the ignition on. The Daimler engine sputtered, straining to turn over, flipping the three prop blades twice, then stopped. Miki glared at the mechanic as if he had not done his job. Maybe the fuel line was clogged. Would they have to unwrap it again and tear off the tape to start over? The mechanics turned the flywheel crank to try again.

The foggy soup in the windshield of the Junkers began to clear and Aaron could just make out the coastline and the churning water of the English Channel. He had been flying low and blind for forty minutes. He had held his breath that they wouldn't run into a radio tower array. He could not tell whether they were too low for radar, he only hoped so. His foot ached on the rudder pedal. He had been trying to use the side of his foot to yaw right to look out the side cockpit so he could see the ground ahead. He checked the fuel gauge, just under a quarter of a tank. He did a quick calculation in his head.

"We just might make it," he said to Lacy over his shoulder. The stutter of the engine and wind whistling in a break in the window frame weather stripping made it a little hard to hear. "How's your swimming?"

Lacy thought about all those laps at the steam-heated Swimbad in Mulheim she had kept herself occupied with while Miki was gone. Maybe it would come in handy.

"I still sink like a rock in cold water," she joked, looking out the window, down to the beach turning to water below. Aaron pushed the throttle to a slow climb.

"We better gain some altitude in case we have to glide."

"In case we have to what?!" Lacy asked.

313

Aaron didn't answer. He didn't need to.

"I thought they'd send the whole defense group after us. Maybe we had some luck".

Aaron shifted his heading toward the south coast at Margate and pushed the plane higher over the channel water, trying to climb out of the small arms range of the spotter barges and channel patrols, but if one of them opened up with a .37 mm anti-aircraft gun, they would be toast. He didn't think he'd mention that to Lacy.

They had passed over the last of land and flown on for several minutes. Lacy looked down to the water as far as the eye could see. There were small vessels floating on the surface in a line. It seemed to be a demarcation barrier of some kind.

"How much farther," she asked.

"About twenty-one minutes to land fall."

Lacy thought, "That doesn't seem like so much." She leaned to look over his shoulder. The fuel gauge was in the yellow line below 1/8. A little red light was glowing on the panel. She didn't know what it was.

Suddenly, a BF109 fighter roared past them, at twice their speed, its wake vortex rocking the little plane.

Aaron and Lacy looked out the window as the 109 zoomed ahead and banked around. Aaron pushed the throttle to full as they watched the Messerschmitt sweep around in a hard bank to come up behind them.

Miki leveled his wings behind the Junkers, not bothering to throttle back. He raced toward it for another pass, closer this time. If they didn't see him before, they would not be mistaken. He swooped right over the tail of the plane, his prop passing through the twin tail boom just missing the wing.

Aaron wrestled with the stick, trying to hold the plane steady, as the 109 swept around again. Aaron didn't recognize the markings. He thought it looked like JG 21, but he easily recognized the flying.

"It's Miki," he said. He pushed the throttle to full open, damn the fuel.

Miki banked around again on the Ju120, reaching down to pull the flap handle and throttle down to match the speed. The flap handle was slippery and fuel was dripping from under the instrument panel onto his boots. With his flaps down to slow flight, Miki settled his 109 behind the slower plane.

Aaron and Lacy could only look out the back narrow window glass as the yellow-tipped prop spinner of the powerful plane seemed to snap at their tail. The 109 jogged to the left, then the right.

Lacy instinctively ducked low as the larger fighter came over the top of them, just over the wing, settling close.

Aaron just kept flying. He knew Miki was trying to force them down. To make them give up.

"Forget it, Miki!" he shouted aloud, "Dover or bust!"

The 109 settled to the side of them, its air cooler just off of the tail wing. Lacy could look out and see Miki in the cockpit without his flight cap, looking at her. His face was filled with anger, and loss. He pointed his finger down, like they should go back and land.

Aaron just kept flying.

Miki dropped back behind the Junker's tail again, flying right with it, tipping side to side. He didn't know what to do. He was a Luftwaffe officer, sworn to duty. Aaron was an escaping enemy. He didn't want to lose Lacy to Aaron, or anyone. She was the only bright breath of innocence in his life. The radio operator had directed him toward the signal of the west heading target. It had gone in and out of signal, but he was able to track its heading. The radio operator was to inform and vector the fighter group that had chased the flock of geese, once the Javelin had made contact with the target, but they would be ten minutes behind.

Miki held his 109 just behind the Junkers and lined up the gun sight, a desperate man. His finger reached to the firing button of the twin MG 17s. It settled there, quivering a moment, then, pressed.

Lacy looked back to the deadly plane behind them as its cowling machine guns flashed. Glowing bullets whizzed over the wing of the Junkers out into the channel fog.

"God, he's shooting at us!" Lacy shouted, clutching at the seat frame.

"If he was shooting at us, he would have hit us." Aaron assured her.

He just kept flying. The English coast was drawing closer, horizontal strips of gray white and dark green through the miasma haze. Aaron looked to the gauge.

"Just about down to fumes. We might have to ditch if he doesn't light us up."

He turned to look back to the 109. Miki was visible in the cockpit. He was shouting at them, but they couldn't hear. He was pointing back to the enemy coast behind him.

"That's it, Miki. That's all that's left!" Aaron shouted, knowing Miki couldn't hear him either. "You can only kill us, now."

Miki hung on the tail of the plane with his wife and his one-time best friend. He pounded his fist on the instrument console of his plane in fury, straining against the belt restraints as if he might somehow leap out of it to catch them but impotent to stop them. He fell back into his seat, crying. He never knew he could care so much about anything.

His finger extended to caress the firing trigger of his control stick, cannons or guns. It hesitated there, shaking. His gunsight was level on the Junkers in the crosshairs.

He cried as he sang the old song, the sweet memory of a distant past and ingrained mechanical habit of countless battles entwined in one.

"Fight for Old Nas-sau," he sang in a hushed whisper, barely able to force oxygen from his lungs, "Fight for our ivy halls..." His finger selected cannons and quivered on the trigger, starting to tighten. "Fight..." He could see Lacy's face looking out at him from the narrow slat of the Junkers with wonder, fear, and a wish for his salvation in her eyes, a wish they could take all of it back.

"Fight... Oh, God!!" he burst out a breath and released his finger from the trigger, not shooting. He couldn't.

"I love you," he mouthed through the glass canopy, across the air. With a last look at her, he pulled back his stick to bank away. To let them go.

Suddenly, bullet hits sparked on the 109's wings and into the fuselage behind him. A Spitfire roared past, bouncing on him from above.

The Spitfire roared around, banking hard to turn back for another pass, flicking the wings to load gas into the carburetors, as Miki's 109 wobbled on the edge of control.

Miki shoved his throttle open to gain fighting speed, caught by surprise. As the fuel pressure ramped, the leaking fuel through connector burst through the rag wrapping, squirting out under the instrument panel onto Miki's uniform pants and boots.

Aaron banked the Junkers toward the approaching high English cliff of white chalk limestone across a wide

317

stretch of watery estuary beach at low tide. The engine sputtered and stammered, starved of fuel. He swung the stick side to side to get the last of the gas into the fuel lines. The engine revved for a few moments more, then quit, out of fuel, the propeller winding in the air uselessly. The high cliff loomed in the windshield. The plane would never make the cliff tops.

Lacy looked out the back slat window of the plane at Miki's 109 and the Spitfire. The British plane was arcing around for another attack.

In the cockpit of the Spitfire, Wilson held his bank to line up on the accelerating 109. He had scrambled at the report of a two flight low altitude coastal raid, but was surprised at the fighter escort for a reconnaissance plane. No matter, he was happy for another check mark for his confirmed victory score.

"Sitting duck, piece of cake," he said to himself and he pushed his stick forward, lining up his sights on the 109 with the markings of JG 21 group. He had heard they were stationed in Holland and thought it was strange they were this far south. He tugged his finger on the firing button. The eight Brownings in his wings rattled his jaw as they fired, tracing out toward the enemy plane.

The 109 exploded in a raging ball of flame

"Miki!!" Lacy shouted, watching his plane burst in a hellfire of fuel, but flying onward like a flaming missile, still following them.

Aaron could not see it, as he was focused on the cliff rushing at them. He could try to pull up with a last ounce of lift and hope for ground effect on the cliff updraft, but he only had that thought that for a second as the cliff filled his view. He threw the stick over at the last instant and floated on the rising draft of air, hanging there a moment, then a snapbank to angle along the cliff in the updraft, like a seagull, to drop to the wet sandy beach.

The Junkers hit hard on the wet soaked broken shells which had gathered for eons at the base of the cliff. It bounced once, then caught in the sand and suddenly yanked around, coming to a standstill in the rising and falling tidal surge.

Aaron forced the bent door open and flopped onto the watery beach. Lacy was looking at him from the plane, banged up and aching, but with the clear bright eyes he had seen behind his closed lids when he had gone to sleep before every mission. He reached in to pull her out. He struggled with her lap belt, but it wouldn't come loose.

The waves of the tide rose to the fuselage, surging as if to lift it from the sand and carry it away into the channel. He yanked at the belt, the latch unfamiliar to him. Finally, it freed.

They looked out over the channel where the burning wreckage of the 109 had tumbled in the sky, breaking into pieces before falling to the waves below and splashing into the sea. Something white appeared in the sky, a chute opening. It drifted downward slowly toward the water. Miki had managed to bail out.

"Thank God," Lacy breathed, clutching a silver crucifix around her neck that Miki had given her.

They could not see from where they stood, but as Miki slowly drifted down in his parachute his legs were on fire, crawling up his fuel soaked uniform, engulfing him. He cried out in agony, like so many he had sent to their fate.

As Wilson banked around toward the drifting chute, following it down, he could see the flames.

"Poor Kraut bastard," he said, sad, but without pity.

He lined up his gunsight and squeezed his firing button.

As Miki hung in the straps, burning, the bullets from the Spitfire whizzed past him, missing him. The water was still far below. He screamed in pain.

"Damned lousy English shot!" he thought, maybe he said it, he didn't know. He couldn't wait for the pilot to make another pass to kill him. He reached a hand to the harness release and pulled. The harness came free and he slipped from it. He could feel himself falling, falling in freedom and agony until he hit the water and all was gone.

Lacy could see the figure fall to the sea until he disappeared beneath the chopping waves. She turned to hide her face in Aaron's shoulder, crying. He held her tightly, stroking her hair, comforting. He looked out at the water, lapping at the shore, holding back his own feelings as he clutched her.

"Absent friends," he said softly to himself as the Spitfire roared over their heads.

The white cloth of the parachute settled on the water of the channel, with nothing else in sight but drifting clouds in the sky.

A shore patrol would find them as an enemy observer plane was reported having been shot down approaching the coast. The soldiers would be shocked to find the Luftwaffe major wearing the medals of a German ace in the company of a young woman, and cursing at them with the bark of a Yank accent to his English, citing his unit number, claiming to be one of them. A coastal trawler had found the parachute of the enemy pilot floating on the channel surface and some wreckage pieces, but no sign of the pilot.

❖

About The Author

Michael January is a writer for film and television as well as a travel writer, photographer, and private pilot. His love of aviation and fascination with history the World War II era was the inspiration for this story. He has traveled extensively, visiting the locations where this story takes place and writing about the history. This is his second historical novel. He lives in Los Angeles.

Other Books by Michael January

"The Secret Memoirs of Mary Shelley: Frankenstein Diaries" is available in print, ebook and audiobook.

Favorites Castles: England and Wales
Favorites Castles: More England and Wales
Favorites Castles: Ireland and Northern Ireland
Favorites Castles of Switzerland
Favorites Castles of Germany

Visit Amazon Author Page
amazon.com/Michael-January/e/B00CJNK16O/

WingedLionPublications.com
PrestburyBooks.com

Printed in Dunstable, United Kingdom

67957904R00188